Praise for *High-Wire Heartbreak*

"Much like the historical heroine swinging on her trapeze bar from one side to another in a death-defying performance, author Anna Schmidt takes the reader on a thrilling ride from the present to the past and back again. The modern-day heroine, despite a looming deadline, can't resist the lure of solving the mystery surrounding her great-grandmother's apparent disappearance amidst a scandal. I couldn't resist turning the pages to discover the revelations from the past and how they affected the present."

–Johnnie Alexander, bestselling and award-winning author of *Where Treasure Hides* and *The Cryptographer's Dilemma.*

"*High-Wire Heartbreak* swings into action to give this cold case fan an entertaining, high-flying mystery. Learning about the Ringling Circus and romance is a double win! I love how the past and present are woven together into a single delightful tale of intrigue and love."

–Mary Davis, award-winning, bestselling author of the Quilting Circle series

T0016605

Doors to the Past

HIGH-WIRE
Heartbreak

ANNA SCHMIDT

BARBOUR
PUBLISHING

High-Wire Heartbreak ©2022 by Anna Schmidt

Print ISBN 978-1-63609-137-2

eBook Editions:
Adobe Digital Edition (.epub) 978-1-63609-139-6

All scripture quotations, unless otherwise indicated, are taken from the HOLY BIBLE, NEW INTERNATIONAL VERSION®. NIV®. Copyright © 1973, 1978, 1984, 2011 by Biblica, Inc.™ Used by permission. All rights reserved worldwide.

This book is a work of fiction. Names, characters, places, and incidents are either products of the author's imagination or used fictitiously. Any similarity to actual people, organizations, and/or events is purely coincidental.

Cover image © Ilina Simeonova / Trevillion Images

Published by Barbour Publishing, Inc., 1810 Barbour Drive, Uhrichsville, Ohio 44683, www.barbourbooks.com

Our mission is to inspire the world with the life-changing message of the Bible.

 Member of the
Evangelical Christian
Publishers Association

Printed in the United States of America.

Dear Reader,

John Ringling was a force to be reckoned with when it comes to the development and history of Sarasota, Florida. He was far more than a "circus man." He owned a great deal of property both in Sarasota proper and on the barrier islands (the Keys) that separate the mainland from the Gulf of Mexico.

If you visit Sarasota today, you will see the Ringling name everywhere: on the sixty-five-acre art and circus museum where Ca'd'Zan (House of John)—the home John and his beloved Mable built—is the centerpiece; a world-renowned school of art and design; and the bridge that connects the mainland to those barrier islands—just to name a few.

In this novel most of the characters are fictional—as is the story. To my knowledge John did not throw a seventieth birthday party for himself and, while there is a cottage on the property where special guests can stay, again, to my knowledge no mystery writer (not even Sarasota resident Stephen King) ever took up residence there. Lillian Leitzel was a performer with Ringling's troupe, but Lucinda Conroy is my creation.

I am indebted to the staff of the Ringling Museum Archives for their assistance in answering my questions and clarifying details for the setting. And I am always a champion for those who see the value of preservation, keeping alive the past so that perhaps we learn for the present and future. I hope you will have an opportunity to visit this wonderful city on the west coast of Florida—it is an often-overlooked treasure trove of art and history and nature.

Until next time...enjoy the story and be in touch: https://booksbyann.com to let me know your thoughts.

All best,
Anna

CHAPTER ONE

Sarasota, Florida, July 2022

CHLOE

*S*weat beaded Chloe Whitfield's forehead and soaked her neck. Her loose-fitting shift-style dress was a mass of wrinkles. Who had ever thought linen was a good idea for clothing? She'd chosen her outfit with the thought of wanting to present herself as the professional and successful woman she was.

But why had she bothered? There was no one she needed to impress. She was an award-winning novelist—her historical mysteries regularly topping the bestseller charts. Why should she care about making an impression? And what on earth had possessed her to consider spending the summer in Florida in the first place? Of course, the grant she'd received allowing her to research her latest novel set on the grounds of circus magnate John Ringling's winter estate had been far too generous to pass up.

Steamy was the word that sprang to mind to describe the midsummer weather as she drove her rental car to the employee parking lot she'd been told to find. The lot was half empty—or perhaps half full depending on one's mood. It was low season, meaning the snowbirds had all flown north, and the museum's trustees had decided this was the perfect time to close the Ringling mansion—the showplace of the museum—to the public for some much-needed restoration. The museum's director, historian Dr. Ian Flanner, was supposed to meet her in the parking lot at ten.

He was late.

Chloe was not surprised. On the phone, the man had sounded preoccupied, and he'd shown zero interest in her or her project. The truth was he'd come across as a bit distracted. She'd pictured a gray-haired, absentminded professor type approaching retirement. A man who saw the clock ticking on his own career and had little interest in furthering hers.

From the back seat of the convertible she'd decided was essential for getting around in Sarasota, she retrieved the shoulder satchel that held her essentials—laptop, phone, pens, and notebook, along with the floppy straw hat her mother had insisted was *de rigueur* to protect her fair skin. Using the side mirror, she checked the angle of the hat and tucked an errant strand of her shoulder-length copper-colored hair behind her ear. Her mother had also advised a shorter cut. She might have had a point, but Chloe liked her hair long enough to pull up or back as she chose.

She turned to find a man standing only a few feet away. He studied her with what she could only translate as a look of decided impatience. He was tall and—*lanky* was the word that came to her writer's mind. He was dressed in shorts, a T-shirt, and sandals. A worn and faded baseball cap covered his dark hair. She assumed he worked on the grounds.

"You'll want to put the top up," he said with a nod toward her car. "It rains most afternoons this time of year."

The sky was a cloudless blue.

She ignored his warning and stepped forward. "I'm meeting Dr. Flanner. Perhaps—"

"That's me, and it's Ian." He glanced at the car again. "Do you want me to handle the top?"

"I'll take care of that later. I'd really like to see the house, if possible. I'm on a tight deadline, and the sooner I have a feel for my setting the better."

He shrugged. "Suit yourself. Have you got everything?" he asked with a nod toward her satchel.

Her luggage was crammed in the trunk. She hoped he wasn't expecting her to drag it out and haul it herself. Certainly not in the high wedge espadrilles that were as poor a choice as the linen dress had been. "I have more stuff in the trunk. Perhaps..."

He cocked his head, his lips twisting into a half-smile. "You like that word, don't you? *Perhaps?*"

Was he mocking her?

His voice held the lilt of a twang—western, perhaps Texas?

"I was just saying that per—that since I am unfamiliar with the location of the guest house where I am to stay, perhaps..." She *did* overuse the word.

"I'll have one of the crew take care of that." He glanced at his phone and frowned. "So, you'd like to see the mansion straight away?"

Kind of why I'm here.

She forced a smile. It had been a long day already and she was out of sorts. "That would be lovely." *Lovely? Where is this primness coming from?*

"This way," he said as he cut across parts of the grounds where the thick roots of a massive banyan tree reached out its tentacles to form unexpected obstacles. Gingerly she picked her way along as her escort forged ahead. Along the way, he pointed out landmarks. "Over there are Mable's roses," he said, indicating a more formal garden in the distance. "Past that and back toward the circus museum is the guesthouse. There's a café nearby, but it's closed for the summer. Tilda Tucker, my assistant, can stock the kitchen once you make up a list."

"I'm a vegetarian," she said, her breath a little short as she tried to keep up with the pace he'd set.

"So is Tilda—at least some of the time. Shouldn't be a problem."

She'd been focusing on the uneven ground, but as soon as they reached level ground she looked up, and that's when she saw the house. It was magnificent—far more impressive in real life than it had been in the photographs she'd researched. Inspired by the Venetian Gothic architectural style they had admired during their extensive travels in Italy, John Ringling and his wife Mable had unwittingly created the perfect setting for Chloe's next novel.

She fished in her bag for her phone. Documenting each moment of her research with photos, sketches, and handwritten notes was second nature to her. She swiped the screen to access the camera and snapped several angles.

"It gets better from here," Ian called out.

He was standing on the walkway that stretched the width of the front of the mansion, his head cocked to one side.

"Could you step out of the shot, please," she shouted, waving him aside. Holding her phone like a guiding light, she stepped forward. Later the photos would remind her of the thoughts and ideas she'd had on first seeing the house. She would discard most of the images once she'd made her notes. But for now, she could not seem to get enough of the pale pink and rose-colored patina of the terra cotta exterior. As she advanced on the mansion, she could see how the facade was highlighted by several colorful tile medallions. Then there were the graceful marble balustrades forming a kind of elegant picket fence…and the colors! Ivory, pastel blues, greens, pinks and yellows…

"It's magnificent," she shouted, her voice filled with excitement. This was so much more than she ever could have imagined. Her mind raced with ideas for scenes—the arrival of her heroine in a 1930s-era roadster—guests gathered on the lawn—that tower! Her research had revealed the presence of a guestroom for very special guests located up there. Word had it that back in the day some of the biggest names in politics and entertainment had spent the night in that guestroom—Will Rogers and even the renowned New York City mayor, Jimmy Walker. Yes, she would need to make good use of that tower. It was perfect for a midnight rendezvous between her hero and heroine. She kept clicking the shutter, her eyes riveted on the house as she fairly danced along the uneven ground.

So engaged was she with having found her novel's perfect setting, she paid little attention to her footing until her shoe caught on a tree root. Desperately trying to find her balance, she fell forward, her phone flying out of her hand as she hit the ground hard.

Ian was beside her in record time. "Are you okay?" He eased her to a sitting position. "Looks like you skinned your knee. We've got a first aid kit. Can you—"

"My phone," she managed, ignoring any personal injuries and the fact the fall had knocked the breath from her. Her phone was her lifeline.

"Right here." He retrieved it and handed it to her.

She gently wiped the screen and tested the functions. The camera still worked, and the photos she'd just taken were intact. Once she assured herself everything was undamaged, she let out a sigh of relief.

Ian watched this with barely concealed astonishment. "You know we have a fairly extensive archive of photos and drawings and such right here at the museum. It's really not necessary—"

"I have my methods," she replied, as she tried to figure out the best way to get back on her feet.

"Here." Ian was standing now, offering her his hand. "Let's get you up to the house and get that knee cleaned up and tended to."

"It's a scrape," she muttered as she accepted his help. But she couldn't help wincing when she tried to put weight on her left foot.

"Your knee is bleeding, and it looks like you might have twisted your ankle. We need to get some ice on that before it starts to swell." He stared at her feet. "Can you walk? Maybe take off those shoes?"

"I'm fine." But if standing was troublesome, the shot of pain she felt when she tried to walk was more significant than she was ready to admit.

"Right," he said. And before she could protest, he wrapped his arm around her back. "Lean on me and keep that foot elevated." They hobbled along like contestants in a three-legged race.

"Really, this isn't necessary."

"Really, it is," he replied. "It seems my crew has run into a problem, and I need to get back up there as soon as possible. So let's at least get you some first aid, and we can reschedule the tour for tomorrow."

Chloe pressed her lips together and hobbled on. She certainly was not getting off on the right foot—every pun intended. Her clothes were wrong, and she was embarrassed by her clumsiness. Clearly she'd made a terrible first impression on this man who was supposed to be her primary connection to the private spaces of the house and the archives he'd mentioned.

"The man has done his homework on this place," Bill Tucker, president of the museum's board of trustees, had assured her when he called to offer her the residency. "He's not just an expert on the architectural details of the property, but he also seems to be a bit of a history buff when it comes to the people who once lived here or came as guests of the Ringlings." Tucker had chuckled. "I think the guy could do a whole new doctoral dissertation on Ca'd'Zan. Never will understand that level of intellectual curiosity."

Chloe had found all of this fascinating. She loved the research piece of writing, especially when she connected with someone with the kind of deep dive knowledge Ian Flanner had to offer. On top of that, it had crossed her mind that a true scholar might just be the person she needed to solve a mystery in her own family. She hadn't yet mentioned that in addition to writing her novel, she hoped to find records that told the story of her great-grandmother, Lucy Conroy. Family lore had it that Lucy had been quite the star in her days with the Ringling Circus—a renowned trapeze artist. But like all family stories, the details had shifted down through the generations. There had been hints of scandal and a bad ending, but no one seemed to know the exact story.

Alice, her grandmother—Lucy's daughter—had been in an orphanage until she was adopted at the age of five by a couple she came to adore. "They may not have been my birth parents, and they certainly had to work hard to put food on the table," Grandma Alice had told her, "but there was love in that house."

"But your real mother, Grams," Chloe had pressed. "What about her?"

"The circus performer?" Her grandmother had sniffed dismissively. "She made her choice—and it wasn't me."

Of course, even though Chloe had no intention of writing about her great-grandmother, Grandma Alice's obvious hurt at what she saw as abandonment made Chloe more determined than ever to clear up the family history. And for that she would need the cooperation of Ian Flanner.

As soon as they reached the level ground of the tiled walkways surrounding the house, Chloe pasted on her warmest smile. "I think I can make it from here. I really hate to hold you up any longer, so if you'll just direct me to that first aid kit and perhaps a restroom where I can wash up a bit?"

Once again, he ignored her, striding up a short ramp to a rear entrance. "Darcy! Got a patient for you," he called out as he pressed the pad that opened the door for the disabled and eased Chloe inside.

"Oh, my stars! What happened?" A small gray-haired woman Chloe guessed to be in her seventies rushed forward and pulled a straight-backed chair closer. "Sit here, honey."

While the older woman hovered, Ian stood aside with his hands on his hips.

"Well, don't just stand there," Darcy instructed. "Get me a wet towel and some ice. There's an elastic bandage in the closet with the first aid kit." Once Ian left the room, the older woman turned her attention to Chloe. "I'm Darcy Prescott and you must be our famous writer. I've read every one of your books, and I could not be more thrilled that you've decided to set your next one right here."

Chloe could hear water running and muttering coming from down the hall. "I'm afraid I'm off to a rocky start with Dr. Flanner."

"Him? Don't mind that boy. Has his head in the clouds about 90 percent of the time—always thinking down the road, that one. Big dreams for this place once he deals with the damage done by hurricanes and other storms these last few years." She gently probed Chloe's ankle. "Pretty sure it's not broke, but you'll be wanting to keep ice on it and keep it elevated." She pulled a second chair closer and propped Chloe's foot on it.

"Perhaps I should have an X-ray—just to be sure?"

The older woman shrugged, but seemed to take no offense. "Suit yourself. I've seen my fair share of such things and pretty much know the signs."

"You're a nurse—or were before?"

Darcy's laugh was a snort. "Nothing so grand. I was with the circus from the time I was sixteen. Part of my family's juggling and tumbling act. Falls and injuries like yours were part of my education." She glanced toward a doorway beyond which Chloe heard ice rattling. "Ian! You gonna bring me that ice or wait for it to melt? This girl's ankle is starting to swell." Gently she removed Chloe's shoe.

"Coming. Keep your shirt on." Ian reappeared, towels and the first aid kit anchored under one arm as he carried a bowl of ice. He set the bowl on the counter and handed Darcy the kit and a wet towel, then spread out another towel. He dumped the ice in its center and wrapped the ends tight around it while Darcy cleaned the dirt from Chloe's knee and applied ointment and a large adhesive strip.

"Okay, I got this," Darcy said, taking the ice pack from Ian.

"That crabby construction foreman has been calling nonstop, says you never answer your phone."

Ian hesitated. "Call Pete. He can get her down to the guest-house. Her luggage needs to be brought from the car and—"

Her?

Chloe bristled. After all, she was sitting right there. She might have made a poor first impression, but there was no call for him to dismiss her.

The phone on the counter shrilled.

"That'll be your foreman," Darcy said. "Go!"

Once Ian left, Darcy's manner softened. "You'll get used to our professor," she said as she expertly secured the ice pack to Chloe's ankle with the elastic bandage.

"Perhaps he should take a moment to get used to me," Chloe grumbled then immediately thought better of it. "Sorry. Bad day."

Darcy arched an eyebrow but made no reply. Instead she stepped behind the counter and picked up a phone. While she connected with whomever Pete was, Chloe took the opportunity to stand and test her mobility. Ian had brought her to a small room that was obviously a visitor's center for the mansion. There was a service counter as well as a rack of informational pamphlets. Through one doorway she saw a unisex bathroom, and through another larger opening, she saw what she assumed was the mansion's kitchen. The walls along the hall leading to the bathroom were decorated with colorful circus posters as well as framed black-and-white photographs. She had her setting but now needed inspiration for her characters. It was part of her process to find photos of real people and adapt them to become her protagonist and villain. Balancing on her good leg, she leaned in to study a double row of photographs—clowns and jugglers and strong men and…

She flicked on the light on her phone and held it closer to an image half hidden behind the door to the restroom. Her attraction to this particular photo was that it was of a woman, and it had a certain aura of glamour to it. She squinted at the neatly typed identification label.

Lucinda Conroy.

Chloe took a step back and nearly fell again. Holding on to the restroom door, she once again studied the photograph. This was unexpected. She peered at the woman—the bobbed, finger-waved golden hair and the wide dewy eyes that stared back at her. The pouty bow of her painted lips. She'd been a beauty all right.

She startled at Darcy's voice calling out from the other room. "Pete's on his way. Says once he has your car key he'll pick up your suitcases and put the top up on that car of yours." She had stepped into the hall and flicked on an overhead light. "Can't predict the rain around here, especially this time of year." Her voice trailed off as she approached Chloe. "Ah, Lucy Conroy. Word is she was the best—a true star and much beloved by everyone in the company."

Then why isn't she in a place of more prominence, Chloe wanted to ask. But instead she said softly, "She was my great-grandmother. I never knew her or saw pictures of her. Just the name and that she was with the circus."

Darcy glanced at Chloe and then back at the photograph. "There's a family resemblance," she said. "Sad story."

"What happened?"

Darcy shrugged. "Before my time, so details are sketchy at best. Something about some money and a missing vase. Lucy was arrested and then she just sort of disappeared. I've heard rumors over the years but nothing concrete—nothing I would be comfortable repeating. The circus—like any small community, can be a gossip mill. You soon learn to believe only about a quarter of whatever you're told." She turned at the sound of the door opening. "Ah, here's Pete. Let's get you over to the guesthouse and properly settled."

Pete was a man of few words and indeterminate age. After

collecting Chloe's luggage and tending to the rental car, he drove Chloe and Darcy to the guesthouse in one of the multi-seat, open vehicles used to transport visitors around the vast grounds of the museum. Darcy seemed used to the man's silence, keeping up a one-sided conversation with him during the short ride. From her position next to him in the front row of seats, her topics skittered from the weather to the construction project to an update on the health of a fellow employee. Chloe sat behind them next to her luggage. She paid little attention to Darcy's chatter as she took in her surroundings.

She'd done enough online research to know that the overall complex was quite something. Two whole buildings devoted to the circus plus the main welcome center that she knew housed a theater that had been brought over from Italy as well as the museum shop and an upscale restaurant. Looking off to her right, she caught a glimpse of a green-tiled building, a newer addition to the campus housing a collection of Asian art. Somewhere beyond that was the museum Ringling had built to house his extensive collection of Italian art. And while she looked forward to exploring all of it, she was here primarily to explore the mansion. Of course, her injured ankle would be a bit of an issue when it came to getting around.

"Pete?" She leaned forward and tapped the man on his shoulder. "Is there any possibility I could get some sort of smaller golf cart or electric scooter to use for a few days? Just until my ankle heals?"

He seemed to not have heard her, and she was about to repeat her request when he spoke. "I reckon I could fix you up with something, miss." He pulled the transport to a stop outside a smaller building, the same salmon pink as the mansion but far simpler in style. "You okay from here?" A short walk led to a covered porch and presumably the front door.

"She can lean on me," Darcy stated as she hopped down and offered Chloe her arm. "You take care of her suitcases, Pete," she added as she pulled a bunch of keys from the pocket of her dress.

After some false starts with wrong keys, Darcy found the correct one and opened the door. "Welcome home, Chloe…is it all right to call you Chloe?"

"Of course. Thank you." Chloe stepped over the threshold and smiled. The space was small—cozy, a real estate agent would have called it—but straight out of the 1930s in ambience and furnishings. Perfectly suited to her needs. Darcy led a tour without leaving the main room.

"Kitchen through there, and that way leads to the bedroom and bath. There's a lovely little patio if you can stand the heat in the day or the no-see-ums in the evening."

"No-see-ums?"

"Florida's mosquito," Pete said as he set her luggage just inside the front door. "So tiny you really can't see them, but boy, do you feel their bite and the itch that comes with it."

It was the most words the man had strung together yet. He grinned at Chloe, then ducked his head and frowned. "I'll just check the electric and AC," he muttered as he hurried off to the kitchen.

"Pete's the best," Darcy announced. "I expect you'll have some kind of vehicle for getting around before sunset." She hoisted one of the suitcases and headed for the bedroom. "I'll just put this on the luggage rack for you—make the unpacking easier."

"Thank you." Chloe took the backpack that contained her research files and journals and set it on the chair next to a small desk. She wished Darcy would go. She wanted to get settled, and she liked doing that on her own.

"I had a few staples delivered earlier to stock the fridge and pantry," Darcy announced, returning to the main room. She glanced around. "I think that should do it for now, but if you need anything, just call." She pulled out a notepad from the desk drawer and wrote down a string of numbers. "That first is for daytime calls and the second will bring you the security guy at night." She turned toward the kitchen. "Pete! Let's go."

Chloe stood at the front door, balancing on her good leg, and waved to them as they drove away. She let out a long sigh, closed the door, and hopped into the kitchen. The refrigerator was indeed well stocked, including a pitcher filled with what she hoped was fresh-squeezed orange juice. She rummaged through the cabinets to find a glass, filled it with ice and juice, and wandered out to the patio. Collapsing wearily onto a chaise, she drank down the juice and turned her face to the sun. For the coming weeks, this would be home.

Well, God, here I am. Now what? Still not sure why You sent me here. Things feel all backwards. I mean, usually I know the plot of my next mystery and then choose a setting. Starting with the setting feels off. So, what's the deal?

As she closed her eyes and gave in to the need for a nap, she wondered if her great-grandmother had ever stayed in this guesthouse—or perhaps the mansion itself. One of the reasons she liked writing historical fiction was the opportunity to walk where others had walked in earlier times. Of course, never had she taken such a walk with a relative. Was it possible Lucy was the reason she'd been led to Sarasota...in ninety-plus-degree heat?

As she fell asleep she imagined the blond, wide-eyed young woman in the photograph come to life. Lucy Conroy had been at the pinnacle of her profession. So what had happened?

CHAPTER TWO

Ca' d'Zan, May 1936

LUCY

*L*ucinda Conroy stood at the window of the room she'd been assigned in Ca' d'Zan, the palatial winter home of John Ringling. It was a mark of her success that she'd been given one of the guest rooms for the weekend. Her view was of the lush tropical landscape and long drive leading up to the grand house. She watched as men and women from Sarasota's elite social set arrived in limousines and fancy automobiles for the all-day and evening event honoring the circus impresario on the occasion of his seventieth birthday. More likely they had come to gawk and gossip, for it was hardly a secret that Ringling was struggling financially. The land investments he'd made on the islands across the bay from the magnificent house, the art collection housed in its own separate building, the private railway car, and even the luxury cars he rode around town in were all rumored to be destined for the auction block.

But the man had a way of rising above adversity. Leave it to Mr. John to throw himself a party, no matter the cost or the circumstances. The circus employees had long ago taken to differentiating between John Ringling and his brothers by calling them by their first names and tacking on a respectful "Mister." Even when Mister John became the sole survivor among the five brothers, the habit continued.

Lucy had no doubt this affair would be grander than any he had ever hosted before. "Flying high, Lucy," he would call out to her as they passed on the circus grounds, after she'd called out a greeting that inquired about his health.

As the star of the current show, she'd been tagged to perform her high-flying trapeze act for the party guests. Her equipment was already in place on the palazzo that faced the aquamarine waters of Sarasota Bay. She and her partner, Bernardo Russo, had rehearsed twice—once after midnight the evening before and again at sunrise this morning. She was ready.

Later, having changed into their finest evening wear, she and Bernardo would join the guests enjoying cocktails and dancing in that same space. This time the background would be the setting sun followed by fireworks. It was going to be a party typical of Mr. John's fondness for flamboyance. Gossip also had it that this might well be his last party at the grand house. But even if that was true—which Lucy doubted—this night was not just Mr. John's grand finale. It would be Lucy's as well—her final performance. Her life was about to change in ways she had only dreamed about until now.

A husband and family…a little house….

As each car paused to discharge its passengers, the guests were greeted by Frank Jefferson, who had served the Ringlings for years and who managed the household staff. Of course, on this occasion that staff had been expanded to include at least a couple dozen others—most of them circus employees—who would serve as waiters and kitchen staff for the event. They all understood John Ringling saw no reason to pay people already on his payroll. The fact that none of the performers had been paid in weeks now had not kept them from showing up earlier that morning and lining the drive outside the servants' dining room to receive their instructions from Mr. Jefferson. That was the thing about Mr. John. The man could sell ice to Eskimos if he set his mind to it.

Lucy turned her attention back to the arriving guests and saw Mr. and Mrs. Rufus Sutherland exit a brown-and-tan Pierce Arrow limo. The Sutherlands were old money from Chicago and close friends of Mrs. Bertha Palmer, whose land holdings rivaled the Ringling assets. Word had it that even with the country clawing its way out of a national financial depression Mrs. Palmer's fortune was not only intact but flourishing. She had declined the invitation to the party—as she had declined every invitation John and his late wife Mable had extended in the past. And while Lucy had no doubt the Sutherlands would also have liked to send their regrets, they were tied to John Ringling through their youngest son, Marty.

To their dismay, Marty had taken a job in the front office of the Ringling Brothers' Circus the day after he graduated college. And a few days later, when his boss invited him and his parents to dine, they had been unable to find a reason to refuse. Usually, their forced attendance at gatherings such as this lavish weekend party was a source of amusement for Marty—and Lucy, but today she felt only raw dread. Today was the day Marty had promised to tell them he and Lucy had secretly wed.

Months had passed since the night Marty had pleaded with her to elope with him. "If we are married," he'd argued, "my parents cannot object."

"Object to what? Me?"

"Not you, darling. They don't know you. But in my world, there are certain occupations…"

"*You* work in the world of the circus," she had reminded him.

"Being on the business end of things is a great deal different from performing, Lucy. Besides, I am speaking of the world I was born into—some call it that blue blood world. It's not fair, but people of that ilk are pretty closed off when it comes to accepting—"

"Me," she said bluntly.

"I was going to say 'those who come from a different background.'

Come on, Lucy. How long do you think a guy like me can hold off? You say not until we're married, so let's get married. I know it may not be the ceremony you dreamed of, but I assure you I'll make it up to you with the wedding night." He'd pulled her close, his lips hovering just a fraction of an inch from hers.

"You'll tell your parents? I mean, I don't want any more of this having to sneak around."

"Soon as I get back from my business trip," he promised. "Say yes, Lucy," he begged, "and let's start our future tonight."

And so, she had been persuaded.

The *oohga* of a car horn drew her attention back to the scene below. She knew that sound. It was Marty's bright red open-topped road-ster traveling far too fast up the drive and skidding to a stop inches from the unruffled Mr. Jefferson. Marty hoisted himself from the driver's seat without bothering to open the car door and tipped his straw hat to the butler. The two men exchanged a few words that ended with Marty laughing as he tossed Mr. Jefferson the car keys and bounded up the steps to the front door.

After checking her hair and makeup in the gilt-framed easel mirror on the dressing table, Lucy hurried from her room and down a short hallway until she reached the mezzanine balcony that over-looked the large main room—the room she'd heard Mr. John refer to as the Grand Court. She bit her lip to keep from calling out to her husband, willing him to look up and see her there. He'd been away now for weeks, and she longed to see that dimpled smile that had stolen her heart the moment they'd been introduced. Oh, how she looked forward to the day they no longer needed to refrain from open displays of affection—the day she could run to meet him and he would lift her in his arms, twirling her around, the two of them dizzy with love.

The Grand Court was filled with guests. Greetings and intro-ductions were being exchanged as circus people threaded their way among the rich and famous, offering glasses of lemonade and orange juice spiked with champagne. Marty crossed the room to where his parents were engaged in conversation with a striking young woman Lucy recognized from photos in the society pages. They were speaking with Julia Gordon, a wealthy socialite whose parents standing next to her had been investors in several of Mr. John's real estate ventures. Lucy smiled, thinking how often Mr. John had praised Marty's instincts for being in exactly the right place with the right people at the right time. The Gordons were exactly the right people, and given the stories circulating of Mr. John's money problems, this was indeed the right time.

She moved along the balcony, hoping to catch Marty's eye. He glanced up, and she had to tighten her fingers into a fist to keep from waving to him and drawing the attention of others. Instead, she smiled and trailed her fingers lightly along the cool marble of the balustrade railing.

But Marty did not return her smile. He gave his full attention to Miss Gordon and her parents with no sign he had seen Lucy. Yet he must have. Yes, she was sure of it. There had been that split second of recognition. But in place of the delighted smile deepening his dimples she would have expected, he had turned away. Even now he was leading the socialite across the room to the Steinway grand piano. He sat, indicating Miss Gordon should share the narrow bench, as he ran his fingers lightly over the keys.

Lucy stood rooted to the spot where she had smiled at him—where she had caught his eye—where he had looked away. Of course, this was business. A large part of his job was to charm potential backers of the Ringling holdings, and the Gordons were certainly part of the circle. Besides, he had been traveling over the last several weeks, setting up dates for the circus's summer tour, so he must be exhausted. Before leaving he'd reminded her that while he couldn't be in touch by telephone or telegram without raising questions about why the company's business manager would need to call or wire her specifically, he would write. Still, in the six weeks he'd been gone, she'd received only one letter, barely a page long and filled with news of the people he was meeting and the parties he was attending with hardly a mention of his work securing bookings for the show. His letter said nothing about them. Nothing about their future or missing her—or loving her.

"Are you checking out the audience?" Her partner in the air, Bernardo Russo, was dressed in an open-collared white shirt and tan linen trousers, his black hair swept back, exposing his deeply tanned features. He joined her at the railing, watching the activity below. "A lot of money down there. Maybe the boss will find a way to make things better?"

Lucy turned her back to the scene, where Marty was now playing a Scott Joplin ragtime melody to the delight of several guests close to the piano. "Perhaps. How is your fancy room?" She gave him a teasing grin. Both she and Nardo understood that it was only because they were the stars of the day's festivities that they'd been invited to stay in the main house. Although she made a handsome wage, had traveled the country and even Europe, and had a luxurious private tent on the circus grounds, there were limits to how far Mr. John could go without upsetting his high society friends. Lucy knew that their fellow circus colleagues would spend the night—what was left of it once they had cleared away the remains of the party—on cots crowded into the small bedrooms of the servants' quarters.

Nardo stood next to her as they took in the scene below. "My mother will never believe we are to perform here on the grounds of Mr. Ringling's estate—and stay for the party to follow. I have written her, of course, but she will admonish me for exaggerating."

"Perhaps at the ball tonight, when you are all dressed up in your tuxedo and looking every bit the suave gentleman, we can find a way to have the newspaper photographer snap a photo you can send to her."

"She'll only believe it if Mr. John himself is in that photo."

"Then we shall make sure he is," Lucy replied. "The three of us."

Nardo glanced away. "And will you dance with me, Lucinda?"

He always called her by her full given name. She knew he was in love with her. Several of the women in the company had told her so and urged her to encourage him. But, of course, she could not. She was in love with Marty, not to mention they were married.

"One dance," she promised, and his shy smile told her she had given him false hope, so she changed the subject. "Have you had time to check our equipment?"

Nardo nodded. "I went over everything after our rehearsal this morning. Still, Lucinda, will you insist on trying the triple today?"

"It's the perfect place and time," she assured him, relieved to be talking about their work. "Mr. John will be delighted."

"But it is also dangerous."

"There's a net."

"There is always a net," he replied. "But that too can pose a danger when you fall from such a height and at such speed."

She knew he was right. If a performer landed the wrong way, the net could cause serious injury. "We've done the triple in rehearsal," she reminded him. "Twice," she added, as if that was an impressive detail.

Nardo arched an eyebrow. For weeks now the two of them had met in secret, late at night or in the darkness of predawn, to practice the feat. Time after time they had come close but failed. Only twice had they succeeded.

He tapped his fingers on the railing. "Martin will not be happy if we try it here in front of these important people and fail, Lucinda."

"I plan *to perform* it here, not try," she corrected.

"But you have not told Martin?"

She knew his concern was for their jobs. While the attraction between Lucy and Marty was hardly a secret, neither Nardo nor anyone else knew of her marriage to the renowned playboy.

"It's a surprise," she said.

"Martin does not like surprises. He has made it clear to everyone that he expects to approve exactly what each act plans for any performance—no matter who they are."

She glanced toward the piano where Marty was swaying side to side as he played, his shoulder brushing that of Miss Gordon. "We will do the triple," she said as she headed for the stairway that would bring her into the midst of Mr. John's guests. Once there she crossed the crowded room to the piano just as Marty completed his performance to applause and stood to take his bow.

His cheeks reddened at the sight of her, but he recovered quickly. "Lucy!" He turned to the socialite still seated on the bench. "Miss Gordon, allow me to introduce you to the star of our show—and today's entertainment."

Lucy met the other woman's smile and cold gaze. Clearly Miss Gordon was not interested in meeting the help, and clearly this was how she viewed a performer in whatever entertainment might be planned. "Charmed," she said before turning to Marty and hooking her hand through the crook of his arm. "If you're done showing off at the piano, I'd love a tour of the grounds, Martin," she said with a teasing smile.

"Of course." As they turned away, he glanced back over his shoulder at Lucy, his arched eyebrows saying, "What can I do?"

Left standing in the midst of those who had little desire to converse with her and one or two friends of Mr. John who leered at her as if she were an item on the menu, she pasted on the smile she wore like a piece of clothing in circumstances like these. Through the open doors that led out to the palazzo she saw Nardo once again checking the rigging for their act. The man was obsessive. She set aside the thought that she wished Marty cared as much about her well-being as Nardo did. After all, what did she expect? Her husband was also in a difficult position—at least until they could finally announce their marriage. He had perfected the role of the carefree bachelor he'd found so useful in charming the wives and daughters of potential investors. What was it he always said?

"It's business, darling."

Well, she would make sure that whatever business might be tied to Miss Gordon ended in short order.

CHAPTER THREE

Ca' d'Zan, July 2022

CHLOE

"*W*oo-hoo!"

Chloe realized she'd been lulled into a much-needed nap while relaxing on a chaise in the garden outside the guesthouse. She pushed herself to a more upright position as she followed the high-pitched sound to where a young woman wearing a floppy-brimmed hat, large sunglasses, and a halter sundress that showed off tanned shoulders and bare arms was coming her way.

"I didn't wake you did I?" The stranger took a seat on a second chaise. "You don't want to be sleeping in this sun, not with your fair skin." She removed her sunglasses and thrust out her hand. "Tilda Tucker," she said. "At your service. Ian sent me to be sure you were settled in and had everything you need." She peered more closely at Chloe. "Oh dear, you're going to have a bit of a burn. Let's get you inside."

Chloe felt like an old woman being rescued by a Girl Scout as Tilda helped her limp back inside.

"You just sit right here, and I'll refill this," Tilda said, holding up Chloe's glass that now held only melting ice. While bustling about in the small kitchen, she kept up a running monologue. "Ian told me about your fall. The man is a godsend for this place. Not that the previous director was bad, but Ian is…well, he sees the possibilities for the future." She returned with a fresh glass filled with orange juice over ice and handed it to Chloe. "You should drink this. In this heat, one can become dehydrated in a flash." She plopped down on a sagging sofa and kicked off her shoes. Somewhere along the way she had abandoned the hat.

"Ian mentioned you. I'll try not to be too much of a bother," Chloe said.

"No bother at all," Tilda replied. "I serve at the pleasure of my good-looking boss."

Taking a long swallow of the orange juice, Chloe took a moment to study Tilda Tucker. Late twenties, the long, styled hair, and perfectly manicured finger- and toenails her generation seemed to prefer. She had a buxom figure that unless watched carefully might one day become a struggle with the bathroom scale.

Tilda released a long sigh as she curled yoga-style into a chair. "The man is gorgeous, don't you think?" Without waiting for a response, she rushed to add, "Not to mention he's single. I mean, seriously, when was the last time anyone saw that combination here in this backwater town?"

Chloe decided it would not be prudent to continue the focus on Ian, so she changed the subject. "From everything I've read about Sarasota, it has an impressive arts community."

Tilda rolled her eyes. "One that caters to retired snowbirds and those in my parents' social circle. Youth—and what is necessary to draw that generation here—is a commodity in short supply."

"I'm beginning to feel I may have passed my sell-by date," Chloe teased.

Tilda blushed. "Oh, heavens. I didn't mean that at all. Following Ian—who I think is about your same age—are what I hope will be a Renaissance of young, hip professionals around here. Wouldn't he be perfect as a character in your novel?"

Chloe thought about the scowling man she'd met earlier. "I suppose he could fit nicely as a sort of brooding hero."

Tilda leaned forward. "A new detective to kick off your new series. Of course. He's perfect. Even better than Detective Rogers in your last series. I was devastated when he and Karina finally married."

"You've read my books?"

"Oh yes. Every one of them. I told Daddy having you on-site and setting your next best seller here would be a boon for the museum. I can just see it. We'll have a grand party to host the launch." She seemed to do some mental calculations and then squealed. "In January, for the grand reopening of the mansion," she announced.

Chloe smiled. It was not unusual for those unfamiliar with the publishing world to assume a book might be written, edited, and ready for sale within a few months. Her draft was not due until September—a deadline she was already pushing, since she had yet to start the novel. "A January release might be a bit ambitious," she said, "but I do appreciate the compliment that you consider my work worthy of such a grand unveiling."

"But—"

Somewhere nearby, Chloe heard the sound of circus music—a calliope.

Tilda fished her cell phone from the pocket of her dress and swiped the screen. "Ian! Yes, still here… She's fine…. Of course, Ian….Can I…" She stared at the phone, and Chloe realized Ian had abruptly ended the exchange. "Well, duty calls," Tilda said. She went to the kitchen and collected her hat and sunglasses. "It's a delight to have you here, Miss Whitfield."

"Chloe, please, and thank you for stopping by."

Tilda grinned. "Text me your shopping list, and I'll be back in the morning. Oh, we are going to have such fun." And with that she waved goodbye by waggling her fingers as she left the way she'd arrived—out the back door and around the side of the cottage.

Chloe had unpacked and was making herself a salad when Pete delivered a golf cart for her to use while her ankle healed.

"Keep it as long as you need it," he said as he backed away from the door. "Boss says to tell you he'll meet you up at the house at eight tomorrow morning if that suits."

"That will be just fine, Pete. Thank you. Can I offer you a lift back?"

His ruddy cheeks turned a deeper shade of crimson. "No, miss. I can walk."

As Pete hurried away, Chloe limped over to the cart. Even without her injury, having wheels was going to be an advantage, given what she had already observed of how spread out the various sites on the museum's campus were. She especially needed to find the archives and get a thorough tour of the nooks and crannies of the mansion. After all, any mystery worth its salt required secret spaces—shadowy corners where her protagonist might hide or discover a clue, or her villain might launch a surprise attack.

As always, turning her thoughts to the project at hand energized her. She had no idea how this story might go, and she had yet to jot down the questions she had for establishing the setting. Presumably tomorrow, Ian would give her the grand tour, and she intended to be fully prepared. Once she found direction for her story, she could spare some time to look for more information about her great-grandmother.

Still, the photograph she'd seen earlier haunted her.

The following morning as she navigated the path between the cottage and mansion, Chloe saw Ian standing just outside the solarium, his face turned to the warmth of the morning sun. He was leaning against the railing that framed the ramp visitors used for entering the house through the solarium. Chloe had to admit he was one good-looking professor. She couldn't imagine he'd been quite so zen when Bill Tucker told him of her arrival—and the expectation that Ian would be at her disposal for anything she might need. Ian Flanner did not strike her as the kind of guy who might be impressed by a celebrity—even one whose books had sold millions of copies and whose name was instantly recognized by millions of readers. She wondered if he was praying for deliverance from this latest intrusion on the work he'd been hired to do.

"Dr. Flanner will personally give you the grand tour of the mansion," Bill Tucker had promised. "I'll see to that."

The sound of the golf cart's quiet motor caught Ian's attention. Chloe saw him straighten, take a deep breath, and then greet her by raising one hand as he started down the ramp.

"Good morning," she called as she climbed out of the cart and hooked her satchel over one shoulder after extracting a notebook and pen. "Lovely day," she added.

As she limped toward him, she was pleasantly surprised to realize she was moving with more ease than had been the case a day earlier. She had dressed in a gauzy peach top and a long gray skirt that skimmed her ankles, revealing the elastic bandage still in place. He gave her outfit—and flat sandals—a once-over and visibly relaxed.

"You seem to be moving with a little less pain," he commented.

"Ice packs, elevation, rest, and ibuprofen," she said. She flipped open the leather cover of her notebook to reveal the page of questions and notes she'd put together for the tour. "Ready to get started? I have a lot of questions."

"And I have some information that just might give you the answers," he said as he led the way to the solarium. He handed her the guidebook to the mansion that she already knew was a best seller in its own right. "This should help," he said. "It's packed with details of the house and its history."

She flipped through it, then tucked it inside the satchel. "Thank you. This will indeed be helpful. Now then, I couldn't help noticing the swimming pool is on this side of the house and not closer to the bay. Why is that?" She pulled out the pencil she'd anchored in her upswept hair and prepared to take notes. "Also," she added before he could come up with an answer, "how deep is it? Was there a diving board?"

He frowned, and she realized he didn't know. "I'll have to ask Tilda to get those details for you," he said as he held the door to the solarium for her.

Chloe paused to jot a note in the margin of her notebook: *Body in pool?*

She saw Ian lift his eyebrows when he saw the note, but he recovered quickly and continued the tour. "Because it was near the pool, the Ringlings often used this room as a respite from the heat. Originally it was open, although even enclosed you can see it had not only the entrance we used just now, but a second access from the north side here." He pointed to doors that led to an outside half-circle patio. "Mrs. Ringling even had a gondola moored in the bay."

"How very Venetian," Chloe murmured as she scribbled yet another note. She turned her attention to the double doors leading to the next room. "Wow! Talk about the Gilded Age." She ran a finger lightly over the carved golden finish, then added another note, turning to a fresh page as they entered the reception area outside the ballroom.

"The Ringlings did a lot of entertaining," he said. "John relied on that to entice investors for his various ventures, and Mable was the consummate hostess."

Chloe sketched a rough floor plan showing the wide opening that led to the main entrance hall for the house and the second opening leading into the ballroom.

It was apparent how much Ian loved this house. Of course,

while she saw the rooms as backdrops for her characters, he looked at the rooms as the sum of their architectural features, pointing out small details she might have missed. For him the house was the spectacle—a work of art he intended to preserve and protect for generations to come.

"And there would be a small orchestra?" She had moved on to the ballroom. "Perhaps there?" She pointed to a corner, then gasped. "The mirrors," she murmured, once again making a note.

She sketched a mirror and then drew a jagged line through it as if it had shattered.

"Did you look up?" He apparently felt the need to redirect her attention, pointing to the coffered ceiling where hand-painted dancing couples were enclosed in thick decorative frames of cypress.

"Oh, what fun! I read about this but seeing it for real…"

"Through that door is the Grand Court—the main room for gathering."

She followed him into the impressive space—easily twice the size of the ballroom—where the ceiling soared up two stories and the massive pipe organ John Ringling had installed seemed as natural a furnishing as the sofas and chairs. She squealed with delight. "Oh, yes," she gasped as she moved slowly around the room. "It's perfect." Again, she began sketching, looking up at the balcony that surrounded the mezzanine corridor. When Ian moved a step closer, she held up her notebook to show him her sketch of a stick figure falling as if it had jumped or been pushed over the railing.

"But where might the body land?" she mused, glancing around the large room for likely spots.

It occurred to her that by now Ian had to be wondering what had ever possessed the board to invite this mystery writer rather than someone more literary. She decided it was time to stop trying to shock him—although that had been fun.

"I love the colored glass," she exclaimed, moving past him to the wall of windows that faced the water where the small lead-framed panes were colored in pastels of blue, pink, green, and gold. "They must filter the strong afternoon sun, and yet, one can see the bay and what a magnificent sight the piazza must be when it's lit at night."

"The windows are one of my favorite details in a house filled with such surprises."

Reluctantly she turned away from the view of the aqua waters of Sarasota Bay filtered through the colorful glass and crossed the room until she was standing in the foyer in front of the large formal entrance doors. "So, as a guest of the Ringlings, I would have come through these doors. Dining room to my left and reception area for the ballroom to the right and straight ahead..." She muttered to herself as she made notes and moved forward, then stopped and glanced around. "So, I understand there is a taproom?"

"It's this way." He walked through the dining room, its table set with crystal and china ready for a sumptuous meal, and on into a short hallway. "There." He pointed and stood aside to let her pass. "Of course, this would have been mostly for the male guests. If your detective is female, she probably would not be invited."

She looked at him with an impish grin. "Why, Dr. Flanner, are you writing my story for me?"

His tanned cheeks flushed. "Not at all," he said gruffly. "Tilda mentioned you might just choose a female protagonist."

"It's a thought," she replied as she squeezed past him, heading for the open door at the opposite end of the short hall. "What's this room?"

He followed her into the large pantry and on to the kitchen, where he checked his phone. Since the moment she arrived, she'd been aware of a growing number of signals coming from his phone. He'd been glancing at the screen off and on throughout the tour. This time he frowned. "Look, I really—"

"Need to go," she said, finishing his sentence. "No worries. We can do the rest this evening."

"Or Darcy should be here any minute and—"

"I'm sure Darcy knows a good deal of the history of the circus, but you are the expert on this house, and that's where the murder will take place, so—"

"Perhaps Tilda—"

She arched an eyebrow. "I met Tilda last night, and she certainly seems competent and…enthusiastic. But I take a lot of pride in getting details correct, and when it comes to this house, I've been told you—not Tilda or Darcy—are the expert." She paused to allow him to consider that before adding, "Of course, I could always wander about on my own."

"That's not an option—not right away," he said. "It's not just a security thing. We're under construction, at least in part of the house."

They both had complex projects to complete, she realized, and decided to propose a compromise. "Look, how about I interview Darcy and Pete, collect their stories, then meet with Tilda to settle on how the two of us will work together. I made an appointment at the archives for tomorrow." She pointed to his phone. "You go deal with whatever fire needs putting out, and we can finish this later."

"Seven o'clock then?"

"Perfect," she said. "And here comes Darcy."

"Keep that ankle elevated," he called as he left. "We'll do the second and third floors tonight."

She waved. "See you this evening," she called. She watched him until he turned a corner and was out of sight, then roused herself. "You are here to write a novel, Chloe Whitfield, not ogle a handsome professor."

After spending over an hour with Darcy, listening to the older woman's memories of days spent on tour with the circus, Chloe returned to the cottage. She did as Ian had advised, elevating her ankle with pillows while she studied the guidebook he had given her. He'd been right that it was an excellent resource for details of the house, but experience had taught her that whenever possible there was no substitute for standing in the actual space.

After catching up with texts and emails from fans and her publicist and agent, Chloe spent the rest of the afternoon trying to come up with an outline for her story. She was tired of always having to include a murder. Weren't other crimes equally as bad? Of course her readers expected a murder, even one that happened "off-stage," and the gorier the better. But perhaps a murder that wasn't a murder, one where the supposed victim lived? Her editor would be skeptical, as would her readers, but she liked the idea. Since in her last book she had married off her hero, she needed a new protagonist to start this series. Maybe female was the way to go. Petite with blond hair and deep-set blue eyes the color of the bay and...

She realized she was picturing her great-grandmother in the role and slammed her laptop shut. *This is fiction, not a biography.*

After a supper of veggies and hummus, she showered and changed into a cotton sundress, pulled her long hair back into a ponytail secured by a barrette, downed another dose of ibuprofen, and headed for the mansion.

Ian was nowhere to be seen as she pulled the golf cart close to the visitor's ramp and climbed out. The solarium door was slightly ajar, which she took as an invitation to enter.

"Ian?" She moved through the rooms as if she'd lived there her entire life. "Darcy?" She walked through the main floor to the visitor's reception area, which was closed up tight. Darcy had left for the day, and why wouldn't she? It was nearly seven. Taking advantage of this opportunity to wander about on her own, Chloe used her camera to snap photos of details she thought might prove useful. And one that had nothing to do with research for her novel.

She wanted a photo of her great-grandmother's framed picture. The hallway leading to the restroom was narrow and fully in shadow, so getting a good image was going to be a problem.

Carefully she lifted the framed photo from its place on the wall and carried it into the pantry where the light was better. She propped it against the backsplash of the long stainless-steel sink.

"What are you doing?"

She hadn't heard Ian enter the room. "I…the light…"

He moved past her and retrieved the photograph, then looked around. "Where was this?"

She pointed to the narrow hallway. "Outside the visitor restroom—on the left wall."

"The one thing we cannot have, Chloe, is anything, even a seemingly insignificant item, being moved or changed," he instructed after he replaced her great-grandmother's picture and returned to the pantry. "How did you get in here anyway?"

He was annoyed.

Well, so was she.

"The door to the solarium was open. You weren't outside, so I assumed you were somewhere in the house. I did call out."

"I was dealing with something. I left the door open, thinking you might wish to wait in the solarium rather than outside."

"And you didn't think I'd be curious?"

"I see now that was a mistake—one I hope will not be repeated."

Has this man ever broken a rule? Ever questioned or defied protocol?

"Understood," she said primly. "May I please see the second floor?" She knew she was being sarcastic, but his reprimand had stung.

"Sorry," he said softly. "Frustrating day, but no excuse for snapping at you. This way." He took her past a back stairway, announcing it led to a room for servants to use when meals were taken in the less formal breakfast room.

"Coatroom," he commented with a wave toward a closed door before rounding a corner. "Stairs or elevator?" He glanced down in the direction of her ankle. "Elevator," he muttered at the same time she said, "Let's take the stairs—I can see more that way."

At the top of the circular stairway, he paused at one corner of the three-sided balcony that overlooked the grand court. "The pipes for the organ are behind this wall," he said, pointing to his left. "Over there are a series of guest rooms. The largest guest room is here," he added, opening a door. "This is where Mrs. Ringling's personal guests stayed."

"Interesting. This is the premier location for a bedroom. I would have thought Mr. Ringling would have claimed it."

Ian shrugged. "I think you'll see that he did quite well for himself—as did Mable."

He showed her the rest of the second floor—Mable's bed, dressing, and bath rooms and then on to John's office with exercise room plus an impressive bedroom and bath. He called the elevator to take them to the third floor.

"Multiple storerooms," he noted before pointing out a vault used for keeping wine and, during the heyday of Prohibition, bootleg whiskey. "And this is what the Ringlings referred to as the 'playroom.'"

Chloe stepped into a room lined with columns, each painted from ceiling to floor in colorful stripes and capped by a character straight out of a Venetian carnival. The ceiling was painted with the Ringlings and their menagerie of household pets that Ian identified for her—Mable's miniature pinschers, John's German shepherd, four exotic birds, and a flock of finches. It was a room that came to life for Chloe as she walked the perimeter, hearing the sounds of music and laughter and seeing costumed couples engaged in card games and charades. Yes, this would be one place she would have to use in her story.

But by far the best part of the house was the tower and guest room with its three-sixty view of the bay and surrounding property.

"Wow!"

"It is a stunning view," Ian replied in what Chloe thought had to be the understatement of the year.

"It's fabulous. You definitely saved the best for last."

"I didn't save it. It's the final space to see—other than the Belvedere tower above."

Chloe realized getting used to his tendency to always look at the logical side of things was going to take some work. That, and the fact that he seemed to struggle to relax or smile or...

"Shall we go?" He was checking his phone again.

"Got a hot date, have you?" She eased past him and headed for the stairs.

"Let's take the elevator," he said. "You've been putting enough stress on that ankle. No sense aggravating it further by walking down steps."

They rode down to the main floor in silence. Chloe took out her phone and checked for messages. Her agent. Her mother. And Tilda.

She clicked on that one.

See you in the morning at eight—we'll get breakfast. My treat.

The elevator door slid open, rousing Ian from his phone to step aside and let her pass. They walked back through the house to the solarium. "I've told Tilda she's to be available for whatever you need." Once they reached the door, he extended his hand. "I hope the tour has been what you need. If there's anything else..."

She accepted the handshake. "Oh, I expect we'll see one another again, Dr. Flanner. I still have a lot of questions, and I'm not sure Tilda—or Darcy for that matter—will be able to answer them. So rest assured you have not yet seen the last of me."

He held the door for her, an indication he would be staying. "If your questions have to do with bodies thrown from the mezzanine or floating in the swimming pool, I suggest you contact the local police."

"No doubt that will happen, but don't think you can be rid of me so easily." She made her way down the short ramp and was surprised to find him still standing in the open door as she reached the bottom. "Was there something else?"

"I'll be doing some work in the archives tomorrow afternoon. If there's anything you'd like me to check on for you, just text me."

"Way ahead of you. I made an appointment before I arrived. Have a good evening," she said as she headed for her golf cart—and tried not to limp.

CHAPTER FOUR

Ca' d' Zan, May 1936

Lucy

$\int$ tanding on the tiny platform high above the gathering of local dignitaries and other guests, Lucy closed her eyes for a moment, taking in the warmth of the late afternoon sun. The triple was her birthday present for Mr. John. He was seventy years old and beginning to suffer the ravages of age. Just over the last two seasons he had been hospitalized, and when he joined the tour at all, the toll his illness had taken was obvious. Lucy felt she owed him the triple. How often had he talked about it being performed at another rival company? She would do it, and she would do it here in front of the monied people who were attending the party. Already she and Nardo had thrilled the guests below with their high-flying acrobatics—stunts that to them were second nature but that still elicited gasps of surprise from those watching.

Far below she spotted Marty deep in conversation with the socialite, while Mr. John was looking up at her. Thinner and paler than normal but with his trademark cigar clenched firmly between his teeth, he gave her a salute. She knew both men expected to see her perform her usual finale—a double somersault, Nardo's catch, all followed by a double pirouette as she returned to her own trapeze and swung to the safety of the platform.

Across from her Nardo waited on a second platform, his dark eyes riveted on her, every part of his lean muscular body pleading with her to forget the triple. She met his gaze, lifting her chin to show her determination, and saw by the subtle shift in his posture that he understood there would be no going back. He was ready. After coating her hands with chalk dust, she unhooked her trapeze and ran her palms along the bar, finding her grip before leaping from the platform. She pumped her legs hard, sending her body into a straight-line high to gain the altitude she would need to complete three rotations. Sunlight flickered over the calm azure blue waters of the bay like the sequins that covered her costume. The world turned upside down, below her a cloudless blue sky. And above her the crazy quilt of the patterned tile of the expansive palazzo.

She swung back toward her platform, pumping her legs again. This was it. On this rise, she would release the bar. Across from her she saw Nardo grip his bar. Timing was everything.

Pump hard.

Rise.

Release.

Tuck and grab knees.

Backward somersault…one, two.

Release knees.

Three and—

She stretched her full length to reach Nardo, saw the hard, set line of his lips as he stretched out toward her, and the relief in his eyes when they connected. She felt his fingers close around her wrists, stopping her free fall. Together they swung back and then forward again. Once he released her for the double pirouette back to her trapeze and the safety of the platform, she exhaled a long breath of pure relief.

They did it.

She felt every muscle in her body tremble with relief and pride.

Far below she saw Mr. John fairly dancing with excitement, and for that moment he was the hale and hearty showman they all knew and loved. He took on the role of ringmaster as he grabbed a mega-phone and shouted to his guests the news of what they had just witnessed. And as realization dawned, the people below applauded and whistled and stamped their feet in appreciation.

All except for Marty.

He wasn't there. She scanned the onlookers for any sign of him. She had just performed the most amazing stunt of her career, and he had missed it.

After acknowledging the applause with bows taken from their separate platforms, first Nardo then Lucy unhooked their trapezes, swung up and out, and somersaulted to the net below where Nardo helped Lucy to the ground. They took more bows as Lucy continued to search for some sign of Marty. Perhaps he had gone inside to have a better view from the second floor. Or perhaps he was across from the rest of the guests, watching from the lawn that stretched between Ca' d'Zan and another Ringling estate. Either way she had expected him to be there, to be looking at her with a mixture of pride and love along with a dash of reprimand for having not told him her plan.

Slowly the guests wandered off, making their way back inside the house, the women fanning themselves and the men running a finger around a collar that had become uncomfortably tight in the late afternoon heat. Across the expanse of netting, she saw Nardo begin to dismantle the rigging for their act. A trio of roustabouts were on hand to help. Marty always insisted that rigging, props, costumes—anything used in an act—be disassembled and packed away, ready for transport to the next performance as soon as possible. Not that they were going anywhere nor was there a need to free the space for setting up the next act. There was no next act. Still, Lucy knew that if any guest wandered out to the palazzo an hour from now, there would be no sign the performance had taken place at all.

"I'm going to change," she called out to Nardo. "See you tonight?"

He blew her a kiss. "*Ciao!*"

She walked along the circular driveway, the shortest route to a side entrance that would have her passing through the kitchen and on to the back stairs that would get her up to her room without being seen by the guests. As she approached the exterior corridor leading to the kitchen, she heard laughter, followed by muted conversation. One voice belonged to a woman.

The other belonged to her husband.

Lucy retreated to the shade of a corner outside the taproom. She felt unable to move, her body as rigid as one of Mr. John's many stone garden statues.

"Naughty boy," she heard the woman say.

There was no more talk, and a moment later Julia Gordon exited the seclusion of the outside corridor and hurried away.

Seconds later Marty strolled into the sunlight. He was lighting a cigarette and smiling.

With any other man, Lucy would have known what to do. She would have made it clear she did not condone his behavior and that she wanted nothing more to do with him. But this was Marty. This was her husband. They had taken a vow—for better or worse. He would have a business explanation. They would laugh about it later. And yet, she stayed where she was until he went back inside the house. The truth was, deep inside she was afraid that what she had just witnessed had little to do with business, and everything to do with Marty's well-known wandering eye. Once she reached her room, she sank onto the bed, her head swimming, her vision blurred.

For the last week or so she had awakened every morning barely making it to the bathroom before vomiting. She was worldly enough to understand this was a good sign that she was pregnant, but she had kept the news to herself, afraid Nardo would insist she not perform and wanting Marty to be the first to know if what she suspected was true. She'd planned to tell him later that evening as the two of them stood together on the palazzo watching the fireworks.

Marty loved children. He was like the Pied Piper, drawing even the shyest to him. A child of his own would surely be good news, would surely seal their union and be an end to any remnants of the carefree playboy he'd been.

Wouldn't it?

CHAPTER FIVE

Sarasota, July 2022

Chloe

*T*he morning after spending her second night in the guest cottage, Chloe woke to a downpour and someone pounding on the front door.

"Coming," she croaked as she reached for her robe. The clock read 8:03. *Either this place better be on fire or someone is bleeding outside my door.*

She opened the door and a bedraggled Tilda brushed past her, pulling her umbrella shut and placing it in the corner as water dripped all over the floor. "Whew! Welcome to summertime in Sarasota," she announced, her smile a bit of sunshine on the otherwise gloomy day.

Chloe shut the door and waited while Tilda removed a rain hat and her shoes. From the large plastic-coated satchel she'd set down with the umbrella, she pulled out a bag.

"Breakfast," she announced as she headed for the kitchen. "I'll warm these up while you make the coffee. They're from the little French café in Burns Court—to die for."

Make yourself at home. Chloe was usually not so grumpy, but she'd been up past two working through a series of ideas for the book—none of which seemed to work. Still, the scent of cinnamon wafting from the microwave lifted her spirits. She set to work making the coffee. "You know, Tilda, you really don't have to bring me breakfast."

Tilda reached for dishes to plate the pastries, then opened the refrigerator and began rummaging around. "Oh, don't think this will be a regular thing. I had planned to take you out. There are so many great places for breakfast in Sarasota. But when I saw the rain—and the forecast that promises to have it coming down most of the day, I figured you might be in the mood for a treat." She set the plates on the table and turned to get cloth napkins from a drawer. "How's the ankle?"

"Definitely on the mend," Chloe replied, realizing the pain reliever she'd taken before going to bed seemed to have helped. She watched as Tilda set about preparing their breakfast. "You really seem to know your way around this place," she said as Tilda opened a drawer to retrieve spoons for the coffee.

Tilda shrugged. "I stayed here for several weeks over the winter. Probably helps to know people in high places," she added with a grin.

"Your father?"

Tilda nodded. "Daddy made the arrangements for me to stay here while I found a place of my own once I moved down from New York after the holidays." Her usual cheery demeanor wavered. In fact, her eyes welled with tears as she sat down.

"Sorry. I didn't mean to pry." Chloe set a mug of coffee by each place and sat across from the younger woman.

Tilda swiped at her eyes and smiled. "It's an oft-told tale. Left at the altar—sort of. The breakup was not amicable, and I needed to get away. So, I came home to Mom and Dad. How sad is that?"

Chloe had wondered how Tilda had landed such a prestigious position at the museum. After all, her position presumed a high level of proficiency, and while Chloe liked Tilda, the young woman did appear to be on the ditzy side. Now she was fairly sure she knew. Tilda's father in his role as chairman of the board had made sure his daughter had a place to live and a meaningful job to take her mind off her troubles. "I hope my being here doesn't mean you've been put out."

"Heavens, no. I rent a little cottage near Burns Court—thus the delicious pastry." She took a bite of hers and closed her eyes in an expression of ecstasy. "Divine," she murmured.

Chloe had to agree and decided she was glad Tilda had surprised her with breakfast. She did hope this would not become a habit though. "Do you really think the rain will keep up all day?"

"Off and on. Why? Do you need to go somewhere? I can drive you."

"I have an appointment at the archives after lunch. I can certainly walk or take the cart, assuming there's an extra umbrella around."

"Front hall closet," Tilda said. She got up to refill their mugs. "Ian's also got the archives on his schedule. Did he ask you to meet him there?"

Chloe laughed. "Not exactly. Apparently, he plans to be there doing some research for his project, and I certainly need to get started on mine."

When Tilda returned to the table there was a definite change in her demeanor. She barely glanced at Chloe as she added cream and three sugars to her coffee and cradled the mug with her palms. "I realize I never...that is, I've read your mysteries, but know very little about you. Now that I think of it, your bio on your website is very brief."

"By design," Chloe replied. "There was a time earlier in my career when I was being stalked online by a fan who wanted his ideas put into the stories."

Tilda eyes widened with curiosity. "What happened?"

Chloe shrugged. "It was a mess. Eventually I was forced to shut down my social media accounts and set up very strict and limited access to my email account. Contact with readers went directly through my publisher. Still, things eventually got so bad that I was forced to move."

"That's awful. You could use that in one of your novels."

Chloe smiled. She had gotten used to people latching on to some incident and deciding it would make a good story with no clue what writing a novel really entailed. "I tend to stay away from anything autobiographical," she replied.

But that wasn't completely true. Ever since seeing the photograph of her great-grandmother, she had found her thoughts returning to the image often. The day before as she walked through the mansion with Ian, she'd thought of Lucy walking those same rooms. Or had she? It was unlikely a circus performer was included in the guest list for any party at Ca' d'Zan, no matter how famous. Of course, John Ringling was the consummate showman. Might he not have delighted in shocking his upper-crust guests by including his employees?

She put the thought aside. Frankly, her great-grandmother was beginning to seriously distract her from the project at hand—the one with the deadline bearing down on her.

She stood and began gathering the breakfast dishes. "Tilda, thank you so much for stopping by and bringing breakfast. I really need to shower and dress and get some work done before I head over to the archives."

Tilda did not get the hint. Instead, she went to the sink and began washing the dishes Chloe had set on the counter. "You go on and get dressed," she said. "I'll take care of this."

Not wanting to be rude, Chloe saw no option but to head back to her bedroom and get ready for the day. After all, Tilda was just trying to do her job. Assuming Ian had assigned her the task of babysitting the famous writer, Chloe had to give the young woman credit for being enthusiastic about her work.

She had a quick shower, pulled on the ankle support Pete had dropped off for her along with some other items Darcy had asked him to pick up at the pharmacy, and then dressed for comfort. She planned to spend the morning transcribing the notes she'd developed on her initial tour of the house before exploring whatever she could uncover in the archives. The truth was, the closest she'd gotten to a beginning for her novel was the possibility of a party. Parties or funerals were always a good start. Lots of potential suspects and victims roaming about. There had to be some record of some grand soiree the Ringlings had hosted.

Certain she would not be hosting any dinner parties, Chloe had commandeered the cottage's dining room to serve as her office. She'd set up her laptop on the table that could seat six, covering the rest of the tabletop with a rainbow of sticky notes labeling the various steps needed to write a mystery: characters, setting, clues, red herrings, etc. Setting was the only place where she had added content—the research she'd found before arriving at the museum as well as the guidebook Ian had given her.

While dressing, she'd thought of a couple more categories she needed to add to her files so went straight to the dining room to post the notes before it slipped her mind. When she rounded the corner, she found Tilda circling the table, reading the notes.

"This is how you do it?" she asked. "This is the start of a new book?"

"Well, it's one way," Chloe said.

Tilda picked up one paper—notes Chloe had made before arriving. "This isn't realistic," she said, frowning at the page. "I mean, after seeing the house yesterday, you realize there's no maze."

Chloe relieved her of the paper and set it back in its stack, all the while trying not to show her annoyance at the younger woman's intrusion. "Yes, I realized that yesterday." She stepped into the entry outside the dining room and retrieved Tilda's umbrella and hat.

"Thanks for the breakfast treat, Tilda, but I really do need to get to work. And I'm sure you have more to do than babysit me," she added. She opened the front door and waited.

"Oh, have I overstepped? I didn't mean to upset you. I'm just so excited to finally meet you, and when Ian said—"

"No worries. It's just that I do try and keep a schedule for my work. And with travel and all, that has fallen by the wayside. I really need to get back to my routine. Thanks again for stopping by, and I'll be sure to let Ian know how attentive you've been." As soon as she saw Tilda had finally put on her hat and picked up her bag, Chloe handed her the umbrella. "Thanks again," she called when Tilda finally took the hint and headed down the path.

"I'll check on you later," Tilda shouted above the rain.

Chloe waved and shut the door.

At last. Now, where was I? Oh, yes. Funeral or party?

CHAPTER SIX

Ca' d'Zan, May 1936

Lucy

*A*fter a long, luxurious bath and a nap, Lucy dressed for the evening's festivities—already well in progress given the sounds of music and chatter rising from the Grand Court and palazzo. When she was ready to make her entrance, she paused at the top of the stairway, taking a moment to observe the scene below. She had already missed the light supper guests had enjoyed, using the time to do her hair and makeup as she prepared for what might just possibly be the most important night of her life to date. She scanned the crowd. She recognized a few of the guests by name or from seeing their photograph on the society pages of the newspaper, although she did not really know any of them other than Marty and Mr. John.

And they do not know me. They have no wish to know me.

But in marrying Marty, she realized, her social standing had changed. He was a part of this world, and as his wife, she would be as well. Oh, she had little doubt acceptance would take time. But she would win them over, and it would begin with Marty's parents. Once they accepted her, the others would fall in line. Once Marty told them of the marriage, the Sutherlands would have no choice. And if she was right about a baby coming…

She made one last survey of her appearance—the beaded beige gown that skimmed her body, pooling around her ankles; the satin high heels; and the white feathered shrug that was perhaps unnecessary given the Florida heat, but was an item she could not resist adding. Her short blond curls framed her face, and she had used a subtle hand in applying her makeup. She imagined the pride with which Marty would look at her as he introduced her to his parents.

Squaring her shoulders, she descended the curved stairway. She saw Nardo in conversation with Mr. John and both men glanced up at her, their smiles wide and welcoming—spotlights that assured her she looked every bit the star she was.

"And here she is at last," Mr. John announced, his booming voice drawing the attention of others gathered near the bottom of the stairway. He stopped a passing waiter and took a glass of champagne from the tray and held it up to her in a toast, then called for everyone to raise a glass. "To Miss Lucinda Conroy, who today performed the incredible feat of not a single or double, but a *triple* backwards somersault while flying through the air. To Lucy—always a star but tonight a luminary in the world of entertainment."

He stepped closer and kissed her lightly on each cheek, while behind him the guests followed his instructions to raise their glasses and then turned back to their conversations. As Mr. John rejoined his guests, Nardo took a step toward her. He had the body of a man born to wear a tuxedo, and she was about to tease him about that when she saw Marty, and her breath caught. He wore a white dinner jacket that set off his tanned features to perfection. The man was so handsome—and he was her husband.

"Excuse me, Nardo," she murmured as she moved past him and made her way through small groups of partygoers. But her step and confidence faltered when she saw Marty lead Julia Gordon to the ballroom.

Smiling politely at congratulations offered by some she passed,

Lucy made her way to the ballroom where the musicians played a tango. A circle had formed around the couple in the center of the room—Marty and Julia—expertly performing the sensuous dance. The dance of love.

She wouldn't think of it that way. It was a show, something Marty enjoyed. How often had Mr. John teased her that Marty was a born performer and should have been a member of the cast rather than a front office man? But Lucy was sure that this, like everything Marty did for the circus, was business. The Gordons had a fortune that might be the salvation of Mr. John's financial woes. Marty was doing what needed to be done. She forced herself to take a calming breath and paste on her showtime smile as she joined the others in applauding when the dance ended.

She waited for him to notice her standing alone at the front of a crowd that had now dissolved into small groups. He looked her way briefly before walking in the opposite direction, hand in hand with Julia.

Lucy swallowed the rage that lodged in her throat as she faced the reality that her husband was deliberately ignoring her—and it had little to do with Mr. John's business. The time for her to be patient was at an end. Then she caught sight of herself in one of the large Venetian mirrors that lined one side of the room, and her heart sank.

How could she not have realized how ridiculous the fuzzy shrug looked in this weather? And the gown. How could she fail to see that most of the women at the party were dressed in the latest fashion of the season while hers was woefully out of style? There had been a time in the not so distant past when she could afford the finest—afford a gown every bit as current as those around her. But having not been paid in several weeks, there had been no funds for shopping, so with the help of the circus's wardrobe mistress she had attempted to restyle an older gown to fit the times. From a distance and under a theatrical spotlight, that might have worked, but not here. No wonder Marty had turned away. She was an embarrassment to him.

As tears welled, she wanted only to make her escape. But as she hurried back toward the stairway, Nardo stopped her. He smiled uncertainly. "I believe I was promised—" He frowned with concern. "What is it Lucinda? Are you unwell?" Without waiting for an answer, he escorted her to a chair near the front door to the grand house—a place where she would be away from the other guests. "You need water," he announced as he flagged a passing waiter. "Rico, bring Miss Lucinda some water."

"I have club soda here," Rico replied. He handed Nardo a crystal glass filled with the bubbly liquid and ice cubes then hovered for a moment while Lucy sipped the drink.

"Thank you, Rico," she said handing him the glass. "I expect it's the excitement of the day," she assured both men.

Rico nodded and went back to serving the guests, but Nardo was not so easily fooled. "You have tears," he said, offering her his handkerchief. "Something has upset you."

"I'm fine, Nardo. It's been an exciting day and I think I just became overly emotional."

"I am getting Martin," Nardo announced before striding away.

Lucy leapt to her feet to stop him, but a wave of dizziness overcame her, and as she grasped for a hold on the wall, everything went black.

When she regained consciousness, she was no longer in the same place. Instead, she was in her guest room on the bed. From across the room she heard whispers. She forced her eyes open and saw Marty and another man huddled together, their backs to her. The low volume of their exchange did nothing to conceal the fact that Marty was upset.

So, he cares after all.

She smiled and allowed her eyes to drift shut.

"You're certain?" She heard the urgency in her husband's voice.

"I cannot be without a complete examination, but I have been at this for a long time, young man, and I feel confident in telling you that Miss Conroy is with child."

Lucy's eyes flew open. Surely, she had not heard that correctly. Surely, she had drifted back into the haze of before and dreamed it. This was not how she had wanted Marty to hear this news.

"Marty?" Her voice was dry and raspy. She pushed herself to a sitting position against the multiple pillows and hand-painted headboard. "What's happening?"

He glanced her way, then said something more to the doctor, who left the room. As he came to her side, his smile looked forced.

"There's my girl," he said, taking her hand as he sat on the side of the bed. "You gave us all a scare."

"What happened?"

"You fainted, darling. Nardo carried you up here to your room, and fortunately, Dr. Rosen was a guest tonight. Apparently a little too much excitement for you today, and if I know you at all, you failed to eat anything."

"I heard him say I might be pregnant."

Marty stood and walked to the window. "That's not possible," he said.

Lucy laughed. "Of course it is, darling. Have you completely forgotten our wedding night? This is wonderful news. Now, when you tell your parents about our marriage plus a grandchild on the way, they will have to embrace our union." She swung her legs over the side of the bed and walked to where he stood, embracing him from behind, her cheek against his back.

His body stiffened, and she released him, stepping around to face him. "What is it?"

He stared at her as if he had no idea who she was.

"Marty?" Cupping his face with her palms, she stood on tiptoe to kiss him. "I know it's a surprise, but it's such wonderful news."

He stroked her cheek with the backs of his fingers. "I have to speak with Father. Perhaps you should lie down. You've had quite a shock."

"I fainted," she said with a nervous laugh. "It's hardly life-threatening. We should go together to speak with your parents."

"No!"

She took a step back, surprised at his tone. But then he smiled and reached for her, enfolding her in his arms and chuckling. "Perhaps I'm the one who has had a shock, dearest. Let me handle this. In the meantime, Mr. John is leaving tonight for New York, and I need to see him off. You get some rest, and I'll see you first thing in the morning."

Following him out to the mezzanine, she realized the party below was breaking up. Mr. John boomed his farewells to departing guests. Those staying in the mansion, including Marty's parents, would soon return to their rooms. She understood Marty would be expected to accompany Mr. John to the depot and that by the time he returned his parents would be asleep. With a sigh of resignation, she kissed Marty's cheek and returned to her room.

Tomorrow, she thought happily. The day when they could be open about their love, their marriage, and—if the doctor was right—their coming baby.

But it was not Marty who sat at the table the following morning when Lucy entered the smaller dining room used for more informal meals. Instead, Mr. Sutherland was just finishing a cup of coffee. He glanced at her and cleared his throat. "We need to talk," he said, indicating a chair without rising to assist her as he would for his wife or any other woman of their social standing.

"Where is Marty?"

"That is hardly your concern."

Lucy felt her stomach lurch, and knew she needed to eat something to stave off the morning sickness she now had a confirmed reason to expect. But she stood her ground. She was tired of hiding, of pretending, of sneaking around.

"I was hoping to have breakfast with my husband," she said. Enough was enough. If Marty had not yet given his parents their news, then she would.

Marty's father barely looked up from his newspaper as he expelled a mirthless laugh. "You would need to have a husband for that to be possible."

Fighting to maintain her calm, Lucy turned to the sideboard and poured herself a glass of orange juice. She had barely taken the first sip when Mr. Sutherland was suddenly behind her. "I don't know who you think you are, but I will not allow you to spread false rumors about my family. And to answer your question, Martin has gone to the beach with Miss Gordon. I expect he might have selected that as a romantic setting for his proposal."

The crystal glass slipped from her fingers and shattered on the floor.

Mr. Sutherland uttered an oath and rang a small bell to call one of the staff. "Clean up this mess," he ordered when Mr. Jefferson appeared. Then Marty's father took hold of Lucy's upper arm and steered her toward the door that led outside. "Miss Conroy and I will be in the rose garden."

She thought of resisting, of insisting she would not have this conversation without Marty, but the man's imperious manner infuriated her. She had far too much pride to make a scene. Still, she refused to be cowed by him.

He set a brisk pace—one she matched step for step after jerking her arm free of his grip. Neither spoke until they reached Mable Ringling's renowned rose garden. In the silence of that walk Lucy tried to plan her strategy for winning over this man who was her father-in-law. She tried to think what someone like Julia Gordon might say to quell his doubts. Of course, someone like Julia would never find herself in this situation. Any parent would be delighted to have her as a daughter-in-law.

As they entered the garden, she realized Marty's father was speaking.

"...prepared to offer a substantial stipend."

She said the first thing that popped to mind. "No amount of money will change the fact that Marty and I are married and have a child on the way."

Mr. Sutherland stopped and faced her. He arched an eyebrow. "And do you have some documentation to prove this so-called marriage to Martin?" When she opened her mouth to reply, he held up a finger to silence her. "Because my son tells me you do not."

She wanted to challenge this as a bluff, but deep down she felt a niggling doubt. Like a silent film, the events of the night she and Marty had eloped flickered through her brain. Had she signed a paper? Surely, she had forgotten in the thrill of the ceremony. Marty had driven her to the home of a friend he'd introduced as "the honorable Edgar Benson." They'd stood in front of the portrait of an older man dressed in the robes of a judge, and Edgar had said the familiar words...

Take this man...
Sickness and in health...
For better or for worse...
Till death do you part...

It all flashed through her mind in an instant as fear bubbled up into her throat that somehow Marty had duped her just to finally get her into his bed. It had just been the three of them. There had been no ring, no flowers, no music. They'd spent their wedding night in the hotel of a neighboring town. And the following day, after dropping her back at the circus grounds in Sarasota, Marty had left on his weeks-long business trip.

She was going to be sick.

Lucy pressed her fist to her mouth and turned away, looking around for a place she might discharge the contents of her stomach without defiling Mrs. Ringling's garden. Suddenly she felt an arm supporting her and leading her to a concrete bench.

"Come sit down," she heard Mr. Sutherland say, his tone kinder than it had been. "You are hardly the first young woman my son has deceived, although admittedly he has never before gone to the point of faking a marriage."

He waited a moment, allowing her time to overcome her nausea, and then he reached inside his coat and produced a vellum envelope. "I believe this will ease the disappointment you are experiencing, Miss Conroy."

Why did he insist on addressing her that way? She was Lucinda Sutherland, Mrs. Martin Sutherland. Marty loved her.

But then she recalled his reaction to the news of the expected baby. At the time she'd chalked it all up to shock and surprise. But now, remembering how he had practically run from the room, she saw his face and the expression of being trapped he'd shown as he hurried away.

She sat, her hands clenched in her lap.

Marty's father stood over her and continued to offer the envelope. "Of course, it goes without saying that Mrs. Sutherland and I will need your assurance that there will be no discussion of this unfortunate matter with anyone—ever. Do we understand one another?"

Lucy clasped her hands together to stop them from shaking as she stood and faced the man. "Your son is the father of the child I am carrying. Married or not, that is not something he can simply wish away."

Marty's father laughed. "I will give you your due, Miss Conroy. You have nerve. If you are indeed with child, I suspect the father could be any one of your admirers. It might even be my son, but once again you have no proof." He moved a step closer. "And I warn you, if you try to create a scandal or come around seeking more payment for your silence, I will personally make sure your life is ruined." He held up the envelope once again.

She ignored it. Let the man and his son wonder what she would do next. Let them be the ones who lived with the possibility that she might reveal her secret. She relaxed and gave Marty's father the smile she reserved for her most ardent fans. Then she looked at the slender wristwatch Marty had given her. "I am afraid I really must go, Mr. Sutherland. I promised the reporter from the *Herald* an interview."

CHAPTER SEVEN

Sarasota, July 2022

CHLOE

The museum's archives, as well as the routine for accessing those materials, were like other collections Chloe had used for research throughout her career. Upon arrival she was asked to store all her personal belongings in a locker. She was permitted to keep her laptop and cell phone and a notebook and writing instruments with her. Next a staff member stood by while she completed a registration form and then reviewed with her the museum's policies for making use of the materials. Her assigned staffer was a short, chubby young man with cherubic cheeks, a ready smile, and a mop of thick blond hair he kept pushing away from his forehead. He'd introduced himself as Toby Jensen, and Chloe liked him immediately.

"You can wash your hands here," Toby said, leading the way to the back of the reading room—the only room she would be allowed to occupy while Toby brought her whatever materials she requested. "Feel free to take a break for coffee, tea, or water. Just be sure you consume any beverage back here."

"Got it," Chloe said as she dried her hands. "What's next?"

Toby led the way to a table where she'd left her laptop and other essentials. He added the usual supplies necessary for examining irreplaceable documents, photographs, and books: white cotton gloves to avoid leaving fingerprints and body oils; squares of Mylar for gently lifting and turning pages; and, specifically for books, foam supports to prevent damage to the binding as well as weights to hold the book open. The reading room also held files and books about the circus and Wild West shows as well as a card catalog for searching out articles and publications about specific topics—performers and other circus companies.

Toby pointed to a pair of silver doors at one end of the room. "Through there we have our processing room and the vault—closed stacks that I'm afraid are off limits for you."

"But not for you?"

Toby gave her a shy smile. "No, ma'am, not for me."

No, ma'am? She suddenly felt older than her thirty years.

"So, where would you like to start?" Toby asked, his excitement to get going on this new project evident in his eager smile.

Chloe had made an extensive list of questions she wanted to explore—questions about the Ringlings and about the mansion itself. Ignoring the list, she asked, "As a start, could you see what you can find about Lucinda Conroy? She was a trapeze artist in the early to midthirties with the Ringling show."

"I'll see what I can find," Toby said and hurried away.

Having failed to charge her laptop the night before, she looked around for an outlet and found the nearest possibility was positioned under a small table next to a cabinet not easily reached from the close quarters. Chloe's reach was too short to connect the plug, so she got down on her knees and crawled under the table.

"Here, let me do that," a male voice offered.

She glanced back over her shoulder and followed a pair of long legs up to see Ian. "I've got it, thanks." She jammed the plug into the outlet and pushed herself out from under the table before awkwardly getting to her feet. She felt the heat of her flushed face and the need to catch her breath. She told herself it was not embarrassment, just the effort it had taken to complete the task. She felt sticky in spite of the air-conditioning. It occurred to her that Dr. Ian Flanner had a penchant for seeing her at less than her best.

Ian made no move to get back to whatever had brought him to the archives. Instead, he handed her a folder thick with articles and labeled *Lillian Leitzel*. "Given your connection to Lucinda Conroy, you might find this of interest," he said.

"I'm writing fiction, not biography," she reminded him.

He shrugged. "Lillian was the headline act until she died from a fall she suffered in Denmark. That's when Lucinda Conroy became the star of the show."

"Toby is looking—"

"I doubt he'll find much about your relative. I just thought there might be some reference to her in Lillian's file."

Her fingers itched to examine the file. Maybe there was something inside that would answer questions she had about her great-grandmother. It seemed unlikely, but experience had taught her there were often surprises to be found in the oddest places. On the other hand, she had a deadline for writing her next novel. She certainly didn't have time to take a deep dive into research about Lucy Conroy. "I'll look through it," she said. "Thank you."

"Well, I'll leave you to it." He gave a wave of acknowledgment to someone coming from the vault area. "Looks like they've found the blueprints I need."

He made his way to another table closer to the vault, and she watched as he spread out the blueprints and bent over them. He jotted a note on a small notepad, then nodded to his assigned librarian, who carefully rolled up the blueprints and carried them back to the vault.

"Happy hunting, Ms. Whitfield," he said as he passed her. He was smiling, so evidently he'd found whatever it was he needed.

He did have a nice smile.

The hours flew by as Chloe became more engrossed in the story of Lillian Leitzel than she'd intended. Lillian came from a circus family. Her mother was a trapeze artist and an uncle had performed as a clown. Lillian and her two sisters performed in companies around the world, and she became known for her aerial act where she spun like a propeller fifty or sixty feet above the audience while holding on to a rope with one hand. It was while performing that act that she fell to her eventual death. She was only thirty-nine.

Moved by the sadness of Lillian's story, Chloe pushed aside the folder Ian had handed her and slowly worked her way through the box of materials Toby had brought her.

"I'm having a little trouble locating the Conroy file," he'd said. "I thought you could get started on these." The box he placed on the table was labeled *Ca' d'Zan*, and it was a treasure trove of photographs and articles about the history of the grand house. Whenever any item or detail caught her attention, she took copious notes, even going so far as to make rudimentary sketches of the details in the photo. As soon as she finished one box, Toby was there with the next—and continued apologies for not yet finding the file she'd originally requested.

"This is more than I can get through today, Toby," she assured him.

"I'll keep looking," he promised.

She was vaguely aware that it had rained off and on throughout the afternoon, and that the single other patron arriving since Ian left had come and gone. As she arched her aching back, she realized she and Toby were the only two people still in the room—even the rest of the staff had gone. "Is it closing time?" she asked, glancing at a wall clock. "It's after five. I had no idea. You should have let me know."

Toby grinned. "I got a kick out of seeing how engrossed you were." He collected the last of the materials, including the folder

Ian had given her. "Lillian Leitzel was quite something. Definitely a prima donna, but also someone who connected with her audiences. The Ringlings paid her a fortune for that time—$250 a week. She had a maid and a butler and traveled in her own private train car."

Chloe wondered if her great-grandmother had ever achieved that level of star power and thought of asking what the file on Lucy Conroy might contain once found. But she decided she had kept him long enough. Besides, wasn't she the one who had determined her latest novel was not about Lucy Conroy—or any actual person for that matter? Bio-fiction was not her brand. She wrote cozy mysteries in the vein of Agatha Christie. And with a deadline fast approaching, she could not afford to get distracted. She thanked Toby for all his help and gathered her things.

"I scheduled you for every afternoon over the next couple of weeks," Toby told her. "You can keep the appointments or not. Just wanted to make sure you were on the calendar."

"How kind of you," Chloe replied. "I'll definitely be back tomorrow."

"And I'll keep looking for that file you need. Have a good evening."

The rain had stopped, leaving everything a tropical wonderland and the grounds of the museum bathed in a late afternoon summer light. The word *muggy* took on new meaning as Chloe followed the winding paths from the building that held the archives to the guesthouse. The distance was not that great, but she was still in desperate need of a shower once she arrived. The cottage had collected the heat of the day despite the ceiling fans left running. Once inside, Chloe dropped her satchel on the desk, turned on the window air conditioner in the bedroom, and headed straight for the bathroom where she turned on the water and peeled off her sticky clothes, leaving them on the floor while she sought the refreshing coolness of the shower. After toweling off and blow-drying her hair, she wrapped herself in the oversized cotton bathrobe provided for those staying in the cottage and padded barefoot into her bedroom.

And that's when she heard the front door click shut.

"Hello?" she called, clutching her robe closed as she went to the front of the cottage. She glanced out the window. It was twilight, and the shadows were more prominent than the light, but she saw no sign of movement. Perhaps she'd been foolish to think there was no need to lock doors when she was staying in the middle of a multiacre museum campus. She turned the dead bolt on the front door and walked to the kitchen where she switched on the light and discovered a bag of takeout food on the counter—a bag that she was sure had not been there when she got home no matter how anxious she'd been to get in the shower. Besides, the contents were still warm.

Tilda?

There was no note. Why wouldn't Tilda stay around? Why sneak in and out? Maybe when Tilda heard the shower, she was embarrassed and didn't want to intrude? But then why not just take the food and come back after a decent interval? Chloe could not deny the younger woman was dedicated to her job, but perhaps a little too dedicated?

Certain Tilda had taken her earlier dismissal to heart, Chloe decided she would talk to her over-eager assistant and set some ground rules. She had far more important tasks for Tilda than grocery shopping. She would go to the grocery store first thing in the morning and stock up so she could assure Tilda there was no need to keep bringing her meals.

And she would lock the door.

The following morning Chloe drove her borrowed golf cart to the parking lot where Pete had told her he'd moved her car. Even though her ankle had healed enough that she could certainly walk, she'd decided the cart made more sense. She couldn't drive the car close to the cottage, and since the temperature promised to rise above ninety by midmorning, she wanted to have some way to transport her groceries from car to cottage as quickly as possible. She parked the golf cart in the shade of a large live oak tree and unlocked her car. The accumulated heat of the last day or so rushed out as soon as she opened the door, so the first order of business was to put the top down. She had never been a fan of air-conditioning, although she understood in this heat, that might change.

She was just leaving the parking lot when she saw Ian drive in. He slowed his vintage beach Jeep as he came alongside her.

"Good morning," he said. "You're out early."

"Going to stock up on food and other necessities," she replied.

He frowned. "Tilda can—"

"Actually, I prefer to do my own shopping rather than try and make a list." She thought of mentioning her concern that Tilda might be overdoing her babysitting role but decided Ian might reprimand his assistant. "Besides, Tilda must have a great many other duties beyond catering to me. I mean, she had a job before I arrived, didn't she?"

To her surprise, he ducked his head to hide a grin.

"What?" she asked.

"I have a confession to make, Chloe."

"A confession?"

He nodded. "Truth is she'd started to drive me nuts just about the time I got the notice you were coming. Truth is I thought you might be the answer to my problem. Tilda's zealous nature can be a bit—"

"What on earth were your instructions to the poor woman?"

He looked up at the sky, avoiding eye contact with her. "Stick close. Meet and even anticipate your every need. I told her you were her full-time assignment for the duration of your stay. I'm surprised she's not with you now."

Chloe couldn't help it. She burst out laughing. "I snuck out early to avoid having her come along," she admitted. "I'm used to taking care of myself, and, well, I was already beginning to feel a little claustrophobic."

"I'll tell her to back off," he offered.

"No, don't do that. She's just doing the job you gave her. I'll talk to her. I can certainly give her some research to do for me."

"Speaking of which, did you find what you needed yesterday?"

"It was a start. I suppose writing a mystery novel must seem so much simpler than restoring a national landmark."

"I suspect you enjoy your work as much as I do mine, Chloe. And by the way, I feel guilty that I pretty much rushed through the tour. I expect you'd like to spend more time in certain parts of the mansion. If you're free late this afternoon, I could ask Tilda—"

"I do have more questions, and frankly I'd rather do that with you," she said. When he frowned, she hurried to add, "This is research vital to getting my story details accurate, and I promise to respect your time." She shifted the car into gear. "See you at four?" She drove away, waving as she went, and heard him shout, "Five."

Downtown Sarasota was a throwback to earlier times, the buildings firmly entrenched in the early-to mid-part of the last century. Main Street was nearly deserted, the heat rising off sidewalks that had been hosed down in preparation for shops and restaurants to open. She navigated one of the town's many roundabouts and then turned left on Lemon, delighting in the street names that heralded the state's reputation for citrus. She easily found street parking outside a chain grocery store that she knew would have everything she needed. Inside she made quick work of touring the outer edges, stocking up on fruits and veggies, a couple of chunks of cheese, a dozen eggs, multigrain bread from the bakery as well as freshly ground almond butter and coffee. She even treated herself to an orchid plant that would last a lot longer than any bouquet of fresh flowers and grabbed a couple of reusable bags the checkout clerk could use to pack everything. She was in and out of the place in under an hour, leaving almost the entire day to work on her novel.

Pleased with herself, she loaded the bags of groceries in the car and drove past the library with its pineapple-shaped columns, a small park, and the opera house on her way back to the thorough-fare that ran along Sarasota Bay and on to the Ringling estate. She decided she liked this town and found herself wondering if her great-grandmother had ever attended a performance at the opera house or browsed through shops on Main Street. And once she'd conjured the image of the young woman she'd seen in the photo-graph out for a night on the town, she had trouble bringing her thoughts back to the novel she'd contracted to deliver.

"That storyline is a mess," she muttered aloud, glancing at the empty passenger seat as if she expected God to be sitting next to her. "Every idea—every word I've managed to write—is like a do-over of books I've written before. I need some help here. I mean, I know You have other things—far more important things, but if You could just give me a nudge…"

Never had she struggled as much as she was now with trying to find a unique direction for a book. The few pages she'd written were like pages she'd crafted dozens of times before—the characters stale and predictable, the plot derivative. Her last few books had not sold well, and her editor had urged her to come up with something completely different—something fresh—for this one. The trouble was she was out of new ideas, and the fact that she seemed to be more focused on Lucinda Conroy than she was on her work wasn't helping. "I really need this new book to come together, God, so if it wouldn't be too much trouble?"

She made the rest of the drive in silence and had transported and unpacked the groceries before she realized there was only one solution. She needed to spend the next few days finding out everything she could about her great-grandmother so she could put that mystery to bed once and for all. Only then would her mind be clear enough to come up with a plot for her new novel.

"Thanks," she whispered with a glance heavenward. With a plan for moving forward, Chloe made herself lunch and then set out for a second day at the archives. When she arrived, Toby was fairly dancing with excitement.

"I was thinking about your great-grandmother last night, and I thought perhaps there might be something more about her in the files related to the seasons she performed."

"You found something," Chloe guessed—not exactly a stretch given his obvious euphoria.

"Yes. There was a party," he continued as he led her to the table where he'd placed the discovered materials. "It was held right here on the grounds to celebrate John Ringling's seventieth birthday, and the entertainment was none other than Lucinda Conroy. She completed a triple somersault in midair for the occasion—first time for a Ringling performer, male or female." He laid a newspaper article on the table and handed Chloe a pair of white gloves.

Chloe set down her laptop and other supplies, pulled on the gloves, and leaned over the table to read the article. The review of her great-grandmother's performance was glowing. John Ringling was reported to have been nearly brought to tears by the accomplishment, and he certainly was not at a loss for words.

Our darling Lucinda…a feat of such thrilling beauty and danger…a moment never to be forgotten.…

And given as he was to hyperbole, Ringling liberally used terms such as *first time in the history of the circus and trapeze,* even though the article noted that a performer from a rival circus had completed the triple some months before.

Toby's delight was contagious, and Chloe found herself wanting more. "There must be other reports about the party if not the performance, and perhaps photographs?"

Toby's smile faltered. "Nothing more, I'm afraid. I looked through all the program notes for that season and the two that followed, and Lucinda Conroy's name never appears—as in, anywhere, and certainly not as a featured performer. It's as if she performed the triple and disappeared." His shoulders slumped. "It's a mystery."

My mystery. In that moment Chloe accepted that her struggle to find a direction for her latest novel was over—at least fictionally, she would solve the mystery of Lucinda Conroy. If her editor was clamoring for something "fresh," here it was. She put aside any notion the story was too personal or that she had come here with no intention of writing about her family. The complete disappearance of her great-grandmother following what had to be the performance of a lifetime was far too enticing to ignore.

"Toby, could you see what you can find about a guest list for the party and who Lucy was working with in her act? There had to be a catcher. Who was he and what happened to him?"

Toby nodded and hurried off to the vault.

Meanwhile Chloe pulled out a chair and opened her laptop. She'd taken care to charge it the night before and felt more ready to get started on writing her next novel than she had since the day she'd first arrived.

Lucinda Conroy—flying high…and then?

Start with the party.

CHAPTER EIGHT

Ca' d'Zan, May 1936

LUCY

*W*ithout the presence of Mr. John and with most evidence of there having been a party removed, the house and surrounding estate felt a bit like a ghost town. Lucy stayed in her room, eschewing the large rooms of the mansion and the expansive grounds, to avoid the Sutherlands and the Gordons. Following her conversation with Marty's father, she had watched for her husband's return, her anger building with every passing hour. From her window, she saw the circus people hired for the party leave and Mr. Jefferson directing vendors who had come to remove extra tables and seating rented for the lavish weekend.

But there was no sign of Marty—or his car.

So the fact that he went off with Julia Gordon had probably not been a lie. But the idea that he planned to marry the socialite? If Lucy knew Marty at all…

But she didn't know him—not really. Theirs had been a whirlwind romance, driven mainly by a physical attraction they were incapable of denying. Their first kiss had kindled a passion neither could extinguish. The need for secrecy had added to the thrill of their affair as had the stolen moments they had shared during the winter tour. And the only thing that came even close to the thrill she felt when flying through the air was the thrill she'd felt when Marty finally made love to her the night they were married.

Or were they?

The seeds of doubt Marty's father had planted took root as Lucy paced the confines of the guest room.

A light knock on her door startled her, and her first move was to the window to see if somehow, she might have missed hearing Marty's car. But the drive was empty.

"Yes?"

"Lucinda?"

Bernardo.

Fluffing her hair and biting her lips to bring color, she opened the door with a flourish and a smile. "Good morning! I thought perhaps you'd left already."

Nardo remained standing in the hall. He was a man of strict proprieties—one who would never consider entering a lady's bedroom uninvited.

"You are feeling better?" He studied her closely.

"Yes, much." She grabbed a wide-brimmed straw hat and stepped into the corridor, closing the door behind her. "I was just thinking of taking a walk around the grounds."

Nardo hesitated, then followed her along the mezzanine to the stairs. "I will accompany you, Lucinda. We need to talk about what happened last night. And about Martin."

He knows. Maybe not the whole of it, but he knows something is wrong.

"Nardo, I need—"

"A friend, someone who truly cares," he said. "We have always confided in one another."

It was true. Theirs had been more than a professional partnership. Nardo was like an older brother. She had never doubted his devotion. "All right," she agreed. "Walk with me."

They left by the side door in the solarium. She caught a glimpse of Marty's mother and Mrs. Gordon sunning themselves by the pool and quickened her step. Nardo took her hand and guided her along the bayfront across the lawn that ran between Mr. John's house and the home of his late brother Charles. The evening before she had heard someone comment about the absence of Charles's widow, Edith, from the party. It was the kind of sniping she knew some people could not resist. Everyone knew of the estrangement between Mr. John and his sister-in-law.

"We should not trespass, Nardo."

He shrugged. "The house of Mr. Charles is vacant. His wife and daughter are visiting friends on the other coast." He led the way to a shaded portico and a carved concrete bench. He waited for her to sit, then took his place beside her. "Will you tell me what has happened?"

"Nothing has happened."

Nardo sighed. "Yesterday you had eyes only for Martin, but his attention was only on Miss Gordon."

"It was business. Miss Gordon's parents are potential investors. Marty's job is—"

Suddenly Nardo was standing—pacing. "How can you think so little of me, Lucinda? I am trying to help you. This morning a note was placed under my door." He removed a folded sheet of stationery from his pocket. "This note."

He handed it to her, and she recognized Marty's handwriting immediately. She felt her breath catch as she unfolded the paper and read:

Nardo, Change of plans. Effective immediately, you will join the Ferrano Brothers in their act. Miss Conroy will not be making the tour. Martin Sutherland, Manager

Lucy slowly refolded the note and handed it back to Nardo. This was a detail she had failed to consider. Assigning Nardo to the

Ferrano Brothers was a huge step down for her friend and partner. At best he would fill in when one of the brothers fell ill or was injured. She had to make this right, first by explaining it to Nardo and then by talking to Marty. She patted the place beside her, inviting Nardo to sit. "Please," she pleaded when he seemed ready to resist.

He did as she asked, his forearms resting on his knees as he stared out toward the bay.

"Marty and I are married, Nardo, and we are expecting our first child." Whatever Mr. Sutherland had said to her, she would never believe him. She had considered the matter from every angle, and of course he would say anything if he thought it would drive a wedge between them—even hint that Marty was off proposing to Julia Gordon.

"You dared the triple knowing you carry a child?"

"I didn't *know* then. It was only after I fainted last evening, and the doctor examined me—"

"But once you knew, you had to realize I would…that we would no longer be partners." Nardo was assembling the facts in the only way he could understand them.

She covered his hand with hers. "No. I mean, I didn't think. It's all happened so fast, and Marty said nothing about changing your position in the company."

Nardo's smile was cynical. "What did you think he would do? I can hardly continue our act alone."

"I didn't…I wasn't…"

"Do I mean so little to you, Lucinda?" His voice was low, and he did not look at her.

The sudden fear that she might lose the one friend she had always been able to count on brought Lucy off the bench and onto her knees in the grass next to him. "Look at me," she said. "You are my dearest friend. I would never knowingly cause you distress, and yet I see that in being so caught up in the secrets Marty and I have kept, I have done just that. I will speak to Marty—remind him that the triple could not have been performed without you, remind him that—"

Nardo stood and drew Lucy to her feet, then wrapped his arms around her. "I can take care of myself, Lucinda. What I need to know is that you have found with Marty the life you want."

His caring had always allowed her to drop the mask of performer and acknowledge her deepest fears. "I thought it would all work out. I thought Marty would return this weekend and tell his parents of our marriage. And once I realized I was expecting…"

"And yet if he knows he is to become a father, where is he?" Once again Nardo's voice shook with anger. "Why is he not at your side? His wife and the mother of his child?"

His outrage fueled her own annoyance at Marty's absence. Why wasn't he here to help her face his parents? Why did she continue to make excuses for him? Never before had she permitted any man to treat her this way. Why Marty? Because his kisses held the promise of a future beyond the circus? Because that had been a worry of hers for the last two seasons? She could not fly through the air forever. She knew of other performers—all female—who had set their caps for some wealthy patron.

"Security trumps love," one friend had told her when Lucy bemoaned the fact that her friend was about to marry a man twenty years her senior. Love had had no part in their plan.

Her relationship with Marty was nothing like that. She loved him—and he said he loved her. How many times had he declared himself as he covered her face, neck, and bare shoulders with his kisses, always pleading for more. But she had understood from the beginning that if their union was to have any chance of succeeding, they must be properly wed before she could grant him that wish. He was so close to his mother and intimidated by his father, always trying to prove himself to the man.

She thought back to her earlier confrontation with Mr.

Sutherland. Hadn't Marty once told her his father would do whatever he found necessary to achieve his purpose? He had chosen a time when Marty was not around to speak with her—to try and intimidate her the way he did his son. Why should she believe anything he said? She needed to talk to Marty, and they needed to go together to face his parents.

She felt tears settling on her cheeks and brushed them away. Nardo offered her his handkerchief.

"I do not mean to cause you more distress, Lucinda. Please do not cry."

"I need to talk to Marty. Together we will make things right again." She kissed Nardo's cheek. "Thank you, dear Nardo. You have made me see what I need to do."

Before he could say more or stop her, she hurried away, back toward the house belonging to Mr. John. She would find Marty. They would devise a plan, and together…

But as she neared the house, she saw Marty's roadster coming up the drive. He navigated the lane with one hand on the steering wheel and the other draped around Julia Gordon, who rested her head on his shoulder. As he pulled the car to a stop, he tenderly kissed her forehead, rousing her. She touched his cheek, then sat up and checked her hair and makeup in the rearview mirror, reapplying lipstick—as Lucy had so often done after being with Marty.

Frozen by the scene she was witnessing and trying to fight the tumble of emotions that raced through her in that instant, she did not hear Nardo come alongside her until he spoke.

"He has known her since childhood. The families are friends."

Business…business…business…

Like a buzzing mosquito she heard Marty's voice—his excuse. But this was not business. This was betrayal.

CHAPTER NINE

Sarasota, July 2022

Chloe

*W*hen Chloe arrived at the mansion and met Ian in the great room beneath the mezzanine, she regretted pressing him to be her guide. If her day had been filled with discovery and answered prayers, clearly his had not. He looked stressed and exhausted. "I won't take much of your time," she promised. "I just want to double-check a few details."

He shrugged. "No worries. What rooms did you want to revisit?"

She consulted the list she'd made—the list she now thought was far too long. What were the essentials she needed to get the story started? "Uh, well…"

He took the notebook from her and studied her notes. "Guest room?"

"Yes. I'm thinking my protagonist would spend the night here, attending a party. Where would she stay?"

He pointed up. "One of the rooms up there—maybe the pink room." He led the way to the stairs, hesitated, and then turned to the elevator.

"I can do the stairs," she said, and started up ahead of him to prove her point. Once they reached the next level, she stepped aside to allow him to lead the way to a bedroom down the corridor from the room he'd previously shown her where Mrs. Ringling's personal guests stayed.

"It's in need of some refurbishing," he said as he opened the door. "But then, it's been twenty years since the major renovation, and every room is in need of something."

"May I take pictures?" She held up her phone. "Sometimes sketches aren't enough."

"Okay. No flash though."

"There's still plenty of light," she assured him before snapping pictures of each item of furniture—a sleigh bed embellished with brass decorations in need of a good polishing, a dressing table missing its chair, a three-paneled gilded dressing screen upholstered in rose brocade that had faded in places, and an oddly masculine marble-topped cabinet flanked by two straight-backed chairs. The walls and draperies were a pale, almost peach-colored, pink, and the wooden floor was bare of any rug.

Ian leaned against the open door, watching her. "So, will this be the scene of the crime?" He was still holding her notebook, open to her list of questions.

"Perhaps." She moved to the window and, with a glance at Ian for permission, opened the blinds. She calculated the room was above the solarium and overlooked the swimming pool and what had once been the drive up to the house. She took a few photos and then carefully closed the blinds. Turning, she stood for a moment, envisioning her great-grandmother seated at the dressing table and then slipping behind the screen for a quick change of clothes.

"There's a bathroom," Ian said, crossing the room. He opened another door. "Each guest room had one, and Mable made sure they were decorated to complement the bedroom. She was unbelievably detailed in her plans for the house. No room escaped her attention."

Chloe took more pictures then returned to the bedroom and glanced around once more.

"Where next?" Ian asked, glancing at her list. "The vault?"

"Yes, if possible. We only walked past it the other day. I'd like to see it."

"This time we're taking the elevator," he said.

She wondered if that might be more for his sake than hers.

The space was tight inside the cage, giving her a chance to study Ian Flanner. There were shadows under his deep-set blue eyes and lines of worry or stress furrowed his brow. His mind seemed to be anywhere but with her or her project, and she felt guilty to have kept him past the end of what had obviously been a long day of work.

"Is my mascara running?" he joked, meeting her gaze.

"Not at all," she replied, smiling. "Is mine?"

"Hm-m-m." He pretended to examine her closely. "Hard to say in this light."

"Not hard at all," she replied as the elevator reached its stop with a slight jerk that caused her to bump against him. "I don't wear mascara."

He reached around her to pull back the cage door and hold it while she stepped out. "And," she added, "neither presumably do you, so how do you explain the dark circles under your eyes?"

"Long days and sleepless nights where the body's willing but the brain refuses to shut down. I imagine you might know a little something about that? Working under pressure?"

She thought about the hours she'd spent trying to plot this novel. She'd been up and down throughout last night, pacing the small rooms of the cottage and downing a pint of Ben and Jerry's in the process. "Deadlines are a beast to be reckoned with," she admitted. "Look, I wasn't thinking. Just give me a tour of the vault and let's both call it a day. I imagine you'd like to get home and have a nice meal and relax a bit."

He glanced at the list in her notebook. "Or we could see the vault and then—since we're both going to need something to eat—share a meal while I see if I can answer some of these questions for you."

"I stocked up on groceries earlier. Why don't you come to the guesthouse?" Was she seriously inviting him to dinner? "I mean, if that would work for you. All my research is there, spread out on the dining room table, and some of the questions I have relate to what I found at the archives."

"Sounds like a plan." He turned toward the entrance to the vault. "Probably the coolest thing about this is the extra door that hid the actual entrance. Ringling had it installed because this is where he stored his liquor during Prohibition, and just in case the Feds came calling…"

"I love that!" Chloe took a couple of photos, but the vault had no windows, so the lighting was not good. She slipped her phone into her pocket and, taking her notebook from Ian, began sketching details. "What else did they keep here?"

"Household items of value. Remember, they only used the house during the winter. The rest of the year they were either traveling or on tour or in New York dealing with their other investments. Railroads, oil…"

"Did anything ever go missing?"

"Not that I've heard, but then, my focus has been on the building itself. Even with the incredible restoration that was completed in 2002, a house this age and size? There's always something going haywire."

She glanced around once more. "I've got what I need for now. Thank you for being so patient. Shall we go?"

They walked down the wide curved stairway and out through the kitchen and visitor area together. Outside the sun was still bright, and the heat was like a moist towel thrown over Chloe's shoulders.

"I need to collect some paperwork from the work site and make sure everything here is locked up," Ian said. "See you in say, half an hour?"

"Perfect," Chloe replied, wondering as she walked down the path back to the guesthouse if half an hour gave her time to shower before she started dinner.

As it turned out she needn't have worried. She was just clearing the dining room table of her paperwork when her phone rang.

"I might be a little longer than planned," Ian said. "Tilda's dad just stopped by and wants to see the work done today."

He sounded frustrated.

"Stop by whenever. I'll be here. I'm not much of a cook, but I have the makings of a salad plus a loaf of artisan bread. I mean, we don't have to work—just have a nice dinner and maybe get to know one another a little better?"

The silence stretched on until she thought they'd lost the connection. "Ian?"

"Yeah. Sounds good. Gotta go."

He arrived an hour later. "Sorry."

"No worries, and certainly not anything you could control. Does Mr. Tucker come by often to—"

"Check up on me? Yeah. I call his visits pop quizzes. It usually means he's come up with some new idea and wants to see how I'll react. He always makes a major deal that he's what he calls a self-made success, which I take to be a dig at my years of education." He shrugged. "Nothing I can't handle." He turned his attention to the salad she'd been mixing when he arrived. "This looks great. Should I slice the bread?"

She pulled a bread knife from a collection and pushed it and the bread on a cutting board across the counter. "I brewed some tea, and I also have lemonade."

"The two ingredients needed for a proper Arnold Palmer."

She set the salad on the table and brought the glasses to the kitchen, filling them with ice and then half tea and half lemonade. "Why do they call it that?"

"Arnold Palmer? Supposedly, he invented the combo and it just stuck."

Once they sat at the table—a formal dining room setting—Chloe smiled. "I feel a bit as if I've gone back in time. I mean, when is the last time you ate in an actual dining room?"

"I have that feeling a lot since coming here to work. Being in the mansion every day, and it being furnished as if John and Mable just stepped out sometimes makes me feel like…"

"Like a member of the family?"

He chuckled. "More like a member of the staff, I think."

"And so you are—in a way. I'm sure the Ringlings are watching over the place, and no doubt checking your work."

Having run out of small talk about the Ringlings, they ate in a silence interspersed with niceties—"Could you please pass the pepper?" "This bread is really good. Where did you buy it?" "The tomatoes here have a lot more flavor than the hothouse option I have in New York."

Finally Chloe could take no more. "Tell me about the work you're doing in the tower. I understand it's been twenty years since the last major work was done, but I would think a place like this might stand the test of time—at least structurally."

"The building is coming up on its centennial. Like any older structure, Ca' d'Zan must withstand the ravages of the weather, not to mention the wear and tear of thousands of tourists tramping through the house and around the grounds pretty much every day of the year. Of course, with the mansion shut down for repairs and it being summer and all, there are very few visitors these days." He pushed his chair away from the table, stretching out his long legs. "Enough about that. So tell me, will your novel open with a party, or a funeral?"

She'd forgotten she'd mentioned that to him. "A party. Toby came across a society page article about a grand affair Mr. Ringling arranged to celebrate his seventieth birthday." She got up to retrieve the copy of the article Toby had given her and handed it to Ian before she began clearing the table. "It seems as good a place as any to start."

After skimming the article, he followed her to the kitchen, bringing the rest of the dishes with him and going directly to the sink. He scraped the plates and then began filling the sink.

"I can do that later," she protested.

He shrugged. "You need to work. Let's get these out of the way." He tossed her a dish towel before plunging his hands into the soapy water.

Normally Chloe kept details of her process and story-building to herself, but she found Ian to be just the sounding board she needed. "I've never included someone who actually lived as a major character, much less the protagonist. But my great-grandmother seems intent on driving me in that direction."

"Tell me her name again."

"Lucinda Conroy. From the little Toby and I have been able to uncover about her, she was a trapeze artist and, at one time, the star of the show. In the article you just read she gets kudos for having thrilled the partygoers with her performance at the birthday bash."

"Nothing more?"

Chloe shrugged. "She seems to have simply disappeared. Some-where along the way she presumably married and had a child—my grandmother, but that's about all I know. Darcy said there was something about her being arrested. She also said rumor and gossip tend to run rampant in the circus world."

Ian handed her the last dish before draining the sink and wiping the counter. "So it would seem you might interview your grandmother."

"Easier said than done. My grandmother is very tight lipped when it comes to her mother. Grams was left at an orphanage as an infant, and although she was eventually adopted by a couple who loved her dearly and gave everything they had to assure her a life of promise, I think she never quite got over that sense of having been abandoned. Over time she's offered several versions of why she thinks Lucy left the circus, most of them dismissive of any possibility that there's more to the story than she simply aged out of a job. Nothing to see here, folks."

"There should be records. Payroll, for example."

She'd thought of that. "I'll ask Toby to see what he can find tomorrow."

"Or Tilda could do that for you," Ian suggested. He leaned against the counter, watching her put the dishes away. "How are things working out with her?"

"Much better now that I've given her more substantial work to do. Having her work with Toby frees me up to start doing the actual writing." She reached to put the pitcher on a higher shelf, standing on tiptoe.

"Let me do that," he offered. Without waiting for her to agree, he stood behind her and easily put the pitcher in its place.

She was far too aware of his nearness, the brush of his arm alongside her face. The moment passed, and he stepped back, allowing her space to turn around. But when she did, he was looking at her in a way that told her he'd also felt something—an arc of attraction neither of them had time to pursue.

"Well, I should get going," he said, but hesitated.

"You never told me about your work," she reminded him.

"Another time," he said. He reached the front door and pushed open the screen. "Look, I had no idea your work is, in many ways, as complicated as mine is. We're both building something, and frankly the more I learn about your work, the more intrigued I am. That said, I have a job to do and a deadline as well. So, for now, maybe use Tilda as a go-between with me as well as Toby. Probably more efficient for both of us," he added.

"Sure. That's probably best." She wondered if it was her imagination that they both seemed reluctant to end the evening and decided she was being silly.

But as he crossed the lawn, he called out to her. "Hey, just to be clear, we both have work to do, but maybe now and again we can just take a break—like tonight?"

"I'd like that," she called back. She stood in the doorway, watching him walk toward the mansion,

After closing the front door, she allowed herself a moment to lean back and enjoy the memory of the evening. Then she pushed herself away from the door. "To work," she muttered. She had a mystery to write. Turning, with the intent of organizing her research on the now-bare dining room table, she gasped when she saw Tilda scowling at her from the kitchen.

"Tilda, you startled me."

The scowl faded to a grin as the young woman held up a carton of frozen yogurt and a large spoon. "Thought we might need a pick-me-up to get us through the evening." She set the carton on the counter and opened a cupboard to retrieve a couple of bowls. "I was thinking perhaps we could get started on that opening. The more I think about it, a funeral seems perfect. The question is, who died? And more to the point, how?"

"What are you doing here? It's late."

"But you still need to work, and I came to help. I brought ice cream—and fudge sauce."

Chloe watched her for a moment and then realized there had been no obvious sign of Tilda's arrival. "How did you get in?"

"Through the back. You must have left the door unlocked."

"That's not possible. I locked it last night before going to bed, and I left by the front door this afternoon."

"To meet Ian, right?" Tilda's back was to Chloe as she dug

into the ice cream with a scoop.

"To do research at the archives. With Toby. I told you yesterday that was my plan."

"But Ian was there and the two of you... I saw him leave just now." She sounded upset as she plopped a large scoop into the first bowl and then started digging again.

"I had some questions about the house. It was nearly seven, and neither of us had eaten and..."

Why do I need to explain myself?

"Calm down. No one is attacking you," Tilda said with a grin that made Chloe even more uncomfortable.

Having filled both bowls, Tilda placed the fudge sauce in the microwave and pushed buttons, then faced Chloe. "I just find it a little hurtful that you would go to him when you know he specifically assigned me to be your assistant."

So she's feeling insecure. Understandable. But still...

The microwave bell dinged, and Tilda retrieved the now molten fudge and began spooning it over the ice cream.

"Tilda, please come sit down. We need to talk. These unannounced visits have got to stop. I really appreciate your zeal, but I need my privacy—I need to be able to rely on having that privacy."

"Are you still seeing that actor?" Tilda sat at the table and took a bite of her sundae.

"What?"

"It was online that you and the actor who played the lead in the movie version of your first novel were an item. He's hot."

Chloe couldn't help laughing. "He's also five years younger than I am and... No, I am not seeing him or anyone else." Once again she had allowed Tilda to shift the topic away from their work relationship. "Look, Tilda, I think you're a person determined to do a good job, and I appreciate that. But we need to set some ground rules, starting with the fact that you and I are in a working relationship.

We are not…girlfriends who share personal details of our lives."

Tilda nodded. "It's because of that stalker, right? I mean, I get it. You have trust issues. Totally understandable."

"This has nothing to do with—" Chloe forced herself to take a deep breath. "I am here to complete a project, and I'm grateful for your assistance with the details that make that work easier. I am simply asking you to wait until I ask you to do something before you take action, okay?"

"But you're always asking Ian."

"Ian is the expert I need to make sure that aspects of my novel are authentic. You, on the other hand, are going to be invaluable in the coming weeks in terms of fact-checking certain details with Toby or at the library downtown or historical society." Realizing she had turned down Tilda's offers to shop or run errands for her, Chloe drew in a long breath and let it out. "In fact, I have an entire list of items I need your help checking up on this week."

Tilda grinned and set her empty bowl aside to take out her phone. "Ready when you are, oh-great-writer-of-mysteries."

Chloe ticked off half a dozen details about Sarasota in the mid-1930s for Tilda to research, and then added, "Let's plan to meet at the archives at three tomorrow afternoon. Have you met Toby?"

Tilda nodded and pocketed her phone. She rinsed her ice cream dish and spoon and set them in the sink before heading for the back door. "Three works fine. See you then." She opened the door, and just before stepping outside, she grinned at Chloe and said, "And don't worry. You didn't forget to lock the door. I have a key—one I expect you'd rather I don't use?"

Chloe held out her hand, and Tilda gave her the key. "See you tomorrow, boss."

CHAPTER TEN

Ca' d'Zan, May 1936

L<small>UCY</small>

*L*ucy stopped short of confronting Marty in front of Julia. She knew he was staying in the cottage occupied by the Ringling's yacht captain a short distance from the main house. The captain and his family were away visiting their daughter, and Marty had taken over the small house for the weekend. Lucy watched him drive back toward the cottage and decided to follow on foot. The cottage would give them the privacy they needed to sort out what she still believed in her heart of hearts Marty would easily explain.

When she arrived, she heard Marty puttering about in the kitchen, chopping at ice and then filling a glass. The door was open, and she could see him through the screen. He was humming as he sliced a lemon into wedges. She moved inside, deliberately allowing the screen door to close with a bang behind her. Marty stepped into the doorway between the kitchen and dining room. "Hello?"

Lucy drew in a long breath—the kind of breath she would take before leaping from the platform eighty feet above the ground. "It's me, darling," she called as she settled herself on the sofa, tucking her feet under her—making herself at home.

"Well, this is a surprise," Marty said, coming into the living room, still holding the glass of ice, lemon, and probably something stronger than water.

"We've hardly had time to talk," she said, patting the sofa, inviting him to sit. "So, let's talk, shall we?"

"Of course. I'll just get you a glass of—"

"Sit down, Marty."

She knew by his expression that her tone had struck home. He assumed a sheepish, schoolboy demeanor as he perched on the arm of the sofa and set his glass on a side table. "Uh-oh, methinks I'm in trouble."

"I had breakfast with your father this morning. He seems to be…misinformed about our relationship." She would get to Julia Gordon later. Marty opened his mouth, but she held up her hand to stop him saying anything. "I'm not finished. Your father tells me neither you nor I have proof of our marriage. He offered me cash—a rather large sum given the thickness of the envelope he waved in front of me—to go away. I declined. So, my first question—and I have several—is: Are we legally married or not?"

Marty stood and stared out the window, refusing to look at her. "I thought you understood, Lucy. Our so-called wedding was a lark. Surely you never believed…that is…you? Me?"

She forced herself to remain calm. "So, a ruse cooked up to take me to bed."

He wheeled around and smirked at her. "Oh, come on, now. You wanted that as much as I did. You certainly didn't hold back once we—"

"I thought I was experiencing my wedding night."

His laugh was harsh and ugly. "Don't play the innocent with me, Lucy. You knew exactly what that was. I give you credit for putting on a good act—enough so that I felt the need to play along with the whole elopement thing."

"That was all your idea. I certainly did not have access to a friend willing to pretend to be a justice of the peace." She flexed her fingers, calming herself. "But that is all water under the bridge. The more immediate issue is what you plan to do about this child I am carrying. Your child."

"Come on, Luce," he sneered. "Don't take me for a fool. That kid—if there is a kid—is more likely Nardo's or one of the roustabouts always fawning over you."

She was on her feet and toe-to-toe with him in a second, her index finger stabbing repeatedly at his chest. "You keep implying I am a loose woman. I slept with one man—you—one time."

He grasped her wrist and squeezed it so hard she was sure there would be a bruise. "Pregnant first time out? I don't think so, Lucy."

Wrenching her hand free, she turned away. "Well, believe it. I am pregnant with your child, and if you're worried about scandal, then I would suggest we find a bona fide justice of the peace today and set things right."

Even as the words left her mouth, she regretted them. A lifetime with a man who would come to despise her if he didn't already? A life sentence for the innocent child? But what choice did she have? She couldn't work—at least not for the next several months. Of course, Mr. John would make sure she was all right. But what if the rumors were true, and the circus was about to fold? Even if they were not true, by the time she could make a return, someone would have taken her place. No, it was past time Marty took responsibility for his actions.

"Are you threatening me, Lucy?"

She hadn't heard him move closer until he whispered the words close to her ear, his breath hot on her neck. He took hold of her shoulders and turned her so she was facing him. "Here is what you are going to do, my dear. You are going to take the money my father so generously offered. I suggest you use it to rid yourself of the situation you find yourself in and continue your career—one that will skyrocket now that you have successfully performed the triple. In fact, I may be able to arrange for the medical procedure."

Lucy was horrified. The man was suggesting she murder her child—*his* child. "Never," she whispered, backing away from him.

He shrugged, retrieved his glass, and drained it. "Suit yourself, darling. But you and I are finished. And if you do anything that in any way embarrasses me or my family—or stands in the way of my actual upcoming nuptials with Miss Gordon..." She saw the grin that spread across his face when he realized this was all news to her. "Ah yes, Julia and I have been headed for the altar for years now. She has been most patient in allowing me time to sow some wild oats before settling down, but the date is set for New Year's Eve in New York. Sounds terribly romantic, don't you think?"

So his father had not lied. There had been no need for him to lie.

Lucy sank back onto the sofa, her hands shaking, her chin on her chest as she fought to hold back the tears she refused to allow him to see.

"You should go," he said, moving to the door. "I'll speak to my father and tell him you've reconsidered. I'll ask him to leave the envelope in your room." He moved to the telephone. "You need to understand the plan here. We are finished, you and me. If you're smart, you'll take the money and get your problem fixed. Now that you've successfully done the triple, you'll be in demand. And believe me, sweetheart, everyone working for Mr. John is going to need to think about finding a new place to work."

Woodenly she got to her feet and forced herself to move. A thousand retorts spun in her brain, but she pressed her lips together and brushed past him.

"It was fun while it lasted," she heard him murmur as he dialed the phone.

She was barely off the front porch before she turned to the foliage lining the path and vomited. The heat and humidity were a blanket she wanted to push aside, but they enveloped her. Sweat ran down her neck and back as she stumbled toward the main house that shimmered in the noon sun like a mirage. She wiped her lips with the back of her hand and lengthened her stride. She needed to get away from here—away from Marty and his father. She would pack her things and be gone within the hour.

To where?

Home. The circus grounds where she could think what to do next.

Once she reached her room, she pulled her suitcase from under the bed and began laying out the clothes she would pack and those she would wear after her bath. She turned on the spigots to fill the bathtub before stepping behind the dressing screen and removing her perspiration-soaked clothes. A nice long soak in the tub would give her time to calm down and figure out what to do. She had just stepped into the warm rose-scented water when she thought she heard someone in the bedroom.

"Hello?" She waited, listening for whatever had caught her attention. But the only sound was the call of the birds nesting outside her window. "You are overwrought," she told herself as she sank into the water and closed her eyes. She placed her palms on her flat stomach and mentally calculated the time she would need to fill between now and when the baby arrived. The money Marty's father had offered would no doubt see her through. But if she refused to end the pregnancy? What then? Better not to take the money at all.

She would go to Mr. John and tell him how Marty had deceived her. He would fire Marty on the spot and make sure she was taken care of until the baby came, and then…

Who was she kidding?

Mr. John no longer controlled the hiring and firings of the circus company. His sister-in-law, Edith, widow of his brother Charles, held that power along with Mr. John's old friend, Sam Gompertz. It was Marty—more specifically his father—who held control here. Mr. John needed their investment as well as that of Julia Gordon's parents, and all Marty or his father would need to do is remind him of that.

You're on your own.

Surely if she was careful, she could perform for another couple of months with no harm to the baby. Of course, Nardo would never agree to that, but Marty would. This was one situation where she still held the winning cards. He needed her to cover while he recruited a new star. Every piece of marketing material featured her. Hers was the act people paid to see. She would tell Marty her terms: she would stay on for six more weeks, but she would not take his father's money; she would not perform the triple; and she would not murder their child.

Satisfied that she had a plan, she finished her bath, dressed in gabardine trousers and a loose cotton top, and began packing her things. She hesitated briefly when she realized the fastenings on her suitcase, the one she'd left open earlier, were snapped shut. She was sure she'd left them open. But then the sound of a siren moving closer distracted her. Pulling aside the curtain she saw a police car speed up the driveway and stop outside the front entrance. Two men, one in uniform, the other in a tan summer suit and wearing a Panama hat, got out and followed Mr. Jefferson inside.

What now?

Whatever it was, she had no time for more drama. Whatever it was had nothing to do with her. She would pack and ask Mr. Jefferson to have a car ready to drive her to the circus grounds as soon as possible. Hastily she removed stacks of undergarments from the bureau and placed them along with her personal effects into the suitcase. On top of all that she placed the carefully folded gown she'd worn the evening before and the feather shrug before closing the lid, pressing down on it with her full weight so the latches would catch. After looking around to be sure she had not left anything, she shoved her bare feet into a pair of wedge-heeled espadrilles and was just about to put on her cloche hat when there was a knock at the door.

"Lucinda?"

Nardo. "Come in," she called as she turned to the mirror to check her hat.

Nardo opened the door and stood in the threshold. "You are leaving?"

"Just going back to the circus grounds."

"The police—"

"Yes, I heard the siren. What's that all about?" Lucy dropped her compact and lipstick into her purse and snapped it shut.

"There has been a robbery," Nardo said. He made no move to pick up her suitcase. Rather, he remained standing in the doorway. "You need to come downstairs. The police wish to have everyone downstairs."

"But—"

"You should come right away, Lucinda. They are quite serious."

She tossed her purse and hat onto the bed. "Oh, very well."

Nardo waited for her to step past him and then closed the door to her room. As they walked the mezzanine to the main stairway, she looked down and saw Marty and his parents as well as Julia Gordon and her parents all gathered in the Grand Court below. The uniformed policeman stood guard, while the man in the suit—a detective, she supposed—consulted a small notebook. Mr. Jefferson and the maid who had been hired for the weekend to serve them all stood at the entrance to the breakfast room.

Lucy glanced at Marty, who looked away.

"Ah, so here we all are," the detective said, pocketing his note-book. "Please take a seat Miss…"

"Conroy—Lucinda Conroy," Lucy replied.

"Ah yes, the aerialist," the detective said. "Mr. Russo here is your partner, I believe?"

"That's right." Lucy saw no cause for alarm. Whatever had brought the police had nothing to do with her or Nardo. She chose a chair that was the greatest distance from Marty, sat, and crossed her legs. "I'm afraid I'm at a loss as to why we are here, Detective…?"

"Taylor." Beyond providing his last name, he offered no further explanation. He turned to Mr. Jefferson. "Other staff?"

"Miss Rogers is a temporary hire for the weekend. When Mr. Ringling is not in residence, there are usually three of us—me and a housekeeper whose position is currently vacant. The third is the yacht captain. He lives in the cottage you passed on your way here, but has been given an extended leave of absence since the sale of the yachts."

Detective Taylor glanced around. "You had quite a party here yesterday and last night, did you not?"

"We did."

"And you and Miss Rogers handled that all on your own?"

"Several of the circus performers were brought in as waiters and busboys, but they all left earlier this morning."

"I see." He turned his attention to Marty's parents. "And exactly when did you notice the missing item?"

"Just after lunch," Mrs. Sutherland replied. "I went to our room to lie down. I suffer from migraines. Mr. Jefferson has kindly provided a small bouquet of lavender since our arrival. The scent helps ease my headaches. But the lavender was not there."

Lucy looked up at Nardo who had taken up a position next to her chair. Was this really about a missing bunch of lavender?

"Go on," the detective urged.

"Well, naturally I missed the lavender before I realized the silver Tiffany bud vase that held it was gone as well."

Marty's father put a protective hand on his wife's forearm. "My wife certainly could not rest once she'd noticed the missing vase. She immediately rang for Mr. Jefferson."

Lucy's heartrate accelerated the way it did whenever she realized something was not right with the rigging for her act.

Mr. Sutherland glanced at her, then cleared his throat and addressed Detective Taylor. "I'm afraid there's more. A rather large sum of cash my wife and I had in our room is also gone."

Lucy turned her gaze to Marty, who refused to look at her. Her heart raced. Her stomach tightened. His father was pointing the finger directly at her when Marty knew very well…

Over the next several minutes—minutes that felt like hours— the detective continued to question each person. Where were they throughout the morning and specifically between noon and two? Which rooms were theirs, and did they object to the uniformed officer performing a thorough search?

When it was Marty's turn to respond Lucy noticed how he carefully avoided saying she had been with him in the cottage. He told the detective he'd brought Miss Gordon back to the house after a morning of golf, then gone to the cottage to refresh himself. "I returned when Dad called to let me know Mother was deeply upset."

Ever the devoted son.

"You were the one to call us?" the detective asked.

"No, that was me," Julia's father announced. "As an attorney, I thought it best we get to the core of this at once, especially once Mr. Sutherland told me of the missing money."

"The vase was definitely there this morning," Julia's mother chimed in. "I'm sure of it. Janine and I had coffee in her room, and I remember admiring it."

The detective turned his attention to Nardo and Lucy. "And the two of you?"

"Mr. Russo was assisting me to transport the crystal and silver used for the party to the vault," Mr. Jefferson said.

"And you, Miss Conroy? Where were you?"

Marty gave her a pleading look, then glanced at his fiancée. He looked so desperate Lucy felt the shift of power revert to her. If she lied for him…

"I went to the cottage."

She was aware that Marty visibly tensed. She waited for the detective to ask her what her business at the cottage had been—and with whom. But he simply stared at her for a long moment before saying, "Officer Chandler, please start your search. Perhaps Mr. Jefferson can accompany you?"

The two men mounted the stairs, and the detective continued gathering information. Why were the guests staying in the house when Mr. Ringling was not on the premises? Why especially were Marty and his parents—who lived in Sarasota—spending the night rather than leaving for their home after the party? He repeated his question to the Gordons. Both couples noted how late the party had gone and praised their host's generosity in insisting they stay over and relax the following day. "The Gordons drove in from Miami for the event," Marty's father said. "We all plan to leave later this afternoon. The Gordons will stay with us for another day or so before returning home."

"And you, sir?" Detective Taylor turned his attention to Marty.

"Me? Well, that is…"

Lucy realized that, as usual, Marty had not thought that far into the future.

"My son and Miss Gordon have recently become engaged, Detective. I'm afraid he's still a little befuddled by the excitement of these past few days."

"Congratulations," the detective muttered as he consulted his notebook and drew a line through a notation. When he looked up his eyes met Lucy's. "So that leaves the two of you."

Nardo moved half a step closer.

"Why did the two of you stay on?"

"It was Mr. John's wish," Nardo said. "Lucinda—Miss Conroy—became ill during the party, and his instructions were to make sure she stayed until she had fully recovered."

"I see." Detective Taylor once again consulted his notes. "I assume your health has taken a turn for the better if you were able to walk to the cottage earlier?" Before she could reply, he glanced up at the balcony. "Find something, Chandler?"

"You might want to come up and have a look, sir."

"Which room?"

"Miss Conroy's."

As Taylor headed for the stairway, Marty's father followed. Then Marty crossed the room as well.

Lucy stood and looked at Nardo. "Go," he urged.

She hurried up the stairs and down the hall, reaching the open door in time to see the four men crowded into the room. The policeman led the detective to her now fully opened suitcase. Her carefully folded clothes were in disarray in a pile on the bed. The gown she'd worn to the party was on the floor, and Officer Chandler was pulling away the lining of the empty case.

Pushing her way forward past Mr. Jefferson, she snatched up the gown. "I see no reason to damage my property," she seethed.

The detective lifted a corner of the lining of the suitcase and removed a thick vellum envelope. "Is this your property, Miss Conroy?"

"Is that our money?" Marty's mother demanded as she rushed into the room followed by all three of the Gordons. "You took this?" She turned on Lucy. "How could you resort to common thievery after everything John Ringling has done for you?"

"Where's the vase, miss?" The detective had continued examining her suitcase.

With nearly a dozen people now in the room, Lucy felt cornered.

She knew nothing of this vase. But she knew that envelope—knew who had placed it there and when. And knew no one would believe her if she tried to explain. If she accused the real culprit who stood by, smirking at her.

"Miss Conroy?"

"That is not mine," she managed.

"Yes, so it would seem. And yet, the envelope and its contents have somehow turned up in the lining of your luggage," Marty's father said, and the smile he gave her was filled with triumph.

"Marty?" Out of habit she turned to the man she'd thought of for months now as her husband and protector. "Tell them the truth. Tell them I was…we were…"

Marty's father stepped between her and the detective, his back to her. "The truth is, Detective, this young woman tried to entrap my son in a faked marriage in order to secure a father for the child she is carrying. Obviously failing that and faced with the fact she cannot perform her act while with child, she was desperate to find some means to secure her future."

Lucy saw Nardo's eyes widen in shock.

Please tell me you don't believe him, she wanted to say. She started toward him, but too late realized her move was viewed as an attempt to run. Officer Chandler grabbed her upper arm and did not let go as she watched Nardo turn and leave.

CHAPTER ELEVEN

Sarasota, August 2022

Chloe

As July turned into late August, Chloe's days fell into an unbroken schedule: up in the morning for a run before the heat and humidity made any kind of physical activity unbearable; shower and breakfast—usually a protein smoothie; walk to the archives or the mansion—whichever seemed the most likely setting to advance her novel that day; work through lunch and the rain that invariably came midafternoon; and then back to the cottage for a second shower, supper, and more writing. The weekends were dedicated to business—keeping up with her fans through her limited social media, replying to emails from friends and associates, working out her schedule of appearances, and readings with her publicist.

To her relief Tilda seemed to have settled into a routine of her own, one that had made her invaluable in taking care of the fact-checking so necessary when writing a novel about a real person, event, and setting. They worked well together. Chloe's interaction with Ian, on the other hand, had virtually disappeared. They exchanged texts and spoke by phone, checking in to see how their respective projects were going. But any plans they made for a repeat of the evening they'd shared after her second tour of the house with him never materialized. Somehow such plans were always inter-rupted by some issue at the mansion or by her growing panic that she had not yet found a solid plot on which to build her novel.

A couple of times she had sent him questions about some detail via text and he had answered within an hour. And she'd seen him around, of course, but he was always with other people—or Tilda's father. Recently Mr. Tucker had started taking his morning run through the grounds of the museum and often fell into step with Chloe, asking questions about how her research was going. He always seemed to wind up at the mansion questioning Ian about the work being done. With Mr. Tucker's oversight added to his workload, she understood why Ian had asked Darcy to orchestrate any need Chloe might have to revisit the mansion. The man simply did not have enough hours in his day. Of course, Darcy was a gold mine of the kind of detail readers loved to savor when entering a book's world, but Chloe had to admit she missed Ian. She'd been looking forward to getting to know him better.

The truth was that like anyone else there were times when Chloe needed a break from her work. Tilda had set up a number of appearances for her—book signings at two local bookstores plus appearances at the main library and a high school. Those helped, but the truth was, she was lonely. The museum grounds, especially at night, were deserted, and the cottage felt isolated from the rest of the world. She'd never been much of a TV watcher, and she avoided reading the works of other authors when she was working on a novel herself. Their voices too easily got into her head, and she had always feared making some mistake that might be seen as plagiarism. Tilda and Toby had struck up a friendship appropriate to their younger age, and while they often invited her to join them in the evenings or on weekends to hear some musical group or try the newest restaurant, she always declined. Hanging out with Tilda and Toby and their friends made her feel like someone's maiden aunt. She had friends, of course, but they were miles away—as was her family. She spoke to them often and even "saw" them via online visits. But it wasn't the same as sitting with someone, enjoying a meal or sunset, and just venting about work or catching up on the latest news. She considered inviting Darcy to see a movie with her, but soon learned Darcy had a large family—and a second job to help support them.

And that left Ian as the best fit for someone to hang out with. He was the right age. Like her, he was also new to the area, so without any obvious family commitments. Of course, he might have a significant other, but surely Tilda would have mentioned that. Besides, she wasn't looking for romance. She and Ian had interests in common. And long gone were the days when a woman needed to wait for a man to call and extend an invitation. She took out her phone, scrolled down to his name, and pressed the button.

Voicemail.

"Please leave a message." *Beeeep.*

Not "You've reached the voicemail of Dr. Ian Flanner."

No promise of a return call.

No "goodbye" or "Have a good day."

Expecting a longer outgoing message giving her time, she couldn't think what to say, so she simply ended the call.

Her phone was barely back in her pocket when it pealed out the ringtone her nephew had installed—Vivaldi's *Four Seasons.*

Ian.

"Hello." She tried to tone down the sudden delight she felt.

"You rang?" He sounded...lighter...less stressed. She hoped this was a sign his work was progressing.

In an instant she considered her options—lie and say it must have been a misdial, or plow forward with her original intent?

"I did. But then I chickened out."

His chuckle, like his voice, was warm and deep, and somehow

comforting. "I intimidate you that much, do I?"

"You never intimidated me, Dr. Flanner. Well, maybe just a bit that first meeting."

Are we flirting? Is this flirting? It had been so long, she could no longer tell.

They both fell silent.

He cleared his throat and started to say something at the same time she blurted, "Do you want to meet me on the terrace at the mansion and watch the sunset?"

Seriously? You lead with that?

"Best offer I've had in a long time. Just give me twenty minutes to wrap something up here and I'll meet you there."

"It's a…I mean, great." She had actually almost said "It's a date."

You really need to get a life, Chloe Whitfield.

Twenty minutes. Walking there from the cottage would take ten, especially in this heat. No time to change. She checked her hair in the mirror. It would probably be nice to bring along wine and glasses. She'd seen people at the beach emerge from their high-rises to toast the setting sun. But she didn't drink, and there was no wine. She pulled two bottles of water from the refrigerator. Water would have to do.

Tucking the water bottles into her satchel and grabbing her keys and sunglasses, she headed for the main house. The wide palazzo featured a row of wicker chairs that faced the bay. Near the end of the terrace where tourists exited, Ian had already moved two chairs so that they faced the sun, now a vivid orange orb just above the horizon. He was dressed in cutoff jeans and a white collarless shirt, the sleeves rolled back to expose his tanned forearms. She found herself appreciating Tilda's assessment. The man was hot.

Get a grip.

He walked toward her, his smile wide and welcoming. "Boy, am I glad you called," he said. "It's been a day—no, more like a week." He brushed his hair back from his forehead. "Shall we?" He indicated the positioned chairs with a slight bow.

Once they were seated, she pulled the bottles of water from her satchel and handed him one. "Sorry. No wine."

"Wine is overrated," he said, twisting the cap off his bottle. He waited while she did the same, then raised his in a toast. "Cheers."

They clicked the plastic together before each taking a long swallow.

"I never appreciated cold water so much," she said. "In this heat, I probably go through a gallon a day."

"Where are you from? I mean originally?"

"Brooklyn."

"Parents? Siblings?"

"My parents are retired. They never made it to being snow-birds here in Florida. Instead, they settled in North Carolina—the mountains. It suits them. Dad has his workshop and Mom sells her handcrafted dolls at several galleries in the area."

"And siblings?"

"One sister—married with three children—still living in New York." She saw he'd already drained his water, and wished she'd thought to bring more. "What about you?"

"Dad died—COVID."

"Oh, Ian, how terrible."

"Yeah. He always seemed like the strongest man in the world—and then…" He shook off his thoughts. "Mom was the one who got us all through it and back on track. She's pretty amazing."

"She lives here?"

He chuckled. "Not a chance. She thinks I'm crazy to have taken this job. She and my two brothers and their families manage the ranch we grew up on near Santa Fe."

The sun slid lower until it was just half an orange ball resting on the horizon.

"So beautiful," Chloe murmured. "Imagine if this was your home and every night you could simply stroll out here and see that."

"Well, maybe not every night. As you may have noticed, Sarasota has an epic rainy season, not to mention it's in the path of hurricanes around this time of year."

"I can't imagine what that must be like—being here in a hurricane." Chloe shivered in spite of the warm evening.

"You might just get your chance. Rumor has it there are a couple of candidates brewing in the Caribbean. The good news is the city has some protection from the barrier islands—Lido and Longboat and the other Keys. Still, the damage from rain and wind can do a number on old houses like this one."

Chloe sighed and leaned back in her chair. "Even so, can't you just envision John and Mable sitting out here watching sunsets in their day?"

"Maybe during the winter months when they weren't off traveling and buying art in Europe. They tended to head north for the summer. They had another home in New Jersey and an apartment in New York. John Ringling was a lot more than just a circus impresario." He pointed across the bay. "At one time all of that land over there belonged to him. He was a very wealthy man—at least for a while."

Chloe knew the history. How things in John Ringling's life disintegrated after the crash of 1929 and after Mable's death. Both she and Ian fell silent as they watched the sun begin to slip below the horizon, coloring the sky around it with streaks of orange and purple. It was not an uncomfortable silence, just two people sharing a moment.

"Have you found any more information about your great-grandmother?" Ian asked.

"Since Toby found the article about a birthday celebration for John Ringling where she performed her act, the well seems to have run dry." Chloe glanced around in the gathering dusk. "Do you think they set up her trapeze out here?"

"Seems like the perfect place, although depending on the weather, the winds might have been a factor."

"Now that's exactly the kind of detail I look for to use in my stories." She gave him a light punch on his arm. "That's why I need to pick your brain. You see things from an entirely different perspective."

"Glad to be of service."

"Really? Tilda said—that is, she inferred that you were really busy and—"

"I'll admit I'm intrigued by the mystery of your great-grandmother, so if I can help, let me know." He stood. "We should probably head out. Now that the sun is down, the bug population will be coming out in force."

"Yes. Back to work for me."

"I'll walk with you."

She almost protested that she felt perfectly safe, but the truth was she was enjoying being with him. "Thanks." She turned for one last look at the dark house and thought of what it must have looked like the night of John Ringling's birthday party. She imagined the palazzo lit with lanterns and the colorful light that would spill out through the windowpanes tinted in soft pastels. As she followed the silhouette of the house to the floors above and on to the tower, she saw a single light—moving.

"Ian?"

He'd taken their water bottles to deposit in a recycle bin near the visitor entrance and was just crossing the palazzo. She pointed to the tower, and he looked up. "There was a light."

"One of the guys must have left a work light on," he said. "I'll walk you home and come back and check it out."

Suddenly the idea of being inside the grand house when it was deserted and dark seemed very appealing—on more than one level.

It would give her new information for her novel, and being in the dark with Ian was not the worst idea she'd ever had. "Or we could check it out together," she suggested.

He chuckled. "I thought you wanted to get back to work."

"This is work." She hooked her arm through his and started forward. "Did I fail to mention that the light was moving?"

Ian's features hardened as he stared up at the tower. "Come on," he said, leading the way to the door. "Darcy keeps a flashlight here somewhere." He searched a shelf under the counter in the reception area. "Here we go." He flicked it on. The beam was weak. "Well, it'll do. We won't be here long."

"We have lights on our phones," Chloe reminded him and flicked hers on.

Together they walked through the kitchen and pantry and on to the stairway.

"You wait here," Ian said as he started up the stairs. "Probably the wind or a short circuit. Just need to make sure the light's out. I won't be long."

"And miss this chance to gather info for my book about the house at night? Right behind you," Chloe countered, following him to the mezzanine—where Ian stopped so suddenly, she bumped into him.

"Shhh."

He pointed to the elevator, and Chloe heard the sound of the motor.

Someone was in the house—on the elevator.

Ian motioned for her to stay where she was as he crept back down the stairs to intercept the intruder. Chloe heard the elevator stop and the door slide open, and then Ian was suddenly running back toward the pantry and kitchen. "Stay there," he called out.

"Not a chance," Chloe muttered as she felt her way down the dark stairway and through the house. When she reached the exit, she heard Ian shout, "Stop!"

Figuring that was for the intruder and not her, she kept going and was breathing hard from excitement rather than exertion when she reached his side. "Did you see who it was?" she managed.

"No. Whoever it was knew the house and used the elevator as a decoy while he got away using the back stairs." He flicked off the flashlight that had gone dead. "It's my fault. I didn't set the security system, thinking I would go back to finish up some work."

"Still, it seems unlikely that someone would know that and choose this moment to do whatever it was they intended." Chloe hated convenient coincidences—in novels and in life.

"I should call it in," Ian said, taking out his cell. "Can you stay? They'll want to talk to you."

"Of course."

The police arrived in what to Chloe seemed like record time. On the other hand, this was probably the most excitement they'd seen since the tourist season ended. They questioned Ian and Chloe separately, taking notes. Then they asked Ian to turn on the lights throughout the house, and several patrol officers spread out to search for any noticeable signs of damage or the intrusion. Ian and Chloe waited in the reception area—Ian pacing while Chloe sat on Darcy's stool behind the counter.

"Doc? You might want to see this," an officer called.

Ian was instantly in motion, and Chloe followed close behind.

The officer, a man who seemed close to retirement in age and weariness, waited by the elevator, holding the door open for the three of them to crowd inside. From the minute the police arrived, this officer had seemed to know—and respect—Ian. While he and Chloe had waited, she'd asked him how he knew the officer.

"Jake? He stopped by one day—used to do carpentry work before joining the force. He's lived in Sarasota his entire life, as did his parents and grandparents. We got talking, and from time to time we get together. He likes telling stories from the past, and I like hearing them."

As the elevator made its ascent to the third floor, Chloe studied the older man. His face and arms beneath the short sleeves of his uniform were permanently tanned, his face lined like cracked leather. He had gray eyes capped by bushy gray eyebrows. His hair—what was left of it—was the white of the surf.

"Not sure what to make of it," he said to Ian. "A real mess."

The elevator stopped with a slight jerk, and the door opened to reveal chaos. The floor of the guest room that Ian had been using as his headquarters was covered in paper—architectural drawings, files, notes, and receipts. Drawers in a file cabinet had been rifled and left open. And everything was soaked, water still dripping from the sprinklers above that the intruder had apparently set off. The two officers who had arrived with Jake were snapping pictures and dusting for prints.

"We checked the main floor and bedrooms, and nothing seems to have been disturbed. Looks like this was the target. Any idea what they might have been after?"

"No clue," Ian said. His voice was soft, and he surveyed the scene as if he couldn't quite believe it. "This sets us back weeks, maybe months." He shook his head.

Behind her Chloe heard footsteps slowly climbing the stairs and turned to see Pete and another officer.

"No sign of anybody on the grounds, sir," the young officer reported to Jake while Pete walked over to stand next to Ian.

"I can stay the night," Pete offered. "Make sure whoever did this doesn't come back."

"No," Ian replied. "You've put in more than a full day already. I've got this." He glanced at Chloe. "Jake, if you have no more questions for Ms. Whitfield, maybe Pete could see her home?"

Jake nodded as he answered a call on his cell.

"I'll be fine," Chloe said, but from the way both Pete and Ian looked at her, she knew protest was useless. "Okay. Thanks." On her way to the stairs, she touched Ian's arm. "Let me know if I can do anything to help," she said.

"Sure. Get some rest."

She followed Pete to the golf cart parked outside the entrance to the mansion and climbed in. He set the cart in motion and seemed inclined to make the short journey in silence. Chloe was not of the same mind.

"Who would do such a thing?"

Pete shrugged. "Kids maybe, looking for mischief. We get 'em sometimes, have to chase them off."

"This was far more than mischief," Chloe fumed.

"I reckon you've got a point there."

"I mean, has anything even close to this ever happened before?"

Pete stopped at the entrance to the path leading to the cottage. "Not since I've been here." He walked with her to the door, and once she'd unlocked it, he followed her inside and did a quick survey of the rooms.

"Thank you, Pete. I'll be fine."

"I expect you will, but keep things locked up in case."

She stood at the door while he headed back to his cart. Suddenly he stopped and turned. "This might interest you, you being a mystery writer and all. I did hear a tale about police being called and arresting one of the circus people back when Mr. Ringling was still alive, but that might just be an old wives' tale."

"What did the person do?"

"Stole some money and stuff, I think. It was a woman…. Linda…Lou…"

"Lucinda?"

"That was it."

"Darcy told you?"

"Darcy? No, I heard it from Jake. Case was never solved, according to him. Well, best be getting back." He waved and headed back toward the mansion.

Three people had now repeated the same story accusing her great-grandmother. But where was the proof?

CHAPTER TWELVE

Sarasota, May 1936

LUCY

The Sarasota jail was not the worst place Lucy had ever been. The cell was cleaner than some of the dressing rooms she'd occupied during her European tour. No, it was not her surroundings that she found intolerable, it was the situation. It was the fact that she had been arrested. Accused of theft. It was the way Marty's parents and the Gordons had looked at her as if her culpability was a foregone conclusion simply because of her occupation. Contrary to the old adage, in her case there seemed to be an assumption of guilt until proven innocent. It was also the hours of questioning by Detective Taylor she had endured since arriving at the jail. How many times did she need to say she had never seen the vase? How many times did she need to explain the offer of the money—which she'd refused?

She had finally been returned to her cell, where she collapsed onto the cot bolted to the wall and surrendered to the exhaustion of the day's events. She wakened to see darkness had come and then heard a door open and close and footsteps moving in her direction.

Please, no more questions. I can't think. I can't—

Officer Chandler sorted through a ring of keys and opened her cell. "Your bail's been posted," he said.

"Who…? I mean, how…?"

The policeman shrugged and led the way back down the hall and on into the outer office where she'd been brought earlier. Nardo was waiting. She couldn't remember when she'd ever been so glad to see a familiar—and friendly—face.

"Nardo," she murmured as she walked straight into his embrace.

"We can go?" he asked Detective Taylor, who was seated at his desk, typing some report.

"For now. Just don't be leaving the area, miss. You've a date for court you'd best not forget."

As if she could.

Another policeman pushed a manila envelope and a clipboard across a counter. "Your stuff," he said. "Check that it's all there and sign here."

Lucy emptied the items onto the counter, put on her wristwatch and the bangle bracelets she'd been wearing when they brought her to the station, then scribbled her name on the sheet of paper and turned back to Nardo. "Let's go."

Outside, dusk had set in, and she realized hours had passed since she'd confronted Marty and returned to the mansion to pack her things.

"Are you all right?" Nardo asked as they walked to a car she recognized as belonging to the ringmaster.

"I thought you left me," she said. "I thought you knew I was lying for Marty and you—"

"I left to get help." He sounded annoyed, and he did not look at her as he opened the car door for her.

She waited for him to come round to the driver's side, get in, and start the motor. "Thank you, Nardo. I'll pay you the bail money."

His grip on the steering wheel tightened, and his jaw clenched. He pulled away from the curb, narrowly missing a collision with a produce delivery truck.

"Nardo!"

"You think it is the money that is important for me? You think I would leave you? You think you know what is in my mind—my heart?"

He had never spoken to her this way—never in all the time they had performed together. They had been friends for years, working their way to the pinnacle of stardom as a team. She knew there had never been a time when he hadn't hoped for more than friendship, but once Marty came into her life...

"Why are you mad at me?"

He pulled the car to the side of the road and turned to face her. "I am not angry, Lucinda. I am frightened—for you and for the baby. You are accused of stealing from Mr. Ringling. An item his wife treasured and that is therefore doubly treasured by him because she is dead. How do you think he will take this?"

"He will believe in my innocence," Lucy replied, but in that same moment she realized she was not so sure. Mr. John was a man who liked others for what they might do for him, not the other way round. And even if he had at times treated her more as a daughter than an employee, everyone knew that the one thing guaranteed to end any goodwill the circus magnate might show was to do something that touched his beloved Mable or her memory in a negative way.

"Why would I take such a trivial item as that?" she demanded. "I have money of my own. What could a small silver vase be worth anyway?"

Nardo cocked an eyebrow. "Apparently a great deal. In such matters it is not the size of the object but the artist creating it that sets the value. As for you having money, we have not been paid in weeks," he reminded her. "It is unlikely we will ever see that money."

She knew he was right. "Still, I had the opportunity to accept the money and turned that down. Not to mention it was Marty who said he was going to tell his father to give me the money anyway. Why not just hand it to me?"

"Because if you are suspected of stealing it and sent to jail, Martin and his parents can move on with their lives."

Of course, Nardo was right. "Do you think I will be convicted?" Her voice sounded small and childlike, even to herself.

Nardo cupped her jaw in his large calloused palm. "I have made a plan, Lucinda. You will not spend another day in jail, I promise you that." He started the motor and pulled onto the road. "And you will not be in court. You will be miles from any courtroom."

"I can't run, Nardo."

"I see no other choice," he said.

There might not be, but still, how would she prove her innocence if she went into hiding?

When they reached the circus grounds, he parked outside the makeup tent where her friend, Violet Evans, the costume mistress and makeup artist, stood waiting. As they left the truck, Violet glanced around. "Quick," she hissed, holding back the tent flap and waiting for Lucy to enter. "There's not much time."

Violet's daughter, Edna, relieved Lucy of her purse and ushered her to a chair. She wrapped a towel around Lucy's shoulders, then retrieved a bowl from the dressing table and began mixing liquids she poured from unlabeled bottles. "Light or dark?" This she directed to her mother.

"The darker the better—and don't forget the eyebrows." Violet busied herself pulling a selection of items from the racks of costumes that lined the walls of the large tent.

"I don't—"

"Cover your eyes," Edna instructed as she pulled on a pair of rubber gloves then picked up a flat brush and dipped it in the mixture. "Sit still," she ordered when Lucy tried to turn away. To Lucy's horror, Edna began painting her hair with the smelly concoction.

"This or this?" She heard Violet raise the question and tried to peek out from beneath the towel Edna had handed her to protect her eyes.

"The blue," Edna replied.

Lucy had had enough. She dropped the towel and spun to face the two women. "What is going on?"

Violet sighed. "Nardo did not explain? No, I see he didn't. We are giving you a new look, my dear. One more suited to the new life you will assume."

Edna gently pulled her back in the chair and rewrapped the towel. "Now either sit still and let me finish dyeing your hair, or go through the next several weeks half blond and half brunette."

"I will not run," Lucy said. "I am innocent."

"No doubt, yet here we all are," Violet muttered. "You think it matters for one minute to those people?"

"Marty will—"

"Will what? Come to your rescue? Proclaim your innocence? Funny, I don't see him around, and I sure haven't heard he was the one who paid your bail."

"If you'll listen to somebody besides those in the high society circles for once in your life," Edna said, "you just might beat this thing and keep that baby safe in the bargain."

Lucy was well aware that Edna did not especially like her. She'd always chalked it up to jealousy. They were about the same age, but Lucy was the star of the show while Edna worked behind the scenes. Lucy had caught Marty's eye. She'd traveled on Mr. John's private railway car. She'd met royalty. And most important of all, Nardo was in love with her—not Edna.

"Why would you care what happens to me?"

Edna leaned in close. "Don't flatter yourself. It's Nardo I care about, and the sooner we get you away from here, the sooner he will stop mooning over you, and the sooner I will be there to mend the pieces of his broken heart." She plastered on the last of the hair dye and set a kitchen timer before leaving the tent as if being in the same space with Lucy was more than she could handle.

"Don't mind her," Violet said. "She's in love, and it's hardly your fault that love isn't coming back her way. Here, try these shoes." She handed Lucy a battered pair of black Mary Jane's. "Make sure they fit. You're likely to be doing some walking."

"I don't know about this, Violet. I mean, it puts you and Edna in danger."

Violet shrugged. "From what we're hearing, it's likely the whole company will have scattered by the time the police realize you've skipped town. Mr. John's been keeping up a good act, but the signs are all there, and he's not the one deciding such things these days."

Lucy couldn't argue the point. For nearly a year now attendance had been down, and even more telling was the choice of locations for staging those performances—no more than a day's travel from Sarasota, and there'd been no official "season" announced. It was a show here or there and then a week or more with nothing on the schedule.

The timer buzzed, and Edna reappeared carrying two buckets filled with water. Lucy knew the drill. She crossed the tent to where a large tin basin had been set on a table, a hose running from the drain to outside the tent. She bent over the basin and allowed Edna to dump the water over her dyed hair, watched the inky liquid flow away, felt Edna's gloved fingers massage her wet curls as she poured more water. When the two buckets were empty, Edna wrapped Lucy's head in a fresh towel. "Let's do those eyebrows," she said with a disgruntled sigh.

An hour later Lucy stood in front of the mirror, staring at herself. Her hair was almost black in contrast to her natural blond, and Edna had put some kind of pomade on it to flatten the curls.

"Dowdy," Violet had instructed. "Don't want nobody looking your way twice."

She handed Lucy body padding to wear.

"I'm pregnant," Lucy protested. "Isn't that padding enough?"

"Nope. Adding weight and age. They'll be looking for a blond with a good figure, not a brunette who spends too much time in the chow line."

Lucy couldn't help laughing as she studied the result. "I look—"

"Stop laughing. And let your shoulders sag, like you're carrying the weight of the world. And if somebody speaks to you, especially somebody with authority, look down. None of your usual sass. You got that?"

Lucy tried the new persona, and was amazed at how it changed her. She felt older, wearier, sadder. "How long do I need to keep this up?"

"Long as it takes." Violet handed her a piece of paper on which she'd written out a name and address. "That's my sister in Brooklyn. She runs a boardinghouse. Story will be that you and her are cousins, and you're staying with her until the baby comes while your husband is at sea."

"And how am I getting to Brooklyn?"

"Nardo will drive you across the state tonight where you'll catch a train out of St. Augustine first thing tomorrow morning."

"Sorry, luv, no private car this time," Edna added.

Lucy ignored her. "Nardo will come with me?"

"No. Once you're on the train, you're on your own." She tucked the paper with the address in the pocket of the cotton housedress Lucy wore. "When the authorities realize you've skipped town, they're bound to question Nardo. We've worked out a way that will explain how he couldn't have had anything to do with you leaving."

Lucy took a deep breath. Too much was happening, and far too many decisions were being made without her. She removed the paper Violet had placed in her pocket and stared at it. Why should she go live among strangers who knew nothing of her? Why would they care what happened to her or her baby? She wadded the paper into a ball and tossed it aside.

"I am not going anywhere," she announced.

"You cannot stay," Edna said. "You put Nardo and the rest of us in danger by staying."

"I will stay. If I am to clear my name, I must stay. I have done nothing wrong."

"You are a fool," Edna argued. "A fool who will end up delivering her baby in prison."

"Tell me you don't plan to make that court appearance," Violet pleaded. "Marty and his family will make sure you're convicted even if they have to pay the judge."

"I will hide in plain sight," Lucy argued. She studied herself in the mirror—the dark hair, the body suit that added not only pounds but years. "I'll need a new name to go with my new identity. Lucille suits, don't you think? Easier to keep something close to my actual name straight, and that sounds dowdy, don't you think?"

Nardo stepped into the tent. "If we are to make the train, we need to leave now," he said, glancing over his shoulder as if expecting trouble.

Lucy extended her hand. "Hello. I don't believe we've met. My name is Lucille O'Connor—Violet's cousin from Brooklyn. And you must be the famous aerialist, Bernardo Russo."

Nardo ignored her outstretched hand as he brushed past her to pick up the carpetbag Violet had packed for her. "We've no time for games, Lucinda."

Lucy perched on the edge of a chair and crossed her legs. "Well, they told me you were good-looking, but even that does not excuse rudeness—and my name is Lucille."

Nardo looked at Violet, who threw her hands in the air and

turned away. "We've done what you asked," she said.

Setting the bag down, Nardo turned back to Lucy. "You cannot do this."

"I can and I will," she replied. "I cannot prove Lucinda's innocence from miles away. Someone planted that money in her suitcase. As for the vase, I'm sure it is hidden somewhere—probably right there in the house, given the shortness of time to come up with some plan for incriminating Lucinda. I find the vase, and Lucinda walks free."

Nardo took hold of her shoulders, forcing her to look at him. "You speak of Lucinda as if she is someone else—*you* are the one charged."

Lucy studied her image in a hand mirror. "No. I am Lucille O'Conner, and tomorrow I will return to Ca' d'Zan to apply for the position of housekeeper that Mr. Jefferson mentioned he was in need of hiring. I will find that vase."

"And even if you do, what is your proof that Lucinda—that you—weren't the one to hide it there?"

Lucy chewed her lower lip. Nardo had raised a point she had not yet considered. She glared at him. "I am not leaving," she repeated.

"Typical," Edna fumed. "Always thinking only of yourself. What of Nardo? What of my mother—and me?" She held up her hands to show traces of hair dye that stained her fingertips in spite of her using gloves.

"Be quiet, Edna," Nardo said. "I need to think."

The three women watched as he slowly walked to the opening of the tent and back again. He stopped for a moment in front of Lucy, studying her new look before retracing his steps. Finally, he faced her.

"Here are my terms," he said. "I will go with you to see Mr. Jefferson. He likes me, and that will go well for you."

Lucy nodded enthusiastically. "And—"

Nardo held up his hand to silence her. "I have not finished. If he does not offer you the position, we will return to the original plan. One day should not make a difference. You will take the train to Brooklyn and stay with Violet's family until the child is born. In either case I will quit the circus and find work here in Sarasota where I can know what is happening with the case."

Edna gasped and seemed about to protest, but Nardo cut her off.

"My guess is that what Martin's family really wants is for you—and your child—to be out of their lives. I suspect once you are gone, they will not press the issue."

Edna could no longer hold her tongue. She turned on Lucy. "Do you see what you have done? You have robbed Nardo of his livelihood—of his ability to build a reputation for himself as a top performer. You have ruined everything."

Lucy walked to Nardo and cupped his face in her palms. "Thank you," she whispered.

"You agree to my terms?"

"There is no need for such a promise," Lucy said. "The man will hire me."

"What do you know of laundry and mopping floors and such," Edna huffed. "You with your fancy clothes—"

"Hush, Edna," Violet said. "You don't know what you're talking about."

Lucy met Violet's look. They had been through a lot together, the two of them. Violet had been like an older sister and even at times a surrogate mother to Lucy. Her support now meant a great deal. It bolstered Lucy's courage.

"But you need to say the words, Lucille," Violet added. "Give the man your promise or I'll turn you in myself."

CHAPTER THIRTEEN

Sarasota, August 2022

CHLOE

Over the next week there was good news and bad—good for Chloe in that Toby not only uncovered a short newspaper article about Lucy's arrest but also found the guest list for John Ringling's party along with the butler's notation of where each over-night guest would stay. Her great-grandmother's name was listed as staying in the "rose room," the very guest room Ian had shown her on their tour. Eagerly she hurried to the mansion to share the news and hopefully have the chance to look at the room again. Knowing Lucinda Conroy had once stayed there gave it special meaning.

But when she reached the house, entering through the back door, Darcy looked up and frowned.

"Not a good time, honey," she said.

"What's happened? Was there another break-in?"

"More like a breakout. The contractor pulled his crew this morning. He said until he got his money, there would be no work done." She shook her head. "Ian's beside himself. He's got nothing to do with paying them—that's Bill Tucker's area."

"But surely—"

"Ian's been trying to contact Tucker all morning. Every day since Ian arrived on the job that man has made it his business to pretend to be out for a run when what he's really doing is checking up on Ian. But today he's gone AWOL? Truth is, I'm not sure paying the contractor will solve the problem. He and his crew can make a lot more working on one of those new high-rises downtown. If you ask me, the contractor saw an opportunity to bail and took it."

"That's terrible," Chloe protested. "It borders on unethical."

Darcy shrugged. "It's the way of things here in Florida. Definitely not the first time it's happened. Ian's been trying to reach the contractor as well, but his calls there also go to voicemail."

"Does all this have anything to do with the break-in last week?"

Darcy shrugged. "Probably. It could have been a warning, but try proving any connection." The phone on her desk buzzed. "Ah, this will be Ian." She pushed a button. "Hey, boss." She listened. "I can try. Chloe's here. Maybe she can get Tilda to get her dad on the phone so you can talk to him?" She listened a second more, then held out the receiver to Chloe. "He wants to talk to you."

"Ian, Darcy told me. How can I help?" It was a stupid offer, but she wanted him to know somebody was on his side.

"Well," he drawled, "that book you're writing—the one you plan to donate all the profits from to the estate? How fast can we get that thing out there?"

"I guess I can call—"

"Chloe, I'm making a joke—a poor one to be sure, but the fact is we're at a standstill, and on top of that I just got a weather update about that tropical storm south of here. It's just been upgraded to a full-blown hurricane. Has its own name and everything." His voice trailed off, then suddenly he spoke again, this time all business. "Have you seen Tilda this morning?"

"I left her at the archives."

"Get her over here, okay?"

"Sure. I—"

"Put Darcy back on, will you?"

While Darcy talked to Ian, Chloe stepped outside and called Tilda. "Could you come to the mansion?"

"Now?"

It had started to rain.

"Yes, please. I…that is, Ian needs you." *That should do it.*

"On my way."

Chloe gave Darcy a thumbs-up and heard her relay the message to Ian. "He's coming down here," she told Chloe once she stepped back inside. "Cup of coffee?"

"No, thanks."

The rain was coming down harder. Chloe turned at the sound of voices. Ian and Pete stood in the kitchen, staring out at the rain. "I'll call some guys," Pete said.

"Good," Ian replied. "By the time they get here Darcy and I can have the small stuff in the grand court removed so you can get the furniture upstairs."

"I can help," Chloe offered. "And Toby—what about getting him over here?"

"He'll be busy helping secure the archives." Ian ran his hands through his thick hair. "But you're right. We're going to need more help." He took out his phone and stared at it.

Just then Tilda burst through the door, and the gust of wind that followed her carried into the kitchen. She shook off her umbrella and closed it, even as she focused on Ian. "Reporting for duty, my captain," she said with a cheerful smile that faded as soon as she saw his downcast eyes.

He rallied and smiled at her. "Can you get your dad on the phone and let him know we've got a situation here that's rapidly becoming a crisis?"

Tilda looked confused. "I could have done that from—"

"And then," Ian continued, "I need your help organizing the move of all the smaller pieces from the court so Pete and his crew can move the furniture. There are crates and packing materials in the vault."

"I can start gathering those while you call your father," Chloe said. She was barely to the door before she heard Tilda reach her father's office.

"Ginny, it's Tilda. Where's Daddy? We need him here at the house."

The house obviously referred to this house—Ca' d'Zan—the House of John.

Leaving Tilda to find her father and at the same time unsure of what the man might be able to offer in terms of the work needed to secure the house, Chloe hurried up the stairs. After she found the crates, loaded several onto the elevator, then hurried down the stairs to meet it on the ground floor, she could hear Tilda still on the phone.

"I'm calling in the media, Daddy. Ian needs help. The workers have abandoned him, not to mention this treasured piece of Sarasota's history."

Tilda listened as she paced from the pantry to the kitchen and back again. "No, Daddy! This can't wait. Have you looked outside? You need to get hold of that contractor and settle things so he gets his crew back here within the hour."

Chloe could not help being impressed. This was a side of Tilda she had not yet seen—the professional woman taking charge. Tilda clicked off her phone, and turned to Ian. "He says he'll make a few calls." She sighed heavily, then brightened as she studied Chloe. "Were you serious about helping?" It was a challenge.

"Of course," Chloe replied. "Whatever I can do."

"I have an idea." She punched in a number and pressed the phone to her ear. "Danny Sutton," she said, "do I have an exclusive for you!"

Ian and Chloe exchanged baffled glances. "Who's Danny

Sutton?" Chloe asked him.

Darcy had come into the room to listen. "He's an event planner and major social influencer here in town. He knows everyone."

Chloe turned her attention back to Tilda.

"You know Chloe Whitfield is here at the house writing her next novel. Well, she's also pitching in to help secure the place in case the hurricane hits as predicted. And I have a feeling that any of your social media friends who might show up in the next hour to fill sandbags and such could easily find themselves working side by side with Ms. Whitfield."

Immediately Chloe began waving her hands to get Tilda's attention.

"Let me put you on hold a minute, Daniel." She gave Chloe an impatient look. "What?"

"I understand what you're trying to do, but really, Tilda, who is going to come out in this weather on my account?"

"I'd get Stephen King over here if I could, but don't sell yourself short, Chloe. You're a name, and people love being able to say they met—and worked side by side with—a celebrity."

Chloe understood that Tilda had hit on a public relations coup. "Tell your friend I'll do photos and provide everyone who comes with a personally autographed copy of my new book once it's published," Chloe said. She had a reputation for never allowing photos and rarely signing autographs.

"Did you get that?" Tilda had switched the phone to speaker.

"Is that her?" the man at the other end of the call demanded.

Chloe took the phone from Tilda. "Mr. Sutton, we haven't met, but I assure you this is Chloe Whitfield, and time is of the essence here. Please do what you can. We need help—now."

An hour later the house was alive with people—most of them outside following directions for filling and stacking sandbags around the doors and windows of the grand house. Inside, Darcy,

Tilda, and Chloe moved through the rooms on the main floor, carefully removing the dozens of small items from tabletops, desks, and mantels and wrapping each before placing them in crates. As soon as a crate was filled, Pete and his crew moved it up to the mezzanine. Then they worked with the men to move the furnishings to safety.

"The danger is not in a direct hit," Pete had explained when Chloe questioned how likely it might be that the hurricane would come ashore without first being weakened by the barrier islands that lay between the estate and the Gulf of Mexico. "The surge of water is the real threat. We're just nine feet above sea level here, and even a slight surge could be destructive. Something more significant could do real damage."

By the time they finished, most everyone was soaked to the skin, but spirits were high. Tilda had managed to persuade her father to authorize passes for admission to the museum grounds as well as the house's Personal Spaces tour—usually an extra cost—once the house reopened. Bill Tucker had finally shown up just as Pete's team had moved the last piece of furniture. He insisted Ian and Chloe join him in a receiving line outside the entrance to the solarium to thank each volunteer. He made a great show of handing each of them the packet of gift passes and the promise of Chloe's book Tilda had somehow managed to assemble. He acted as if he—and he alone—had saved the mansion, and Chloe realized she didn't much care for Bill Tucker.

CHAPTER FOURTEEN

Ca' d'Zan, Summer 1936

Lucy

*M*r. Jefferson hired them both. Nardo had presented Lucy as his widowed cousin, telling the butler there was no longer a job for him with the circus.

"As part of your pay, Mr. Russo, you may stay in the cottage." Mr. Jefferson explained that the captain had taken ill and was not expected to return any time soon from the visit with his daughter. "Mrs. O'Connor will have a room in the servants' quarters here."

He gave each of them a list of their responsibilities. Lucy was to clean the house and polish the silver. "And be assured, Mrs. O'Connor, that since the day I first came to work for the Ringlings, I have kept a detailed inventory of every item in the house from the utensils and crockery in the kitchen to every stick of furniture."

"Yes, sir," Lucy replied, remembering to keep her eyes downcast as Violet had advised.

Mr. Jefferson turned his attention to Nardo. "Your responsibilities are groundskeeping and security. I expect you to make regular patrols around the property throughout the night. Is that clear?"

"Begging your pardon, sir," Nardo said, holding his cap submissively with both hands and not looking directly at the butler. "Might it not be best if Miz O'Connor takes the cottage, her being the only woman living here?"

Oh, Nardo, stop trying to take care of me before you mess up everything.

"Excellent idea," Mr. Jefferson said. "Mr. Russo and I will take our meals there at the cottage with you. That saves having to use the kitchen here. I presume you can cook?"

She could practically hear Nardo begging her to say yes although they both knew very well it had been years since Lucy had prepared anything more complicated than scrambled eggs and toast.

She glanced at Mr. Jefferson and smiled. "I can do simple meals, Mr. Jefferson. But my cousin here is quite the chef. He's Italian, you know."

For the first time since they'd arrived, Mr. Jefferson smiled. "Mrs. Ringling was very fond of Italian cuisine."

And Mr. John still is. Lucy had to bite her tongue to stop herself from adding this detail.

The butler tapped his forefinger against his upper lip. "Very well. Mrs. O'Connor will occupy the cottage and take responsibility for breakfast and lunch. Mr. Russo, you will prepare our evening meal. There's a limited household budget for the purchase of food and supplies, so please keep that in mind. Simple dishes well made." He picked up a ring of keys from his desk and passed them to Nardo, then handed a single key to Lucy. "Welcome to Ca' d'Zan."

Over that summer, Lucy settled into a routine that she was surprised to realize suited her. By day she was surrounded by the fine things in the massive house—beautiful antiques and *objets d'art* that she took pleasure and pride in maintaining. Each morning she prepared a hot breakfast for the two men, and while they ate at the table in the dining room of the cottage, she packed a lunch for each of them to eat at the mansion. Mr. J, as Lucy called Mr.

Jefferson in private, addressed Nardo by his given name, although he maintained a certain formality with her. As summer turned to fall, Lucy abandoned the padding Violet had provided as her own body swelled with her pregnancy.

Before leaving to head back to Wisconsin where the circus had their summer headquarters, Violet had made sure Lucy had a bottle of hair dye to touch up her roots. But Lucy preferred wrapping a colorful scarf around her hair, and Mr. Jefferson had approved. "Dust balls and threads of hair seem to multiply no matter how carefully we try and maintain things," he commented.

He was especially protective of the massive area rug that took up much of the floor in the Grand Court. The beautiful Aubusson carpet dated to 1870, and had been specially chosen by Mable Ringling for the space. It was evident that Mr. Jefferson had been enormously fond of Mrs. Ringling, and, listening to his stories, Lucy found herself admiring the woman as well. Living in the cottage gave her a sense of home she had really never known, and in many ways she, Nardo, and Mr. J had formed a kind of family.

"Ah, there you are, Mrs. O'Connor."

She was standing at the windows of the Grand Court lost in thought as she looked out through the pastel colors of the glass at the calm bay and had not heard her employer enter the room.

She turned quickly, feather duster in hand. "Did you need something, sir?"

He was holding a folded copy of the society section of the *Herald Tribune*. Lucy's heart skipped a beat. It had been four months since she'd been arrested. Earlier in the summer there had been an article about her failure to appear in court and presumed disappearance, but nothing since. The butler crossed the room and held the paper out to her. "I thought you and Nardo might find this of interest."

She set down the duster and accepted the paper, opening it to reveal a large photograph of Marty with Julia Gordon. Lucy scanned the headline.

Socialite Eschews Holiday Nuptials in Favor of Elopement

And then the caption of the photograph of the couple.

"We simply could wait no longer," *Miss Gordon gushed when asked why.*

She was keenly aware that Mr. J was watching her closely, so she swallowed the emotions stirred by the photograph—and the news, and as she returned the paper to Mr. J, said, "Nardo worked for this man, but they were not friends."

"But you and this Martin Sutherland were." It was a statement, not a question.

Lucy retrieved her feather duster and began dusting a small table.

"I know who you are, Miss Conroy." Mr. Jefferson's voice was quiet and calm. There was no accusation in his words. "I am a keen observer of detail. In my work that is an advantage." He moved a step closer, and instinctively Lucy took a step back, nearly upsetting the items on the table.

"Please, come and sit down, Miss Conroy," the butler said, pointing to one of a trio of chairs that faced the fireplace.

Just then they heard Nardo enter through the solarium, and Lucy realized it was lunchtime. On his way to the kitchen where the three of them gathered to open their packed lunches each day, Nardo crossed the foyer that opened onto the Grand Court. When he saw Lucy seated, he stopped, his eyes riveted on her. "Are you…? Is everything—"

"Please join us Nardo." Mr. Jefferson indicated a second chair and then sat between them in the third. "As I was just saying to Miss Conroy, it would appear we are on the horns of a dilemma, my young friends." He passed the newspaper to Nardo, who glanced at the article, then let the paper fall from his fingers as he sat back in the chair.

A kaleidoscope of images passed through Lucy's head—being

caught and arrested again and this time taken directly to prison, her child being born in a narrow dank cell, Marty dancing with Julia at their wedding in New York, Marty's father laughing, the Tiffany vase magically discovered and returned to its rightful place.

Suddenly Nardo sat forward and turned to Mr. Jefferson. "Lucinda did not do the things of which she was accused. She could never—"

"Calm yourself," the butler said. "It was obvious to me that day something did not ring true in the story being told. And then when the elder Mr. Sutherland spoke of Miss Conroy attempting to dupe his son into marriage by claiming pregnancy, things began to come together for me." He turned to Lucy. "You may not realize this, but Mr. Ringling has always been quite fond of you, in a paternal way, of course. He once confided his concern that you had become involved with his business manager. 'She is out of her league,' were his precise words."

A wave of relief at not having to continue the ruse with Mr. Jefferson swept over Lucy. She felt suddenly lighter and more in control of her future. "Mr. John's concern was well placed," she admitted. "But the truth is, even if he had spoken to me directly, I was too far gone to listen."

"Yes, well, the young Mr. Sutherland is a natural charmer."

For some reason his words made Lucy think of a snake charmer and the coiled reptile rising slowly from a basket. The image made her smile.

"And so," Mr. Jefferson continued, "here we are, and what are we to do?"

And as quickly as it had arrived, the relief she'd felt dissipated, replaced once again by the constant fear and anxiety she'd been living with for months now—fear of being discovered and turned over to the police. "Please," she whispered.

The butler reached over and covered her hand with his. "For

now, we can manage. The police seem to have allowed the matter to lapse, at least as long as the key players—Mr. Sutherland and his parents and the Gordon girl—are all away enjoying their lives in New York. But they will return, Lucy, and even before that happens there is the matter of the child you are carrying. What will you do once you deliver?" He glanced at Nardo. "Would it not be best if you—and Bernardo—left Sarasota and began a new life elsewhere?"

"I have tried to persuade her of this, but to no avail," Nardo said.

"I cannot prove my innocence if I am not here."

The older man sighed and sat back in his chair. "Dear girl, you cannot prove your innocence regardless of where you are. It is your word against theirs. I have no doubt about what happened that day—no doubt at all that you were framed, but I am also afraid there is little you can do to change the perception of guilt."

"If we could find the missing vase... I'm sure it's hidden somewhere here in the house. Surely that would show the authorities—"

"What the authorities would see is you having come back here in disguise. In their minds your purpose would have been to retrieve the vase *you* hid."

Lucy's heart sank. Of course he was right. She looked at Nardo, whose expression was as grave as she imagined her own to be.

"We should make a plan for settling elsewhere," he said.

Mr. Jefferson stood. "Yes, that would be wise."

She felt panic rising. To try and find work in these times while settling in a new town where they knew no one? To deliver her baby in a strange place?

"However," Mr. Jefferson continued, "for now, we will press on. The fact is, I cannot manage without you, and furthermore, I will not be responsible for sending you off to have this innocent child in a place where your health and that of the baby might be compromised." He faced the two of them. "Make your plans. Meanwhile, I will, with your permission, bring my friend Dr. Rosen into our little circle of secrecy."

Dr. Rosen had been the one to attend Lucy the night she fainted at Mr. John's party. Over the years he had also come to the circus grounds on more than one occasion to treat someone in the company who had fallen ill or suffered an injury. He was a man of integrity, who took his oath to do no harm seriously. Lucy believed his loyalty would be to that oath, rather than to Marty or his parents. And once again she was overcome with a renewed sense of hope.

She was not aware of the tears that had spilled over until Mr. Jefferson pulled a crisp white handkerchief from his pocket and Nardo untied the bandanna he wore round his neck and both were extended to her in unison.

CHAPTER FIFTEEN

Sarasota, September 2022

C͟HLOE

*A*s if in answer to the prayers Chloe and the volunteers had shared, the hurricane never materialized but was downgraded to a tropical storm as it hit land on the Keys. Still, she soon realized a tropical storm was nothing to ignore. With it came torrential rains and winds significant enough to bring down tree branches and electrical wires. Power still went out, and Ian reported that because the outage was widespread, restoring power to the mansion—or the cottage—was not a priority for the city. He was able to secure a couple of generators and set one up for Chloe at the cottage and the other larger one at the mansion.

"One of the greatest threats with the heat and humidity and dampness is mildew," he told Chloe. "Are you sure you wouldn't like to take Tilda up on her offer to come stay with her parents until this gets sorted?"

The idea of trying to write anywhere but on the grounds where she could have ready access to the mansion was not appealing. Also, once she'd settled in and accepted that Pete was more than willing to pick up whatever she might need or give her a ride to the farmer's market or grocery store, she had rarely used her rental car. She probably should return it. It was an added expense—and responsibility—she didn't need, and not having access to it also helped her stay focused on the task at hand—finishing the book.

You mean writing the book, don't you?

She had quickly realized that documentation of what had actually happened to her great-grandmother was unlikely to materialize and she would need to create facts to move the plot along. She told herself that her great-grandmother was really just the model for her protagonist, but the truth was she longed to know the real story. After spending the first several years of her life in an orphanage in Tampa, Grandma Alice had been adopted by that wonderful couple from New Jersey who had filled her life with love and laughter. But how had she ended up in the orphanage in the first place? The last news of Lucinda Conroy had been her performance at John Ringling's seventieth birthday gala, followed by a short item about her arrest—and then nothing.

Chloe started building a timeline—the date of the party plus the date her grandmother was born—and came to a startling realization. Lucinda Conroy had to have been pregnant when she performed the dangerous triple somersault and pregnant when she was arrested. She also had seen a copy of the paperwork from the orphanage showing that her grandmother's residency there had begun when she was an infant. If the trail led from Ca' d'Zan to an orphanage in Tampa, then perhaps it was time to head north to Tampa.

"I don't understand," Tilda fumed. "I thought you were stressed about needing to finish the manuscript. Not only that, but there's so much we need to do for the opening gala. What's in Tampa?"

"It's just an overnight trip to do some research," Chloe assured her, once again wondering what it was about Tilda that made her feel she needed to explain her decisions. "Ian has—"

"Ian is going?"

"He has business there, and since we both need to go, it seemed silly for me to have to deal with renting another car and driving separately."

"I could drive you," Tilda said.

"You could, but then that would take you away from the important work you have here trying to pull the gala together."

"Or Toby could," Tilda suggested.

"The plan is made," Chloe said, hoping her firm tone would close the subject.

But she had learned there were times when Tilda could be like a dog determined to suck every morsel of marrow from a bone. "What's in Tampa that you can't find here?"

Chloe was not about to discuss her great-grandmother's private life with Tilda. "The entire story cannot take place here on the grounds of Ca' d'Zan, Tilda. I need other places, other details, to move the plot forward."

She was doing it again. Explaining herself.

"But—"

Chloe forced a smile. "Tilda, I love your enthusiasm for my work, but it is, after all, *my* work, and I really need you to respect that."

If she had expected a contrite apology, Chloe realized Tilda was not one to let go of that bone she was determined to conquer. "Just trying to do my job," Tilda muttered as she slung her bag over her shoulder and left the cottage.

Being on the road away from the now familiar grounds of the museum felt like an escape. Ian also seemed to have relaxed with the change of scenery. He'd chosen to take what he called the "back way." "I enjoy taking it slow, seeing what I'm passing, and I'm definitely not a fan of expressways," he'd told her. He wore khakis and a short-sleeved polo shirt in a salmon color that complemented his tanned arms and face. The breeze ruffled his thick coffee-colored hair. "Also not a fan of air-conditioning, if that's okay," he'd added with a grin.

"Me neither," she'd agreed. "Give me fresh air over artificial any time, but if we want to talk…"

He grinned. "Okay, you've got a point."

They talked easily of their individual projects and the progress—or lack of—they'd made.

"The crew is back at work," he told her.

"They caught the person?"

"Actually it was the contractor. Payback for not being paid. Needless to say, he's no longer on the job. I found someone else who seems to be working out."

"I'm sure that's a relief."

"It is. Of course, the storm damage has added to what needs to get done, but we're making good progress. I think we may not yet be out of the woods though. Bill Tucker has hinted at a serious lack of funds."

They rode in silence for several moments.

"Speaking of finances," Chloe said, "Toby brought me some information about John Ringling's financial troubles. I mean, he went from being one of the wealthiest men in the country to having just over $300 in the bank when he died. How does that happen?"

Ian shrugged. "Priorities would be my guess. Some folks have a tendency to put the emphasis on the wrong things. In Ringling's case it was *things* that led to his undoing—that and a second marriage that was a disaster pretty much from day one. Of course, it was also the times. He and Mable, who was his first wife and the love of his life, moved into the house in 1926. She died just three years later, and that same year the stock market crashed. Men like John

Ringling watched helplessly as their investments in land and such pretty much disintegrated."

"There are so many treasures in the house alone," Chloe said. "Why on earth didn't he sell some of it? Or the art in the galleries?"

Ian shrugged. "Times were tough for everyone, and even had he been willing to part with anything, who could afford to buy it?" He chuckled. "As for me? Give me the simple life."

"I completely agree," Chloe said, and it occurred to her she and Ian Flanner had more in common than she'd first thought. She was looking forward to this little getaway, both in terms of the research she hoped to do and in spending more time getting to know Ian.

After they'd checked in at the hotel, Ian dropped her off at the historical society before going on to his meeting. Chloe had arranged a meeting with Alan Helton, the society's director who, after welcoming her to Tampa, gave her the bad news. "I'm afraid the orphanage closed in the early 1950s, and as with so many landmarks, the building was torn down and is now a strip mall."

"That's disappointing. But there must have been files, records…" She could tell by the man's expression that this was unlikely.

"What there was has been stored here for decades now. I'm afraid there were more pressing priorities. We've intended to scan the documents but just haven't had the time, or finances, to do so."

"May I see them anyway?"

He smiled and indicated a small conference room off the main exhibit area. "I anticipated that might be your request. Regrettably there's not much, and from what I've been able to ascertain after a cursory review, there are a number of gaps in what is there."

On the table sat two large file boxes.

"This is it?"

"I'm afraid so. The orphanage had a fire early in the twentieth century, so that explains the lack of anything much before 1910."

But Chloe was not interested in earlier. Grandma Alice had been born in the fall of 1936, and she was relieved to see one box was labeled 1930-1950. "Thank you. I'll start with this."

By the time she walked back to the hotel, Chloe was hot, tired, and disappointed. She hadn't discovered anything new about her great-grandmother's time at the orphanage. Oh, the record of her years there existed, but the details were sketchy or merely verified what her grandmother had always claimed. She'd been brought to the orphanage by a doctor, Evan Rosen. The one piece of new evidence Chloe had managed to uncover in the file was a tattered note attached to Grandma Alice's record of admission that read:

Girl Infant:
Home delivery Sarasota Florida: October 12, 1936.
Mother: circus performer; hospitalized postdelivery with puerperal fever—unlikely to survive.
Father: unknown.

So that was it? Lucy died after giving birth, and the doctor took Grandma Alice to the orphanage? End of story? It was an important bit of news to be sure—but still disappointing.

She had asked for and received permission to scan Dr. Rosen's note, and she studied it now on her phone before sending it to the tablet she'd left back at the cottage. The files had yielded nothing more until five years later when she found the water-stained record of Alice's adoption. The signatures of Alice's adoptive parents were unreadable, but there was nothing in the document that was new, and of course, once the adoption was finalized the trail ended—at least as far as the orphanage was concerned.

So, did Lucy Conroy die giving birth? And if not, where did she go?

A rustling sound at her door brought her back from her reverie. "Who is it?" she called out.

No answer.

She noticed a small white card on the floor half in and half outside the room. The message read:

Can't make dinner. Sorry.

Immediately Chloe suspected a ruse. Ian would simply have texted her. She opened the door and looked up and down the deserted hallway. In an alcove two doors from her room, she heard the elevator bell ding. Barefoot and still holding her phone, she ran down the corridor, but she was too late to see who boarded the elevator—and she was now locked out of her room.

She considered taking the stairs but knew she would never make it in time to see who came off the elevator. Instead, she texted Ian with a proposed time to meet in the lobby to go for dinner, and then called the desk to send someone to let her back in her room so she could shower and wash away some of the day's frustrations.

If her day had been irksome, Ian's had been a complete success. As they walked to the restaurant he'd selected, he talked excitedly about meeting an artisan who was exactly the person he needed to repair the balustrade columns in the tower. "His credentials are those of a man twice his age," Ian said. "We hit it off right away, and his price will certainly please Bill Tucker."

They'd reached the restaurant, and the *maître d'* had shown them to a table on the outside terrace with a nice view of the city's skyline. As soon as they'd been given menus, Ian continued telling her about his day. "I'm sure Bill will question the man's youth and equate that with inexperience. I may have to avoid introducing them until he has a chance to get started and I can show Bill his work, and by then…" He gave her a wry grin. "Sorry. I'm making this all about me, aren't I? How was your day?"

"Let's order, and then I'll give you my story. I'm famished, and everything on the menu sounds fabulous."

"I can definitely recommend the Oaxacan bowl. It's on the spicy side. Or the Peruvian burritos are also great—stuffed with roasted sweet potato and fresh corn. How about we start with an order of spring rolls?"

"Clearly you've been here before," Chloe said. "So on your recommendation I'll have the Oaxacan bowl."

Ian shrugged. "Finding a top-notch restaurant can be worth the drive." He motioned for the waiter, who seemed to know him, and placed their orders, then gave her his full attention. "Now, tell me how things were for you today."

She told him what she'd found—or rather been able to verify—about her great-grandmother's stay in the orphanage.

"I can understand why you'd be disappointed," he said as the waiter delivered their food.

"And then later there was this," she said, pulling out the handwritten note that had been slipped under her door earlier.

"Okay, that's weird." He laid the note on the table. "Did you think it was from me?"

"No. I figured you would just text me if you'd run into a delay or problem."

Ian continued to study the note as he ate his food. "Could have been meant for someone else and delivered to your room by mistake."

"That makes sense," Chloe agreed, and she wondered why that hadn't occurred to her as well. "I guess it's a bit of an occupational hazard for me to see shadows in any event I can't readily explain." She picked up the note and placed it back in her purse. "I'll let the front desk know it came to me by mistake."

"Have to feel bad for whoever's feeling stood up," Ian said. "Just glad it wasn't me." He raised his water glass in a toast.

Chloe felt her face flush. This was beginning to feel more like a date than two colleagues having dinner—and the truth was, she kind of liked that idea.

After they'd finished their dinner, Ian suggested ice cream. "I know a place," he said with a teasing grin.

"For someone who hasn't lived in the area that long, you apparently know all the places," Chloe replied with a laugh. It seemed only natural to link arms with him and add, "Lead on."

The ice cream shop was a tiny hole-in-the-wall with limited seating. But the scent of the waffle cones they made on site was irresistible, and the assortment of flavors made choosing difficult.

"I can do a half and half, even on a small," the clerk offered.

And with that in mind, Chloe ordered a raspberry and chocolate mix while Ian stuck to the single flavor of cashew caramel. With cones and plenty of napkins in hand, they strolled down the street, peering in windows of galleries and small shops and forgetting how fast their treat would melt in the summer heat.

"Okay, this is out of control," Ian said, stopping to lick the sides of his cone. "Let's sit over there on that park bench and finish these."

Chloe agreed and, once they were seated, each focused on the job of eating their ice cream before it became soup. She laughed when Ian's began leaking out the bottom of his cone and he slurped it up. Once she finished and had wiped her mouth, he reached over with a clean napkin and gently dabbed her chin.

"Missed a spot," he said, his voice husky.

Their eyes met and held.

"We should start back." She busied herself with gathering the used napkins and looking around for a trash container. She was uneasy with the sudden rush of feelings washing over her—feelings she had no idea how to manage. Surely this was just a matter of it being a long time since she'd been alone with an attractive man. She was out of practice. She was—

Ian stood and held out his hand. "Give me those," he said. "There's a trash can over there."

She watched him walk across the street. She thought of how easily she had linked arms with him earlier—how that had seemed like two old friends on their way for ice cream. *You're being ridiculous. Nothing has changed.*

She was still seated, as if rooted to the park bench, when he returned. He held out his hand to her again. "Come on. Let's walk."

She took his hand. It would be rude to refuse. And when he intertwined his fingers with hers and didn't let go, she had to admit that what had started as dinner with a friend had most certainly evolved into something more.

CHAPTER SIXTEEN

Ca' d'Zan, October 1936

LUCY

𝒟r. Rosen began making regular calls, often joining Lucy, Nardo, and Mr. Jefferson for dinner in the cottage. The dual relief of having his assurance her baby was healthy and no longer having to hide her true identity from Mr. Jefferson gave Lucy a sense of contentment she had not known in some time. She laughed often and freely. She went about her duties at the mansion with more confidence. And most of all, she began to realize how much she had underestimated Nardo's devotion and friendship. She trusted him as she had never trusted any man in her life, and she could not think of a single person she would rather have by her side once her baby was born.

"There is much to think about, Lucinda," he said one evening as the two of them strolled the paths of Mrs. Ringling's rose garden. "We cannot stay here forever. We need a plan."

"I have a plan," she insisted. "Once the baby comes, I will continue working."

"Doing what? Where? Here? And who will care for the child should you find work?" He ran his fingers through his thick black hair. "You do not think, Lucinda."

He had a point. Since being freed of the need to keep her

identity secret from Mr. Jefferson and Dr. Rosen, Lucy had relaxed. She had allowed herself to imagine continuing to live in the cottage, continuing to work in the mansion. She had envisioned her child running across the property—even learning to swim in the pool. She had thought in time the whole nasty business of having been falsely accused would simply go away—and to that end she had stopped thinking of finding some way to prove her innocence. She was certain Mr. John would return to Ca' d'Zan. He would be so happy to see her—and he loved children.

"I have news," Nardo said, interrupting her thoughts. "It is not good for either of us." He led her to a bench in the garden. "Mr. Jefferson told me this morning that he has received word from Mr. John's attorney that Ca' d'Zan is likely to be put up for sale. Mr. John is quite ill, but beyond that he has no money left. Mr. Jefferson will stay on for the time being out of loyalty, but it is not likely Mr. John will be returning—ever. The estate is to be foreclosed on, Lucinda."

Every fear Lucy thought she had conquered came racing back at her. She felt as if she were flying through the air, had released her trapeze and spun, only to find no one there to catch her. She saw Nardo's lips moving, knew he was speaking—pleading with her— but she could hear nothing more than the roar of her own thoughts.

Where would she go? How would she manage? And the baby— what of the baby?

She wrapped her arms protectively around the mound of her pregnancy and began rocking back and forth. She felt Nardo's palm on her back, but there was no comfort in his touch. She squeezed her eyes shut and moaned. The pain she'd felt as emotional was now physical, gripping her like a vise. She tried to stand and collapsed back onto the bench and into Nardo's arms. She heard him calling for help, felt him lift her and carry her from the garden as she clung to him and prayed the pain would stop.

Once inside the house, Nardo carried her up the back stairs, calling repeatedly for Mr. Jefferson to send for the doctor. He laid her on a bed in the servants' quarters, grabbing pillows from other cots to support her head and shoulders.

"I'm all right," she managed, realizing the pain had eased. She pushed herself to a half-sitting position and noticed everything she wore below her waist was soaked. She recalled how Dr. Rosen had explained the delivery when she had asked, "How will I know when it's time?"

His words had made no sense—a flood of water followed by labor pains that would begin probably in her lower back and wrap themselves around her, coming and going, but then coming with increased frequency. She had thought he did not know her—did not know what pains she had endured in the pulled muscles, the dislocated joints, and the falls she'd taken over the years of performing. She could stand pain far better than most.

Mr. Jefferson entered the room, bearing a stack of freshly laundered towels and an empty basin he handed to Nardo with instructions to fill it with water. "The doctor is on his way," he told her.

"I'm fine—" But before she could complete the sentence, the pain returned. Nardo dropped the basin and rushed to her side, grasping her hand in his. Her suffering was reflected in his eyes. He was every bit as terrified as she was. How could this be what was supposed to happen? Something was surely wrong.

"The baby," she whispered.

"*Our* child, Lucinda," he replied. "I will not desert either of you. Marry me, and we will be a family. We will—"

The tentacles of her discomfort tightened so that she cried out in agony.

"Where is the doctor?" she heard Nardo shout, and this time she was the one to hold tight to his forearm.

"Don't leave me," she managed.

There was a commotion at the door, and then the doctor was at her side, calling out orders like a sideshow barker as he removed his suit coat and rolled back his sleeves. While Nardo and Mr. Jefferson scurried to do his bidding, Dr. Rosen focused on Lucy. "Well now, young lady, it would seem your child wishes to make an appearance. You show people have a way of demanding to be seen—and heard, and in this case, it is this baby who wishes to take the spotlight. So I need you to try to relax and follow my instructions without question or debate. I assure you I have not lost a mother or baby yet, and I do not intend to start with you."

Lucy had no idea how much time passed. Hours? Days? She faded in and out of consciousness with the pain. She was vaguely aware of the tone of Dr. Rosen's voice—a tone that told her something was not as it should be. The light outside the small window changed from day to night. She was exhausted, and still the baby had not come. Whispers haunted her as she tried to focus on what was happening…too soon…breech…infection…

The next time she woke the room was quiet. The light in the window could be dawn or dusk. Slowly she realized someone had bathed away the sweat and stench of her fear and dressed her in a cotton gown before covering her with crisp sheets. Gradually she accepted that the pain was no longer a factor. And finally, she realized she was no longer pregnant. She pushed herself higher on the pillows and looked around. The door to the room was closed, but she could hear voices. What she did not hear—what she was desperate to hear—was the cry of her baby.

"Nardo!" Her voice was no more than a raspy whisper, her throat raw, her mouth dry. She coughed and tried again. "Nardo!"

She threw back the covers and moved to the edge of the bed. A wave of dizziness overcame her, driving her back against the pillows. And then she saw it—a tiny fist waving at her from the open drawer of a wooden chest pushed into the tight space between the bed and the wall.

A baby...*her* baby...swaddled in a blanket she had laundered herself while cleaning the rooms of the grand house.

Tears filled her eyes and for a moment she found it difficult to breathe. Then she scooted to the edge of the bed so she could reach her baby. She opened the blanket, and realized it was like unwrapping a fabulous gift. A girl—a beautiful daughter. She traced the tiny lips with her little finger. When the baby opened her mouth and sucked on Lucy's fingertip, Lucy laughed.

The door opened, and Nardo stood there, a tired but relieved smile on his handsome face. "You are awake," he said, coming to stand beside the bed. "She is awake," he called out, and Dr. Rosen and Mr. Jefferson crowded into the room.

"The baby," she managed.

"A girl as beautiful as her mother," Dr. Rosen said. He lifted the child from the drawer and handed her to Lucy. "And, I might add, every bit as willful."

The doctor was smiling, but Lucy did not miss the way his eyes didn't reflect that smile.

"She is all right?"

"She had a long journey, but she will be fine once she puts on a bit of weight."

The trio of men stood around the bed, watching as Lucy met her daughter. She resisted the urge to count the baby's fingers and toes, settling her attention instead on the mass of golden hair and the dark blue eyes that looked up at her. She was so beautiful...so perfect...so...

Suddenly she was overcome by chills so severe she felt the baby slipping from her grasp and felt as if she herself were falling. She fought to hold on as someone took the baby from her, eased her back onto the pillows, and stuck a thermometer under her tongue. She heard voices, panicked and talking over one another.

And then nothing...blackness...followed by a series of episodes where she felt as if she were falling…followed by more blackness. Chills unrelieved by extra covers, and at the same time fever that left her soaked in sweat. She had a sense of being moved…of female voices added to those of Dr. Rosen and Nardo. She fought to find her way back to consciousness—to her child who surely needed her.

"She's coming around. Nurse! Come quickly!"

Nardo.

Nurse? There had been no nurse.

Lucy fought to open her eyes. Her lashes felt crusty, as if there was the need to pry them free of her cheeks. She managed a slit, then immediately closed them again against the sudden light. She tried to raise her hand to block it and found she was too weak for even such a simple task. Her lips were cracked and dry.

"Wait outside, Mr. Russo," a woman instructed, her voice reminding Lucy of Violet's when she was being rushed to finish a costume.

She felt someone lift her wrist and take her pulse. "Mrs. Russo? Come on now. Time to wake up."

Mrs. Russo?

She opened her eyes to a slit and saw the blurred image of a heavyset woman in white bending over her.

"That's a good girl. Doctor is on his way." She slid a thermometer between Lucy's lips and then poured water into a glass on a bedside table—a table Lucy did not recognize, just as she didn't recognize the rest of her surroundings. The window was gone and in its place were cloth-covered privacy screens similar to those she used in her dressing tent. The nurse pulled the thermometer free and held it up to the light. "Now, that's better. The fever has broken finally."

"Where…?" Lucy swallowed and tried again. "Where am I?"

"Hospital, dearie. You gave us all quite a fright. Here, take a sip—just a sip. Wet your lips, and I'll get you some salve to ease the dryness." She cupped Lucy's head with her large palm and tipped the glass to her lips.

Lucy sputtered and coughed but managed to swallow a little of the cool water before the nurse eased her back on the pillow.

"Nardo?"

The nurse, whose features were becoming clearer, grinned. "That man is devoted to you. Hasn't left your side since he brought you here. I can't say my husband would do the same, that's for sure."

"My baby?"

The nurse's expression softened. "Ah, yes, the other nurses said you kept calling for a baby while you were out. I'm sorry, dear. There is no baby, my dear. As sick as you've been though, there's no telling what you might have imagined or dreamed." She turned to a sound outside the curtained screens. "Ah, here comes Doctor."

Someone pulled one of the screens open, and she saw the man turn back to say something to Nardo, who looked around and over the man's shoulder at Lucy. Behind him she saw another woman in a bed and realized she was on a ward of several patients.

"Wait here," the man told Nardo before stepping inside and pulling the screen back into place.

Where's Dr. Rosen?

Lucy tried without success to form the words as the doctor conferred with the nurse. After the nurse left, he turned to Lucy. "I am Dr. Harris," he said as he studied the chart the nurse had handed him. "It's nice to finally meet you, Mrs. Russo."

There was so much she wanted to say—to ask. *I'm not Mrs. Russo. Where am I, exactly? Why aren't you Dr. Rosen?* And most of all, *Where is my child?* Instead, she simply stared at him, waiting for him to finish reading her chart.

"Much improved," he said. He hooked the chart on its place at the foot of the bed—a bed different from the one she'd birthed her daughter in. He took the stethoscope from around his neck and listened to her heart and lungs. He took her pulse, probed her neck with gentle fingers, and then probed her stomach. "Any pain?" he asked.

She shook her head. "Could I speak to Nardo, please?"

"Of course." The doctor rehung his stethoscope around his neck and made a couple of additions to the information on her chart. Then to her amazement, he smiled at her and winked. "We should be able to have you home in a few days," he promised and left.

Lucy heard him share that same information with Nardo, and then Nardo was there with her, heavy bags of worry and weariness under his dark eyes, his face unshaven. He wore clothes that were different than those he'd worn on the day of her delivery, but still looked as if he hadn't changed in days. But he was smiling as he moved to her side and took her hand between his. "I thought I had lost you," he managed, and then surrendered to the tears he'd tried to blink away.

To her surprise, Lucy also started to cry. "Where am I? What has happened to my baby? Why am I here?"

Nardo pulled a metal chair closer to the bed and sat. "You have been very ill, Lucinda. There were times…" His voice caught. "Times when the doctors said there was no hope you would recover."

"Where is my daughter?" Lucy felt her inborn strength returning.

Nardo let out a long sigh. "I will tell you everything, Lucinda, but you must allow me to finish before you say anything."

"My daughter—"

"Is safe and being cared for," he assured her. "Will you let me tell it?"

She folded her arms across her chest and scowled at him. "Go on."

"After the delivery you developed a sickness—I heard the nurses call it childbed fever. Dr. Harris called it something else. Per-per-al or something like that. I heard the nurses talk of sepsis. Dr. Rosen was very worried. He had Mr. Jefferson and me bring you here and assured us he would get the baby to the care she would need." When Lucy started to protest, he continued. "She needed food and care, and neither Mr. Jefferson nor I could provide that. There was no other choice, Lucinda. By the time we got you here, your fever was much higher. The doctors gave us little hope you would make it through the night."

"How long have I been here?"

"Almost two weeks. At one point they gave you a blood transfusion, and they kept trying different medicines to fight the infection they told me was running uncontrolled through your body. I told them you were strong and would beat this, but they were not so sure."

Lucy felt a flicker of pride that Nardo had been right, but then her thoughts returned to her daughter. She recalled holding her, feeling the baby's lips part and suckle Lucy's fingertip as she traced the perfect bow mouth. But she had not nursed her child—had not offered her a mother's milk.

"Where is she?"

"Dr. Rosen took her to an orphanage near Tampa. He knows the sisters there and assured me they are kind and even have a wet nurse who can nurse infants."

Lucy was quiet for a long moment, her mind racing with plans. First, she needed to get out of this hospital, then go and collect her child, then…what?

"There's more," Nardo said softly. "Mr. Ringling has had to close down Ca'd'Zan. It's now a matter for the courts to decide his future and that of his home and art collection. He's sent for Mr. Jefferson to come to New York and serve him there."

"But surely even the courts would need someone to look after the property," Lucy said.

Nardo was shaking his head before she even got the words out. "We cannot go back there, Lucinda." He studied his hands. "The truth is we have no home and no means of supporting ourselves."

"We have our act," she protested. "We can certainly find work with that. Once I get out of here, we can get the baby…." It struck her suddenly that things had deteriorated so quickly she had not even had a chance to name her daughter.

As if reading her thoughts, Nardo said, "She is safe where she is. The sisters have given her the name Alice. They wanted to christen her in case she also got sick."

Lucy had not thought of that. The baby she'd held had been so perfect, the idea she might take ill had never entered her mind. But, of course, if she could be brought down without warning, how much more vulnerable was a newborn?

"But the nurse said there was no baby," she said.

"She wasn't on duty when we brought you here. I think Dr. Rosen asked the other doctor to be…discreet. He feared questions being raised that might bring the police into things. So, you were registered as my wife. I am sorry, but it was the only way."

The police. That whole business seemed so long ago now—so much had happened and changed. She doubted Marty would even care that he had a daughter.

She placed her hand on Nardo's unshaven cheek. "I am not sorry at all," she said softly. "Lucinda Russo is a lovely name. Thank you, Nardo."

He leaned into her touch, then turned his mouth so he could kiss her palm. "I do love you, Lucinda," he whispered.

She realized she had never witnessed the kind of love Nardo offered her. After her mother died, her father had raised her alone— teaching her the craft he knew, but otherwise distant and removed. Her family had been the circus people, a series of women like Violet, who had stepped in when needed. Nardo was the first person in her life who had been, was now, and would likely always be there for her.

She'd be a fool to walk away from that.

"We will get through this, Nardo—together," she whispered, and this time when she saw the hope that he could not hide, she realized at last she was making the right decision for herself and her child.

CHAPTER SEVENTEEN

Sarasota, September 2022

Chloe

The morning after Chloe and Ian returned from their trip to Tampa, Tilda did not show up for work. She also did not call, text, or respond to voicemail. Concerned, Chloe called Ian.

"She called," he said. "Did the two of you have a disagreement?"

"Not at all. Why?"

"She says she doesn't want to work for you anymore." His voice was tight, not at all the casual, easygoing man who'd walked her back to the cottage late the night before. And definitely not the man who had leaned in and kissed her lightly on her forehead.

"Technically she works for you—and her father," Chloe reminded him. "What's going on?"

"I have no idea, and frankly no time to sort it out. So, if you could—"

"I have a meeting with the historical society here," she reminded him. He had been the one to suggest she talk to the director there. He'd made a call during their drive back from Tampa and set up the meeting himself. She'd planned to catch a ride there with Tilda, but that wasn't happening.

"Just call her, Chloe, okay? She's at her place, claiming she's not feeling up to coming in. She comes off as confident, but the truth is from what I've been able to tell, she's pretty fragile, especially when it comes to trying to impress her father. You coming here was all her idea, and Bill's fully on board with that. But he's made it obvious that his daughter has a habit of coming up with grand ideas and then dropping the ball. He's giving her a hard time about the gala, questioning her every idea. She's had a lot of disappointment and distress in her personal life to deal with recently."

Chloe was feeling her own share of stress these days and failed to see how Tilda's was her problem. She was about to say so when Ian added, "I'm sorry to dump this on you, but I'm pretty sure whatever is going on has to do with you, so, please?" All the charm of the evening before was back.

"You owe me," she said, but she was laughing.

"More than willing to pay the price," he said. "Dinner tomorrow?"

"Somewhere expensive and elegant," she bartered, glad to be back to the flirting they'd both engaged in the day before.

"I've got just the place," he said. "Thanks, Chloe." This time his tone was filled with genuine appreciation.

As she pulled up Tilda's number, she glanced at the clock. Her appointment at the historical society was set for late afternoon. Hopefully plenty of time to settle whatever was happening with Tilda and perhaps even get some work done before she had to leave.

Tilda's number rang once and then went immediately to voicemail. Either she was on another call, or she had seen Chloe's name and declined the call. Chloe left a message, asking Tilda to meet her at the historical society. She made no reference to having spoken to Ian or knowing Tilda had said she no longer wanted to serve as her assistant. Instead, she filled her message with compliments. "I don't know these people at the society, or really how they might be of help. I've come to rely on you to be my guide in these matters. So, if there's any way you could meet me there at three thirty... Call or text me when you get this. I'm here at the cottage working.

Would love to go for coffee after the meeting if that works for you." She deliberately took a tone of uncertainty as she signed off. "Well, that's it, then. Hope you can make it—you always know the right questions to ask. Hope everything is okay. Call me."

She clicked off the phone and set it aside. If Tilda took the bait, Chloe would be grateful and appreciative throughout their meeting at the society, but the minute they went for coffee, she would shift gears and demand to know exactly what was going on. She did not have time to play games.

Sitting at the small desk in the parlor of the cottage, she opened her tablet and brought up the file for her manuscript. Suddenly the screen went black, and then it went haywire—filled with repeating images swirling around a black box that announced:

YOUR DEVICE HAS BEEN INFECTED. ALL CONTENT WILL BE DESTROYED UNLESS YOU PAY THE RANSOM WITHIN THE NEXT 12 HOURS. CLICK HERE!

Chloe rocked back in her chair, a flood of disbelief followed by the nausea of terror washing over her as she read the message again. Her forefinger hovered over the mouse, instinctively set to follow the instructions and click on the link. Like a child about to touch a hot stove, she jerked her hand away.

Please, God, this can't be happening. I need help.

She grabbed her phone and was about to call Ian when the thought occurred that her phone, and tablet were linked. If she dialed Ian, would she be spreading the virus to his devices—destroying his work? Pocketing her phone, she hurried from the cottage and ran the short distance to the mansion.

Please let him be there—and know someone who can make this right.

She had completed close to half the novel but knew it wasn't fresh or new.

I can't deliver another mediocre story, God. But what she'd written so far was all she had, and at least she could fix that. Starting from scratch was unthinkable.

She ran around the side of the mansion, sweat already pouring down her cheeks, her hair damp against her neck. "Darcy!" She shouted the woman's name before she even had the door to the visitor area open.

Darcy hurried from the kitchen, her expression one of shock and concern. "Heavens, child, you gave me a start. What on earth?"

"Is Ian here?"

"Of course. He and Pete just went up to the game room."

Chloe hurried past Darcy, heading for the stairs. "Someone has hacked into my computer and—" She realized she couldn't run up the stairs and explain at the same time. "I need help," she said and heard Darcy's footsteps behind her.

"Ian! Pete!" Darcy's shouts echoed up the stairway. "It's Chloe. She's been attacked."

Both men came running to meet them. Ian reached Chloe first, took hold of her shoulders, and studied her closely. "Are you injured?"

"My computer—tablet," she managed, gasping for breath. "A virus and a ransom demand."

Ian handed Darcy his phone, then wrapped his arm around Chloe and ushered her to a chair in the game room. "Call administration and tell them to get the tech over here immediately." He turned back to Chloe. "Where's the tablet, Chloe?"

"At the cottage, on the desk."

"On my way," Pete said as he started down the stairs.

Darcy handed Chloe one of the bottles of water Ian kept on hand and then opened one for herself. "A ransom? I know they've done that with big companies and such, but you're just one person."

"One very famous person in certain circles," Ian said, his voice tight with anger.

Chloe sipped the water as she mentally ran through everything that was on her tablet—research notes, manuscripts, contacts, ideas for future projects—essentially her whole career. Of course, she had backups for most of it, but what about her personal information— her financial information? A backup was no comfort if some hacker already had her private data.

"Chloe, let's go downstairs and wait for the tech to come there," Ian said.

Both he and Darcy were hovering over her as if she might pass out at any moment. Pulling herself together, she stood and drank the last of the water. "Good idea," she said, leading the way.

Pete had just arrived carrying her tablet plus the satchel she always took wherever she went. "Thought you might want this," he said. "I put your phone in there and that little thingamajig you showed me once—you called it a driver or something?"

"Flash drive," Chloe said, relieved to have her belongings in hand. "Thank you, Pete."

A golf cart pulled to a stop, and a man—more like a fresh-faced kid—climbed out. "Where's the patient?" he asked as he entered the reception area.

After a quick examination, the tech decided he needed to take the tablet with him. "Could take some time," he said, never once looking at Chloe, but rather keeping his focus constantly on whatever he was seeing on the screen and clicking through multiple functions.

"Hours? Days? Surely not weeks," Chloe said.

"Couple of days should do it." He faced her for the first time. He was so young. "I can get you a laptop you can use in the meantime, if that'll help."

"It would. Thank you. Can I use my flash drive?"

"That should be okay. I'll just check it first to be safe and get it back to you later today."

Chloe glanced at the wall clock and immediately regretted her decision to return the rental car. "I need to call a cab. I have that meeting." At the moment the last thing she wanted to do was try and concentrate on fresh research for the book, but there was something about the young man holding her tablet that gave her confidence. "Will I be able to have that borrowed laptop and hopefully my flash drive today?"

"Yes, ma'am. Gotcha covered."

Darcy handed her a set of car keys. "Take my car," she said. "Pete can take me home after work."

"You're sure?"

"She'll talk my ear off, but maybe I can get her to agree to stop for a burger and fries someplace along the way," Pete said with a wink at Darcy.

She thanked Pete and Darcy and saw Ian on his phone. She felt guilty for having made her troubles part of his day. "Sorry," she said and turned to leave.

"Wait up," he called. He caught up with her on her way to the parking lot. "I could drive you."

"I'll be fine," she assured him. "I left a message for Tilda to meet me there."

"You let me deal with Tilda. You've got enough to sort out."

"Nope. Got a plan. Besides, whatever is going on is between the two of us. I can't imagine what I've done to upset her, but whatever it is, I need to fix it so we can both get on with our work."

Ian opened the car door and waited for her to get in. "We're still on for dinner tomorrow?"

She grinned. "Now, don't think for one minute I plan to let you off the hook for that one, Dr. Flanner."

His smile exposed the dimple she'd only noticed the night before. He was one good-looking professor.

"Gotta go," she said.

He nodded and shut the car door, then watched as she drove away.

To Chloe's surprise, Tilda was waiting for her outside the historical society offices. "You're here," she said before she could temper her shock.

"Ian called," Tilda replied, her tone chilly.

So did I.

But, of course, Tilda would answer any call from Ian. It didn't take a mind reader to understand exactly what Tilda's problem with her was. She was jealous.

"Well, I'm glad you're here. I've had a problem with my tablet, so I'll need your help taking notes."

Tilda's eyes widened. "Can it be fixed?"

Chloe couldn't help wondering if Tilda might possibly be behind the cyberattack.

Stop it. This isn't some spy movie.

"It's in the shop, so we'll see. In the meantime, we have a meeting." Chloe led the way through the door to report to the receptionist.

She had trouble concentrating on the information offered by the society's director. A lot of it was research she already had, thanks to Toby. She had reached the point where she needed to know what had happened to her great-grandmother. She'd had Tilda search records through southwest Florida, hoping to uncover a death certificate for Lucinda O'Connor, but nothing had turned up. Of course, she was writing fiction, so she could make it up, but she'd come this far and wanted to know the real story.

"This is all so interesting," she said when the director seemed to have warmed enough to his topic that getting away from him might be difficult. "As I mentioned when we spoke, I am very interested in learning anything I can about my great grandmother—the aerialist, Lucinda Conroy. She was part of the Ringling company in the—"

"Midthirties," the director said with an excited smile. He moved to a cabinet and flipped through a series of color-coded files. "Here."

He handed her a scanned copy of a newspaper article.

The headline was one of those *Whatever Happened To...?* columns that had grown in popularity over time. This one was from the 1950s, and immediately Chloe's eye settled on her great-grandmother's name.

Lucinda Conroy, a star performer with the Ringling circus until her arrest in 1936, disappeared shortly after being released from jail on bail pending a court hearing. In a scandal that involved the son of Clive Sutherland—a prominent Sarasota business man and philanthropist at the time, she was rumored to be expecting a child. It has long been assumed her partner, Bernardo Russo, was instrumental in aiding in her escape. Mr. Russo left the circus shortly after Miss Conroy's arrest. He worked for a time on the Ringling estate in Sarasota until that property went into foreclosure, and he was last known to have served during the war, where he was part of the Normandy landing. There is no further record of Miss Conroy or her child.

Chloe read through the article a second time, and realized Tilda had moved closer and was reading over her shoulder. "My grandmother's maiden name is Sutherland," she said softly.

The director shrugged. "Sarasota is at its roots a small town. Chances are your grandmother was part of this Sutherland family. Her father would have been Martin Sutherland, son of Clive, who married a woman from another wealthy family, Julia Gordon."

When it came to Sarasota society, the man was a walking ancestry.com, Chloe thought. "Tilda? Could there be a connection?" she asked.

Tilda frowned. "I can't imagine there is. If you think my Dad is an old fogy, he can't compete in the same league as my great-grandmother. She was something else."

The director closed the drawer. "If you think it might help, keep the article—it's a copy, of course. Now, let's see what else we have...."

Chloe was practically trembling with excitement. The idea that Tilda's family might in some way be connected to hers was exactly the kind of unexpected coincidence she'd been searching for. Not that she put much stock in coincidence, but in this case…

"You've been so helpful," she told the director as she folded the article and slipped it into her satchel. "I have so much to think about—and unfortunately my deadline means little time for doing so. May I call you with any further questions?" She extended her hand to shake his.

"Of course. Any time."

Once they were outside, Chloe turned to Tilda. "Do you have time for coffee?"

"I—"

"We need to talk, Tilda."

Tilda rolled her eyes. She sometimes had the demeanor of a spoiled teenager, and it was all Chloe could do not to say that out loud.

"Why don't I meet you at that coffeehouse in Burns Court you mentioned once? The one with the fabulous cinnamon rolls?"

"I suppose you aren't going to rest until we do this."

This was delivered with an exasperated sigh that made Chloe wonder why she was even bothering to work things out. On the other hand, the news she'd just received made it imperative that she stay on good terms with Tilda—at least until she could find out if Tilda's parents knew anything more about what had become of Lucinda Conroy.

"That's right," Chloe replied with a laugh as she headed for her car. "See you there."

By the time Tilda arrived at the café, Chloe had secured a table outside and ordered for the two of them. After all these weeks of working together, she felt confident in ordering a cappuccino for Tilda along with tea for herself plus a cinnamon roll for each of them. The air was humid and heavy, almost as if she could feel it draped over her bare shoulders like a shawl. But they were the only ones outside, and that would allow them to talk more freely.

Tilda arrived and frowned at Chloe's choice for seating but managed a sweet smile when the waiter delivered their order. "Is the AC not working inside?" she asked as she cut her roll in quarters.

"It was a little crowded inside, and I thought we could talk more comfortably out here." Chloe leaned forward, forcing Tilda to meet her gaze. "What's going on, Tilda? Ian tells me you prefer not to work with me?"

Tilda's cheeks flushed, and she gave her attention to adding three packets of sugar to her coffee. "You spoke to Ian?"

Chloe sighed. "Yes. I often speak to him. He's in charge of the museum. The mansion. The setting for my novel. He's a valued resource that I intend to use to the fullest advantage to get this project completed."

"You like him."

"Well, of course I like him. I like you. I like Toby. I've been pleased to meet a number of people here that—"

"But you *like* Ian."

Chloe's patience was reaching its breaking point. "Oh, for heaven's sake, girl, grow up already." She popped a piece of her sweet roll in her mouth, already regretting her outburst. Tilda's lower lip was twitching. Chloe swallowed. "Look, I'm sorry for that. It was… unnecessarily harsh. But really, Tilda, may I remind you I write mysteries, not romance novels?" She hoped her attempt at a bit of humor would lighten the moment.

"It's just…" Tilda bit her lip.

"I get it. You have a crush on Ian—completely understandable. But the question in any situation like this is whether or not he returns your feelings."

"He's always nice to me."

"He's also nearly ten years older," Chloe reminded her gently. She gave Tilda a moment to consider that before adding, "But, there's more to whatever is going on with me than Ian. You've indicated in other ways that you're struggling with the role I've given you."

"It's not that. I heard Daddy on the phone the other day. A big chunk of the money for the renovation he's been counting on isn't coming. He went out on a limb to convince the rest of the board to support the project. That's why he's been on Ian so much, and then when the contractor got arrested…"

"I don't understand what all that has to do with your treatment of me."

Tilda stared up at the sky and then down at her lap. "Neither do I. Can you understand that with you and Ian getting closer and Daddy's problems, it just seems like once again I'm losing everything? I mean, if the money's not there, then Ian will likely move on, and I'll be out of work—again. I guess I thought if you were the one to leave, then maybe…" She shook her head. "Saying it all out loud makes it all seem so stupid." She looked up. "I don't suppose there's a chance you'll forgive me?"

Chloe drew in a deep breath. "So, what you're telling me is the money to pay the workers is not there—yet."

"It's not there, period," Tilda corrected.

"Then this gala you're planning becomes incredibly important, Tilda. That is the source of funding the project, not me or my book, although that will help."

"Forgive me for bringing it up, but your book seems to have stalled. You've spent a lot of time having me look for stuff about this trapeze performer. I mean, is she the one who gets killed or solves the mystery? And honestly, what are the chances the published novel will be ready for the gala?"

Chloe ran her finger around the lip of her tea glass. "The problem with this work is it's gotten a bit personal for me, and I'm frankly struggling with how to tell a story that's directly related to my family."

Tilda's eyes widened. "Lucinda Conroy?"

"Yes, my great-grandmother," Chloe said. She leaned back in her chair. "I had no thought of writing about her when I began. I mean, I knew there was some family tie to the circus, but I thought, if I had time…" She let out a mirthless laugh. "Of course, time is what I do not have, but I just can't seem to look away, so to speak. She haunts me."

"Well, of course," Tilda said. "Now all those wild goose chases you had Toby and me running make sense. You know, my grand-mother grew up in Sarasota. She knew everybody—or at least everybody who was anybody."

"I'm guessing the circus was long gone by the time she was old enough to pay attention," Chloe said, keeping the obvious fact that Lucinda was not exactly in the league of people Tilda described.

"Can't hurt to pick her brain. I'll set up a lunch." She fished around in her bag for her phone. "Is that really why you and Ian went to Tampa? He's helping you?"

"As I explained before, Ian had some business up there related to his project. It just seemed to make sense for us to go together."

Tilda's face flushed, and, to Chloe's shock, she appeared on the verge of tears. "I guess I thought it was something more…romantic. I'm so sorry," she murmured. "I mean about the whole Ian thing—the green-eyed monster sometimes gets to me."

"No harm done," Chloe assured her.

This time the tears flowed. "Oh, you're going to hate me, Chloe, and Ian will probably fire me, and—"

"Whoa. What on earth?"

"Last night, did you get a note saying dinner with Ian was canceled?"

"Well, it didn't say Ian specifically, but—"

"I called the hotel and asked them to put that under your door," Tilda admitted. "And your tablet? It's fine, really." She reached across the table and grabbed Chloe's hand. "Please, don't tell Ian—or my father."

Tilda was sobbing now. "I don't know what came over me, Chloe. I was so devastated by the breakup in New York, and I guess when I met Ian and he was…well, Ian, I just thought if maybe we became a couple, Daddy would be proud of me for once. I've always been a disappointment to him. He so wanted a son to carry on the name and such. And then when it became obvious Ian wasn't interested, I hit on the idea of bringing you here, and Daddy seemed to take note of that, and…" She let out what could only be called a wail.

Chloe could hardly sort through the many emotions she was feeling. They ran the gamut from shock to anger to pity for this woman who thought so little of herself. "Tilda, get hold of yourself." She handed her a fistful of napkins from the dispenser on the table and waited while Tilda blew her nose and mopped away her tears. "Now you listen to me," she continued, sounding like the big sister she'd been to her own sister in another time. "You've done good work for me, and I will definitely tell your father that. Just the planning you're doing for the gala—my stars, do you think I would know the first thing about how to go about that?"

"I like planning parties and events," Tilda said, sniffing back the last of her tears.

"And you are clearly good at it. So do that. Stop trying to build your life around what you think your father expects. You are far too bright to allow some man—even your father—to shape who and what you are." Chloe couldn't help wondering why she was the one telling Tilda this, and not the young woman's mother. And then she had an idea.

She thought of the threat of the hurricane, and how Tilda had gone into action and saved the day. "Tilda, what if you work exclusively on planning the gala. Toby can help me with whatever I might need. We both know your true talent lies in organization, so why not put that to work for your father? This gala could raise a lot of money—in small increments to be sure, but sometimes smaller donations add up to more than one large gift. He would be so proud of you—and so grateful."

Tilda's eyes widened, and it was almost as if Chloe could see her brain slipping into gear. "Maybe I could do that."

"And in the meantime, I'll drop a hint to Ian that you would be fabulous in the role of event planner for the entire museum."

"There used to be someone on staff, but once the mansion began showing signs of wear and tear, the board decided all events had to be held outdoors. But think of the money we could raise if we offered small elite gatherings in the house that John and Mable built?"

"That's a great idea."

"Will you really talk to Ian for me?"

Chloe hesitated. "I'll be happy to let him know I think you would be perfect for such a position, but you need to do the work, Tilda. Develop your plan and then present it. Consider all the pros and cons and be prepared to address them. My guess is anyone who can figure out how to slip a note under a hotel door and stage a sham virus on my laptop is more than capable of drawing up a simple business plan." She winked at Tilda, whose usually flawless complexion had suddenly turned a blotchy red.

"Can you ever forgive me?" Her voice had dropped to a whisper, and she kept her focus on her hands rather than meeting Chloe's eyes.

Chloe covered Tilda's hand with hers. "That depends. Are we done playing these childish games?"

Tilda nodded. "It was because I saw Ian getting interested in you that I got so carried away."

"Ian has the right to be interested in anyone of his choosing.

That's not your decision, Tilda."

"I know. I was a five-star idiot." She glanced up and gave Chloe a half smile. "He is a little old for me."

Chloe smiled. "Us older codgers prefer the term 'mature.'"

"Mature then, but come on, you have to admit he's a real hottie."

"That he is—in that professorial way of his," Chloe agreed and realized she was the one blushing.

"Ah ha!" Tilda's voice carried so that a passing pedestrian looked their way. She quickly lowered her voice to a conspiratorial tone as she leaned closer. "I can help you. In college I was known as the matchmaker. I cannot tell you how many unsuspecting couples I put together and—"

Talk about jumping from the frying pan into the fire!

"Just focus on putting your plan for the gala together, okay? Focus on yourself for a change, Tilda."

Tilda blinked as if this idea was a foreign concept to her. Chloe's heart went out to her, and she decided she would do her best to make sure Tilda was a success on her own terms for a change.

CHAPTER EIGHTEEN

Newark, 1936-1938

Lucy

$\mathscr{I}$f Lucy thought life had finally started to right itself, she was sadly mistaken. Once she left the hospital, she realized she and Nardo had nowhere to go and no way of supporting themselves. She had been so intent on getting to the orphanage and reclaiming her baby that the realities of what that entailed had escaped her. She could not present herself as Lucinda Conroy or the police would be called. She could not even say she was Lucille O'Connor, because she had no identification. Mr. Jefferson had moved to New York to serve Mister John. The circus was now completely under the control of Mister John's sister-in-law and his business partner—he had no say.

Nardo could not find work, and his continued presence in the area raised suspicions, especially once the Sutherlands returned from New York and pressed the authorities to reopen the case against Lucy. Twice Nardo had been certain someone was following him, and once Detective Taylor had brought him in for more questioning. And then the news broke that John Ringling had died.

"We have to get away from here," Nardo told Lucy one evening as they sat outside the makeshift shelter he had built for them on the now-deserted grounds of Ca' d'Zan. So far no one came to check on the house, which had been boarded up and abandoned until such time as the courts could figure out what to do. Mister John had left all his property, including his priceless art collection, the furnishings of the mansion, and the mansion and land itself, to the state of Florida. In the end, the showman had tricked them all, and Lucy, having witnessed the toll his financial troubles had taken over the years, rejoiced. Until Nardo pointed out that with Mister John's death, their last hope for someone who might stand with them and champion Lucy's innocence was gone. "We have to leave here, Lucinda."

"Not without the baby."

"Yes, without the baby. She is safe where she is—fed and clothed and cared for."

"You can't know that."

He hesitated.

"Nardo?"

"I went there, Lucinda. I went to the orphanage. I pretended to be there because of a report of an infestation of rats. I was able to get the young sister on duty to show me the nursery, telling her the youngest children were the most defenseless and at risk."

"You saw her?"

He nodded. "Yes. There was a bassinet labeled 'Baby Alice.'"

"Wait. How could you be sure—"

"She was the only girl, and the sister said she had only been there a few weeks. She was quite intent on giving me details to prove there was no need for concern. The child has gained weight. And the sister herself took special care to make sure Baby Alice was properly dressed and taken outside for fresh air every day."

"I am her mother. I can feed her and dress her and take her out for fresh air." But she knew Nardo was right. They could barely feed themselves, and keeping themselves clean and presentable had become increasingly difficult with the outdoor lifestyle they were living. "Where would we go?" Her voice quavered, and she could barely sound out the words.

Nardo removed a flyer from his pocket and handed it to her. "This is a government project, Lucinda. They are hiring—men and women. There is but one problem."

"It's in New Jersey," she said after reading the text of the flyer headed **WPA Needs YOU** in large letters. "You should take it."

"I will not go without you." His square jaw was set with determination.

Lucy let out a weary sigh. Since her illness following the delivery of her child, she was always so very tired. She had none of her usual energy. And not just physical energy, but she struggled with trying to think clearly as well. If Nardo left, she had no idea what she would do, how she would manage. And most of all, how she would ever see her baby again.

She felt Nardo's arms fold her into an embrace and rested her cheek against his chest. She could hear the steady rhythm of his heartbeat. How would she survive without him?

"Marry me, Lucinda," he whispered.

She pulled back and looked up at him. "And how will that solve anything?" And yet, for the first time, she realized marrying him would bind him to her forever. They would face the future together.

"It's a beginning," he said. "This paper speaks of work that is available. We know Alice is safe for now. We can leave here and settle some place where no one knows of our past. We can find work and save our money and before you know it, we can present ourselves at the orphanage to claim her."

"They will never believe she is mine—ours," Lucy protested.

"No, but they will welcome a loving couple come to adopt her."

It's so far-fetched, it might just work.

"And what if, in the meantime, someone else adopts her?"

"That might happen, and if it does, we will decide then what we do. But we should not create problems that do not yet exist."

"I can't have other children—our children," she reminded him. "The doctor said—"

"Just say yes, Lucinda. I know you do not love me, but my love is more than enough for two—or three once we are reunited with Alice. Say yes."

Tears filled Lucy's eyes and refused to be contained. She found herself sobbing against Nardo's chest, soaking his shirt. "I have been such a fool, darling Nardo," she finally managed. "I have spent so much time seeking love, and it has been here all along."

He frowned. "Does this mean yes?"

"This means yes."

Over the next weeks Nardo found enough odd jobs to provide the money they would need for train tickets north. Lucy swallowed what was left of her pride and stood in long lines wherever food and clothing were being offered for free. She watched especially for the warmer items they would need immediately on their arrival in New Jersey. On Christmas Eve she and Nardo were married. They attended services at a local church, and afterwards Nardo persuaded the minister to perform the simple ceremony. Having enjoyed perhaps more than his share of the sacramental wine, the minister had misspelled both Nardo's names on the certificate of marriage, and so they became Bernard and Lucille Russell.

It seemed a good omen for the future.

"We have the proof we need, Nardo," Lucy said as they lay next to each other that final night in Sarasota. "And once we have everything settled in Newark, we can return and adopt baby Alice."

She could not recall the last time she had felt so happy.

But although once they arrived in Newark Nardo found work with the WPA right away, Lucy's strength did not return. She was often ill, and there were doctor's fees they had not counted on, plus everything was more expensive than they had planned. Lucy's uncertain health as well as WPA rules preventing a wife from working if her husband was with the agency prevented her from holding a steady full-time job. A year passed and then two, and Lucy sank deeper into a personal depression—one rooted in the realization that her dream of one day returning to Florida and reclaiming her daughter might never come true.

Do something!

Over the next several days she found her thoughts wandering back to her days of performing. How had that adventurous young woman turned into this person seemingly incapable of making a choice about her future? One morning she gazed at her reflection in the small bathroom mirror. She looked haggard and gaunt, her beauty faded almost to the point of never having been.

What's the matter with you?

She lifted her hair off her neck and examined the tangled thickness of it. Taking a pair of scissors from her sewing basket, she began cutting. Short hair was in fashion. Maybe not the really short cuts of the '20s, but the film star Loretta Young wore a style similar to the style Lucy had worn when she did the triple at Mister John's party. How beautiful she had felt that night! Not just beautiful, but remarkable in some way. She had completed the triple—a feat only one other woman had accomplished. She recalled the thrill of that day—the way the trapeze had carried her higher and higher until she'd released it and spun once—twice—three times through the air. That was a woman determined to prove herself, undaunted by uncertainties. She cut through the thick strands, then washed her hair and watched with delight as it sprang into waves as it dried. She felt lighter—more like her old self.

Inspired, she rummaged through the closet until she found a

bright blue rayon dress she'd been unable to resist when accepting free clothes from the church collection in Sarasota. She put it on, cinched it with a belt, and twirled around. Shoes! Well, her old Mary Janes would have to do. She added lipstick and used a bit of that to rouge her cheeks, then topped it all off with a black cloche hat that featured a short rolled back brim.

Now what?

She needed to find steady work—if only part time. If they were ever going to achieve their dream of returning to Florida and bringing Alice home with them, they needed to start adding to the meager savings they'd managed so far. She spread the newspaper on the kitchen table and turned to the classifieds. Running her unmanicured finger down the column, she quickly rejected every listing requiring secretarial skills. She certainly could not type or take dictation. She paused at a brief listing for a salesclerk in a bookstore she passed almost daily on her way to or from the market. She was certainly not a reader, but applying would be good practice. She'd noticed the older man who owned the shop and had exchanged greetings with him in passing. He seemed a kind soul, and she felt as if he might understand her need to use his advertisement as a test.

Grabbing her clutch purse, she hurried down the stairs from their fourth-floor walk-up and out into the street. It was uncommonly warm for March, and there was a hint of spring in the air despite mounds of snow still piled along the sidewalk.

With each step she felt new courage. She could do this. She *would* do this.

A bell over the door chimed as she entered the shop. The proprietor glanced up and smiled. He was with another customer, so Lucy wandered the rows of shelves stuffed to overflowing with books. The shop was tiny—barely larger than the small apartment she and Nardo shared. And yet the way the light came through the large window and reflected the colors of the stained glass in the transom over the entry door made Lucy feel at home, as if this was a place she knew—a safe place.

"Hello. May I help you find something in the chaos?" The shopkeeper was a wiry older man of indeterminate age. He wore trousers with suspenders over a shirt with rolled black sleeves and a bowtie. He wore thick eyeglasses that magnified his hazel eyes and a smile that made him look a bit like a leprechaun. She liked him at once.

"I…my name is Lucille Russell. I live down the street and—"

"And I am Seymour Fisher, proprietor of this little archive. Call me Seymour, please." He offered her a handshake, which she accepted. "Yes. I've seen you pass the shop…often. I'm so glad you finally decided to come inside. Your husband is a bit of a regular. Likes to sit over there and read a chapter or two on his way home most days." He motioned to a corner in the back of the store where there was a small sitting area next to a table with a hot plate and things for making tea.

"Nardo?"

"Bernard—yes. He came in shortly after you young folks moved to the neighborhood. I quickly realized he was never going to buy anything, but he had a love of reading, so we made a bargain."

She thought of the old days when she often saw Nardo off by himself reading after a performance ended. And when they worked and lived at Ca' d'Zan, he borrowed books from Mr. Jefferson and sat on the terrace reading until it got too dark to see. "We can't afford extras," she began, but then stopped as it hit her that Nardo had kept this from her. "A bargain?"

He removed the eyeglasses and wiped them with a handkerchief he pulled from his trouser pocket. "My eyesight is not what it was once. Your husband has agreed to read aloud to me in exchange for borrowing books he can read on his breaks at work. He didn't tell you?"

"No. I—" She thought of the evenings Nardo had been late getting home for supper—evenings when she'd been so wrapped up in her misery she had barely noticed. "Thank you. I'm afraid I haven't been the most attentive wife."

"Bernard tells me you've been quite ill. He worries a great deal about you. I'm delighted to see you looking so, well frankly, vibrant." He indicated the sitting area. "Now perhaps you will join me in a cup of tea and tell me what brings you in after all this time."

While he prepared their tea, Lucy told him of the advertisement she'd seen. "I don't know a thing about books, I'm afraid. But I know how to talk to people, and I am very good at organizing and cleaning." She realized she was no longer using this as a trial run. She wanted this job. She wanted to spend some of her day in this cozy shop with this delightful man who had been so kind to Nardo.

"One of the requirements will be managing the ladders," Seymour said. He pointed to a rolling ladder that ran along the shelves. "Invariably the book needed will be up there somewhere, and that means using the ladder."

She was about to reveal her past as a trapeze artist and assure him heights did not bother her in the least but decided against it. "I'll be fine," she assured him.

He poured tea into two stained and chipped cups and handed her one. "Then shall we give it a try?" He raised his cup in a toast.

"When do you want me to start?"

"I believe you have already, my dear. We'll finish our tea and then I can give you the grand tour if that suits." He leaned closer. "I can hardly wait to see the expression on your husband's face when he stops in later."

The man actually giggled, and Lucy found herself joining in.

CHAPTER NINETEEN

Sarasota, Fall 2022

CHLOE

*I*n the days following their heart-to-heart talk, Chloe was pleased to find that she and Tilda fell into a pattern of work and friendship that made both their lives easier and more productive. Tilda's improved self-confidence gave her the courage to bypass the usual step of allowing her father to veto her ideas and instead send out a detailed proposal for the gala to every member of the board of trustees. She held meetings and secured corporate sponsors ready to foot the bill for the gala itself, leaving any funds raised through ticket sales or by other means as pure profit, and the evening promised to be the highlight of Sarasota's annual season of charity balls and benefits.

Meanwhile Chloe had realized that, even with an extension on her deadline, she needed to stop chasing clues related to her great-grandmother and write the story she could create from what information she'd gathered. That meant hours alone at the computer with far too many breaks to check emails and texts—until one email got her immediate attention and set her heart racing. It was from the records department of the city of Tampa.

Per your recent request please find attached the information available associated with the adoption of Alice Russell.

She clicked the first link, and up popped a grainy black-and-white photo of a man in uniform, a woman wearing what had possibly been her best Sunday dress and sporting a small hat with a half veil set on her unruly curls, and a girl of five or six standing between them. The background was clearly a train station, and the date on the photograph was December 1941.

The second link was a legal document showing the adoption of Alice Smith by Bernard and Lucille Russell of 111 Sussex Avenue, Newark, New Jersey.

She already knew all this.

She glanced at the photograph, and then she studied it more closely, focusing first on her grandmother. She smiled at the image of a little girl who was dressed up like Shirley Temple. How Grandma Alice must have hated that, given her fashion choice these days of jeans and a flannel shirt. Her gaze shifted to the woman holding Alice's hand and looking down at her. It was one thing to see a likeness between her grandmother then and now, but she was seeing a likeness between her grandmother and this woman in the picture who was not her real mother.

Or was it possible…?

Rummaging through her research papers, she found the copy she'd made of the photograph of Lucinda Conroy she'd seen the day of her arrival at Ca' d' Zan and placed it next to this new image. Was it her imagination, or were they the same woman? Was it possible Lucinda Conroy had changed her identity and waited years to come back and claim her own daughter?

Chloe had never missed a deadline in her career, but she was going to miss this one. She was going to put aside the proposed novel and once and for all solve the true mystery of her great-grandmother's story. Who was this woman with the doll's features? A fugitive from justice? A thief who had stolen from her employer? A mother determined to reconnect with her child? All the above? Or might she have been innocent of the charges brought against her?

Please, help me find the truth to this story, she prayed. *And if it wouldn't be too much trouble, maybe a happy ending?*

Chloe thought of her grandmother and mother—both hard-working women who never met a problem they couldn't solve, even at the risk of their own happiness. Both women who had come from Lucinda Conroy. As had she. Down through the generations she could trace similar characteristics, and no one could tell her that her great-grandmother had ever resorted to stealing from her employer to solve her problems.

She grabbed her phone and called her agent, who was less than pleased with the news but assured Chloe she would handle things with the publisher. Next, she called Tilda. The proposed novel was a centerpiece of Tilda's plans for the gala. Chloe owed her an explanation. She kept her explanation vague—something had come up. She hoped Tilda understood.

"But I don't understand. I mean, how can you just abandon a novel?"

"Because sometimes real life takes precedence. Let me just assure you that if I can accomplish what I need to, you are going to have a far better shocker to offer as the highlight of the gala. Do you trust me?"

"Well, sure, but—"

"Great. Do me a favor and call Toby. I want the two of you and Ian here for a brainstorming session—and supper—tonight. We've got a real case to crack."

"Can't wait," Tilda said and hung up.

When Chloe called Ian, she gave him a more in-depth overview of her idea. "Then Darcy needs to be part of this meeting tonight," he said. "I'll make sure she's available. And I'll ask her to order in for us. No need for you to add preparing a meal to your list."

"Ah, you just don't care for my cooking," she teased.

"Jury's still out on that one—hard to mess up a salad," he joked. "See you at six."

Darcy had outdone herself in the catering department. Shortly before six Pete arrived with coolers filled with freshly made salads, fruit bowls, shrimp, and an assortment of beverages. Once he had placed the coolers on the patio, he returned to his cart for bags of chips, kettle corn, pretzels, and a large box of brownies, lemon bars, and mini cupcakes.

"Well, we've certainly got enough food to see us through," Chloe said as she and Tilda set out plates, glasses, and flatware. They added pitchers of iced tea and lemonade and waited for the others to arrive. Ian and Darcy were right on time, but Toby was so late and not answering texts that they feared he had forgotten. "We might as well eat," Chloe suggested. "I'm sure he'll be here."

They had just filled their plates and gathered around the metal patio table when they heard the *putt-putt* of a motor scooter.

"That'll be Toby," Tilda announced before hurrying around to the front of the house to meet him. When the two of them returned Toby carried a canvas bag stuffed full of papers.

"Sorry to be so late," he said. "I had to wait for everyone else to leave so I could make copies of all this stuff without raising eyebrows. Thought they might help."

"What on earth?" Chloe made room on a bench for him to set the materials.

"These are the records Frank Jefferson, the butler, kept in 1936—the year of the party and the theft."

"We looked at these," Chloe reminded him.

"*Au contraire*, my lady." Toby's grin bordered on triumphant. "We studied only the entries made before and after the party, but later Mr. Jefferson hired two people—a couple." He presented her with a paper-clipped packet of papers as the others gathered round to read over her shoulder.

The report showed evidence of a man and woman being hired—the man as a groundskeeper and the woman as housekeeper. They were listed as Lucille O'Connor and…

"Bernardo Russo." Chloe could hardly manage the words.

"Lucinda Conroy's partner on the trapeze," Toby added.

"So, who was this Lucille O'Connor?" Darcy asked.

Chloe continued scanning the pages. "Lucille O'Connor? Lucinda Conroy?" She stopped at the page for the month of October. "Look at this. A Dr. Rosen was called to the estate…on October 12th!"

Ian shook his head in amazement. "Well, Jefferson was known to document everything with a thoroughness rare for those times. I've referred to his files often in working through my project."

Chloe resumed sorting through the documents. "Mr. Jefferson left for New York in November when the mansion was shut down, and there's nothing about what happened to the others." She sat at the table, holding the files as she tried to make sense of what Toby had brought them. "We know Lucinda was arrested in May and never showed up for her court hearing. We—and everyone else—assumed she ran away or died in childbirth, but this tells a different tale."

"She never left Sarasota," Tilda said.

"But then how did she and this Russell fella end up in New Jersey of all places?" Darcy voiced the question on everyone's mind.

Chloe smiled. "I don't know, but I'm willing to bet this 'Russell fella,' as you call him, is none other than Bernardo Russo."

Encouraged by these new discoveries, Chloe asked Tilda if there was any chance she could meet with Tilda's grandmother. The offer

Tilda had made at the café hadn't worked out, and in truth, Chloe had been fine with that. She had had enough on her plate without adding extraneous social events. But now… The woman's parents had been on the guest list Toby had found. Perhaps through the years there had been stories of that party and the aftermath.

"Of course," Tilda readily agreed. "She'd be thrilled. She's such a fan of your books. I'll ask Mom to set up a luncheon. In the meantime, I have a new idea for the gala. What do you think of a silent auction?"

"That seems like a lot of work, Tilda. I mean, you have to find businesses and individuals to donate something at no cost to them."

Tilda laughed. "They get plenty out of the deal. For a business, it's putting their product in front of people who are well known as influencers when it comes to what ordinary beings like you and me buy. As for individuals? One more feather in their charitable-giving cap that carries all sorts of warm fuzzies."

Chloe recalled how Tilda had used the opportunity to meet a real celebrity and the promise of gift cards from the museum as enticements for people to come out in a storm just to say they worked side by side with her. She grinned. "You are so good at this, Tilda."

The younger woman beamed with pride and pleasure. "I have this friend who set me on the right track, and now nothing can stop me from making this gala the best Sarasota has ever seen. People will be tripping over each other to buy tickets at $300 a pop."

"Okay, so put me down for a donation for the auction."

"I already did," Tilda admitted. "Now, let me call Mom and set up this meeting with Nana Rose."

When Chloe arrived at the home of Tilda's parents for the lunch meeting, the house itself was exactly what she would have thought would be Bill Tucker's style—sleek and modern. Tilda's mother,

Nora, warmly greeted Chloe at the door. She was dressed in tailored white slacks and a crisp blue-and-white striped shirt, the collar turned up to frame her tanned and heavily Botoxed features.

"Mama is so excited," she gushed as she led the way through the house to the Olympic-sized pool.

Rose Sutherland Adams—who Tilda assured Chloe always went by her full maiden and married name—was seated in a high-backed wicker chair and dressed in a lavishly embroidered caftan. "Ah, Miss Whitfield," she said, extending her hand, "this is indeed a pleasure."

Her voice was husky, and her smile was as warm as the day itself. Her face was deeply lined, and she'd definitely never bothered to make any attempt to conceal her age. Chloe felt an instant connection—one she had not felt with Tilda's mother. It occurred to her that Nana Rose, as Tilda called her, and her granddaughter had a great deal in common. Furthermore, there was something about the woman that made Chloe think of her own grandmother. She had the feeling Rose Sutherland Adams and Alice Russell would get along famously, and decided she would bring her grandmother to town for the gala.

"The pleasure is mine," Chloe replied as she squeezed the woman's hand. "Tilda has been singing your praises, and I'm so glad we have this opportunity to get better acquainted."

Rose leaned forward. "It will go much better if you share your latest plot with me, my dear." Then she winked, leaned back in her chair, and laughed.

"Mother, really," Nora said in a low voice.

Rose waved her away. "Pay no attention to my daughter, Chloe. My son-in-law lives and breathes by what others might think, and unfortunately, Nora has adopted that same habit. May I call you Chloe?"

"Of course."

"Splendid. Ah, here's lunch. I'm famished."

Rose indicated the chair next to her own, and Chloe sat.

The four women made small talk throughout the meal served by a maid dressed in black slacks and a white shirt. Tilda chattered on about the gala and her latest plans for a silent auction. Every utterance from Nora was something about "my husband" to the point Chloe began to wonder if Tilda's mother saw herself as anything more than an extension of Bill Tucker. Rose made no spoken comment to her daughter's tributes, but her expression of disgust whenever her son-in-law's name came up spoke volumes.

"Tilda, darling," Rose said, "I want you to sign me up for a table at the gala."

Tilda whipped out her phone. "Great, Nana. The tables seat eight, so who will you have with you?"

"Chloe, of course, and that handsome Dr. Flanner…and what about that lovely woman who manages the reception area at Ca' d'Zan? Doris?"

"Darcy," Tilda said, and added the name.

"And her plus-one, of course. Oh, and that shy man who gave me the ride from the visitor center to the mansion that time?"

"Pete?" Tilda added the name. "Plus-one," she said as she counted up the tally. "That leaves one more. How about Toby from the archives? He's really been such a help to Chloe."

"Perfect," Rose announced.

Chloe was fascinated with the struggle Nora was having to maintain her silence. "Mother," she finally said, keeping her voice low, "I really don't think Bill will approve of—"

"Have I ever once asked your husband for his approval, Nora?"

"I know, but…these people—"

Rose held up a finger. "Do not even think of finishing that thought, Nora. *These people* have as much right—possibly more—to enjoy this event as we do. Now come down off that high horse and remember how your father and I raised you and perhaps who *you* are for once." She turned to Tilda. "Toby makes eight. Be sure he's seated next to me. I need a plus-one for the evening as well."

The server brought dessert—key lime pie, the best Chloe could remember having. She would have to tell Ian about it.

Finally Nora stood and faced her daughter. "I'll just… Perhaps we should give Chloe time with Mother?"

"Sure. I've got calls to make, so take your time." Tilda leaned down and kissed her grandmother's cheek. "Thanks, Nana."

"Oh, Tilda, as long as you're here, I have a few items for this silent auction you mentioned last night. I set them aside on my dressing table. They're mementos from your great-grandfather's days as business manager for the Ringlings."

"You're the best," Tilda replied and kissed her again.

Chloe could not help feeling a little sorry for Nora Tucker. First, she was married to a control freak, and second, her own mother seemed far more comfortable with Tilda than she did her daughter. "Nora, thank you for a lovely lunch and for arranging everything," she said as Tilda's mother turned toward the house. "I look forward to seeing you again."

Nora hesitated, and for an instant Chloe was afraid the woman might burst into tears. "Thank you, Chloe," she managed. "I'd like that very much." She had just reached the open sliding doors when Rose called out to her.

"Nora?"

With obvious reluctance, the woman glanced back at her mother.

"I…that is, I can see where Tilda gets her talent for effortless entertaining. It's been a delightful afternoon. Thank you, darling."

Nora's features softened, and in that moment, she looked like the younger woman she obviously strove to present through cosmetics and surgery. "Love you, Mums," she whispered and left.

"Now then, my young friend, what is it you think I can tell you?" Rose was all business as she gave Chloe her full attention.

CHAPTER TWENTY

Newark, December 1941

LUCY

*A*s the country slowly clawed its way out of the Depression, another problem darkened prospects for the future. On September 1, 1939 Adolph Hitler invaded Poland from the west, and within two weeks Great Britain and France declared war on Germany, and Russia began an invasion of Poland from the east. Lucy and Nardo tried without much success to check on their friends from their years in the circus, many of whom had come from Europe and still had family there. Nardo was further alarmed when his beloved Italy was taken over by the dictator Benito Mussolini—an ally of Adolf Hitler.

By 1940 the WPA had switched gears from focusing on rebuilding America's infrastructure to gearing up for a possible attack from the outside. Nardo often worked long hours and sometimes was away for weeks working on some defense project. And then came the shock of the attack on Pearl Harbor. Suddenly the country was not just preparing for war—it was at war on two fronts. The possibility that they would be able to get back to Florida and adopt Alice became more remote by the day.

"If she's even still at the orphanage," Lucy said as she and Seymour took their traditional tea break late one afternoon in early

December. In the time that had passed since Lucy began working in the bookshop, she and Nardo had become so close to the elderly shopkeeper that eventually they had confided everything to him.

"Is there no way you can find out?" Seymour asked, offering her a cookie from the tin they kept on the shelf above the hot plate.

"We are afraid of asking too many questions," she admitted. "Because of the police."

"It's been five years, dear. Surely the case against you has been dropped by now."

"Perhaps." She shrugged even as she recalled the smirk Marty's father had leveled at her when the police arrested her. The expression of victory he had shown her that day still haunted her. "Nardo thinks that with the prospect of war, he might be called to serve."

"And that makes you nervous?"

"It would mean more delay. It would mean—"

Just then the bell over the shop door rang. Lucy set aside her tea. "I'll go," she said.

A portly middle-aged man dressed in a suit and tie and wearing a matching fedora stood just inside the entrance.

"Hello, sir," Lucy greeted him. "How may I help you today?"

"Are you Mrs. Lucille Russell?"

There were times when Lucy thought she might live to be ninety and never get used to that name, but for once she didn't hesitate. A stranger…asking for her by name… Her heart skipped a beat. "Has something happened to my husband?"

"Not that I know of, dear lady. It is you I have come to see. Your landlady was kind enough to steer me here. I hope it is not inconvenient for us to speak on a rather delicate matter in your place of employment?"

Lucy heard the tap of the cane Seymour used to guide him through the maze of shelves and books. "Mrs. Russell may speak to whomever she chooses here," Seymour said. "Perhaps we might make some proper introductions? I am Seymour Fisher, proprietor of this shop. And you are?"

The man removed his hat and extended his hand to Lucy. "My name is Donald Leggett. I have come about a letter you wrote to the Sisters of Saint Monica, several months ago." Once she accepted his handshake, he pulled an envelope from his inside coat pocket.

It was an envelope Lucy recognized—more to the point, she recognized her own handwriting in the address.

"Is there somewhere we might sit and discuss this matter?" he asked, directing his inquiry to Seymour.

"The kettle is still on. Perhaps a cup of tea, Mr. Leggett?" Seymour took hold of Lucy's arm and led the way to the back of the shop. "I'm right here," he murmured. "No need to be afraid."

Lucy pulled a third chair into the circle for the man still holding his hat—and the envelope, although the three of them remained standing. "I don't understand," she said softly, her eyes riveted on the letter she had written late one night after Nardo was asleep. A letter she had never intended to send—but one she had sent. A letter asking the sisters if a baby brought to them in the fall of 1936—a girl they named Alice—had been adopted. She had made up some tale to explain her interest—something about having met the mother who was quite sick with worry over her child.

"I sent this over a year ago," she whispered. Mr. Leggett had set the envelope aside to accept the cup of tea Seymour handed him. Lucy picked it up and ran her fingers over the address. "There was no reply."

"Yes. My apologies for that, Mrs. Russell. There was a fire at the orphanage, and it has taken us some time to get reorganized."

"A fire! Was anyone hurt? Was—"

"Everyone got out safely, but afterwards the building itself was uninhabitable. The children have been living with foster families in the area while we rebuild. Unfortunately, funds for the rebuilding have been slow to accumulate, so there have been delays and—"

She was so tired of waiting for answers. "What happened to Alice?"

"Alice?"

Lucy waved the envelope at him. "The child I inquired about in this letter. Was she adopted before the fire?"

"Oh, of course. No, Alice was temporarily placed with a family in Tampa after the fire. And that is the reason for my visit."

"You came all the way to Newark?" Seymour asked with an incredulous lift of his bushy eyebrows. "Forgive me, sir, but that seems odd."

Mr. Leggett nodded. "I see your point. The fact is that the orphanage is unlikely to be restored or reopened. The sisters and the board advising them were adamant that permanent homes be found for those children who were placed in foster care after the fire. One of the sisters recalled your letter, Mrs. Russell."

"That still does not explain your personal visit," Seymour insisted.

Mr. Leggett removed a second envelope from his pocket and handed it to Lucy. "This should reassure you that I am not trying to predicate some scam on you or the child, Mrs. Russell. This is a letter from the board and Mother Superior stating that if you and your husband are still interested in Alice, then I am to bring you to her with all haste. As you can see, the letter has been properly notarized as to its authenticity."

Lucy read aloud the message in the letter, then handed it to Seymour, who ran his thumb over the embossed seal of the notary. Her hands were shaking so badly she clenched them into fists and thrust them into the pockets of the apron she wore for working in the bookshop.

Alice. My Alice…

Her pulse hammered in her throat, making speech impossible.

"Mrs. Russell?" Mr. Leggett's voice came from somewhere far away, as if Lucy were hearing it from underwater.

"This way," she heard Seymour say and felt herself being led to a chair. "Breathe, my darling girl," Seymour urged. The shop bell jangled and Seymour called out, "Have a look around, and I'll be with you in a minute."

Mr. Leggett offered her a glass of water and the advice to take small sips, and when she looked up to thank him, she saw Nardo. He pushed his way past the other two men and knelt next to her. "What has happened, my love? Are you injured? Ill?" He glanced at Seymour for answers.

"Nothing so dire, my young friend," Seymour said. "Allow me to introduce you to Mr. Leggett. He has come here with the best possible news."

Nardo stood and extended his hand. "Bernard Russell," he said.

"Donald Leggett," the man replied. "I have just informed your wife that if the two of you are still interested in adopting the child known as Alice who was placed in care with the Sisters of Saint Monica five years ago as an infant, I have the authority to accompany you both back to Tampa to finalize the adoption—all expenses paid, of course."

Nardo's expression was something between suspicion and disbelief, and the combination was a bit comical. Lucy felt laughter bubble in her throat and calm her racing heart. Seymour handed him the letter and explained about the fire and the desire to make sure all children who had been placed in foster care found permanent homes.

"As you can see in the letter," Mr. Leggett continued, "the money for my travels and yours comes from a fund originally intended for the rebuilding of the orphanage. Once the board and the sisters decided that was not feasible, they came up with the idea of using the fund to make sure the children were settled." He hesitated as he glanced from Nardo to Lucy. "You are still interested in providing a permanent home for the child?" For the first time since his arrival he seemed uncertain.

Nardo drew Lucy to her feet and held her close at his side as together they faced Mr. Leggett. "We are more than interested, sir," Nardo said, his voice breaking as tears filled his eyes. "You are fulfilling a dream we have never dared hope might come true."

"Well, then, Mr. and Mrs. Russell, if you can arrange to leave the day after tomorrow, I think I can truthfully say that you and Alice will be a family by the end of the week—barring any unforeseen circumstances, of course."

Lucy stiffened and felt Nardo's hold on her tighten. "What sort of circumstances?"

"Rest assured we have already thoroughly investigated your preparedness to take this on. Your superiors at the WPA have certainly sung your praises, Mr. Russell. There was some concern about Mrs. Russell's health, but that seems to have improved. You have an established home here in the city.... Shall I go on?" He chuckled. "Frankly, if this were a wedding, we would have arrived at the point of 'if anyone can show cause why...' and so forth."

He picked up his hat, preparing to leave. "I am staying at the Montclare should you have further questions. I'll be in touch with the time for being at the station day after tomorrow. You may want to bring along an empty suitcase to pack Alice's clothing and toys," he advised. He made his way back to the front of the shop and they heard the bell jangle and the door close.

There was a moment of stunned silence and then the three of them began talking and laughing and—in Lucy's case—dancing. Seymour insisted on closing the shop early and treating them to a celebratory dinner at the Italian restaurant across the street. After sharing the news with Maria and Luigi, the proprietors of the restaurant, they stayed late into the night planning the life they would share with their beloved Alice. Seymour agreed to act as the child's godfather, looking out for mother and child while Nardo served his country.

By the time they reached their apartment building and stopped to collect their mail, Lucy was still bubbling over with plans for rearranging the apartment to provide a room and play space for their daughter. "Seymour says I must bring her to the shop…of course, she will be in school next fall. Oh, Nardo, we must find the school and—"

Nardo had opened the single envelope in their mailbox and was staring at it. "It's my orders, Lucinda. I am to report for duty one week from today."

The news was certainly not unexpected, but to have it arrive on this night of all nights crushed every spark of excitement and anticipation they had shared from the moment Mr. Leggett left the bookshop. Suddenly it felt as if everything had shifted. Once again, they faced unknowns that were terrifying. What if the sisters and Mr. Leggett changed their minds, knowing Nardo would not be available for Alice—knowing there was every possibility he would not come back from the war? As they climbed the stairs to their fourth-floor apartment, they were silent, their hearts heavy with worry that the fantasy that was finally within their reach might be cruelly snatched away—for good.

The train ride to Tampa was far more comfortable than the one they had taken years earlier to Newark. Their tickets included a sleeping berth and meals in the dining car. As they approached their destination, Mr. Leggett filled them in on what needed to happen. "Given the circumstances," he said with a nod toward Nardo, "arrangements have been made for us to go directly to the courthouse once we arrive. There the judge will meet with you and

Alice's foster parents. I must warn you that despite our—the sisters and board members—belief that going through with the adoption is in Alice's best interest, the final decision rests with the judge. I have no idea how he will react once he learns of your imminent deployment, Mr. Russell. He could view that as essentially placing Alice in a situation of being raised by a single mother—not ideal in our society. The foster parents are older, and there is no reason to believe he will be called to serve. In addition, they have two children of their own, meaning Alice would be part of a family."

"We are a family," Lucy objected. "Nar…Bernard and I are a family, and Alice would be loved."

"I've no doubt of that, Mrs. Russell. I am simply trying to prepare you for the worst."

"We have faced many challenges, Mr. Leggett," Nardo assured him. "We will find our way."

"Trust me, I plan to do everything in my power to sway the judge's decision in your direction."

But when they finally arrived at the station, a young woman hurried to meet them. Mr. Leggett introduced her as Sally, his secretary.

"The judge has rescheduled the meeting—we have to go right now," Sally said as she led the way to a line of waiting taxis. "As it is we will likely arrive late."

"But our luggage—" Lucy had planned to change into something more presentable after traveling.

"I'll take care of all that," Mr. Leggett said. "Go!"

Sally was standing by a cab, holding the rear door open. She waited for them to get in, then followed, giving the driver the address as she closed the door.

Lucy pulled her compact from her purse and opened it.

"You look fine," Nardo assured her.

"Maybe a touch of lipstick," Sally advised as the cab lurched around a corner. "But wait until we are at a stop," she added with a smile.

When they arrived, Sally thrust money at the driver, adding a blithe, "Keep the change," before leading them inside the courthouse. "The judge's chambers are down this hall," she said, her high heels clicking on the marble floor. She stopped in front of a pair of tall polished wooden doors at the end of the hall. "Here we go," she said, lowering her voice to a whisper as she turned the ornate brass doorknob and opened the door.

A woman looked up, peering at them over the tops of her wireless glasses. "These are the Russells, I presume?" She looked anything but pleased to see them, reminding Lucy of a teacher she'd had as a child. "You've kept Judge Anders waiting," she announced. She pressed a button on her desk and said, "The Russells are here."

She stood and indicated they should follow her down a short carpeted hall leading to yet another impressive set of doors. She knocked lightly, opened the door, and stood back to allow them to enter.

The room was massive—high ceilings and walls lined with bookcases. Lucy could not help noticing these books were precisely arranged, unlike the stock in Seymour's shop. Dominating the room was a large carved desk, and seated behind it was the man she presumed to be Judge Anders—the man who held their future in his hands. She registered a gray-haired man with a couple who looked to be in their fifties all seated, all looking back to watch as they entered. Sally led them to a pair of chairs across from the couple. Another man—younger than anyone else in the room—stood to greet them.

"Dennis Leggett," he said in a low voice. "My father asked me to represent you today if that's all right?"

Do we have a choice?

Lucy's nerves were making her annoyed and irritated at the entire situation. This Leggett boy looked barely old enough to be out of knickers, while the man seated with the couple she assumed to be the foster parents had a seasoned confidence that was difficult to miss.

Judge Anders cleared his throat. "Well, now that we're all here, let's get started."

Where was Alice?

Lucy realized she had thought her daughter would be in the room. She had imagined seeing her for the first time in five long years. She had practiced how she would react and what she might say and—

"Mrs. Russell?"

The judge—and everyone else—was staring at her. Had he asked her a question?

"I apologize, Your Honor," she murmured. Nardo reached over and grasped her hand.

"My wife and I have hoped to bring a child into our family for some time, sir," he said. "Circumstances prevented that until now...."

"And now you are about to be shipped off to Europe or the Pacific, young man," the judge interrupted, "and while we are all indebted to you for your service, that deployment does raise the issue of what is in the best interests of this child. Mr. and Mrs. Perkins here are willing to continue their foster care for her until such time as—God willing—you return safely."

Suddenly Lucy found her voice. Alice was *her* daughter. She stood and faced the couple opposite her. "While my husband and I are grateful for the care Alice has received from you since the fire and before that from the sisters, those were always meant to be temporary arrangements. We are here to take Alice home—to a permanent home, one where she will finally begin the life that has been on the horizon for her all these years. We will clothe, feed, and educate her, of course, but more than that, we will love her with all our hearts. We have loved her from the day we first knew of her. We have prayed for this day—the day when Alice could become our daughter legally, for she is already that in our hearts."

In the silence that followed, Lucy took her seat, but kept her eyes on Judge Anders. Dennis Leggett stood, "Your Honor, if I may—"

"Sit down, young man. I believe Mrs. Russell has pleaded the case far more eloquently than you ever could." He studied a sheaf of papers for so long that Lucy began to wonder if he had forgotten why they were all waiting. Finally, he leaned back in his chair and steepled his fingers. He looked from the foster parents to Lucy and Nardo, then back at the top document on his desk, which Lucy suddenly realized was a photograph—of Alice.

"This will not be easy for this child," he said slowly, tapping his finger on the photograph. "While you know of her, she knows nothing of you. I assume you plan to take her back to Newark with you, and that also is something to be considered. A new family in a strange town."

He's going to deny the adoption.

Lucy's heart was like a drum in her chest. Hearing him work through the details of the situation, she realized she wouldn't blame him. He was right about much of it, but if he knew Alice was hers? Desperate, she was halfway to her feet when the judge continued. "Still, she is young, and Mrs. Russell makes a strong argument for allowing this young lady to get on with her life—to have some certainty in her life."

Lucy realized she was holding her breath.

Say the words.

Judge Anders tipped his chair forward and rustled through the papers until he found an official-looking document. He opened a drawer in the desk and removed an ink pad and wooden stamp. "This adoption is approved," he said as he brought the stamp down firmly on the document. "Congratulations." The judge stood and came forward to shake hands with Lucy and Nardo.

Suddenly the room erupted as Mr. and Mrs. Perkins offered their congratulations. "She's a lovely girl," Mrs. Perkins assured Lucy. "You'll have your hands full," Lucy heard Mr. Perkins tell Nardo. As they left the chambers, Lucy saw Sally and a nun walking toward the room—and between them was a girl with curly blond hair, huge eyes, and a perfectly bowed mouth.

"Alice," the nun said once they stood before Lucy and Nardo, "remember how on your last birthday you told me you made a wish when you blew out your candles? A wish for a Mommy and Daddy of your very own?"

Alice nodded, her eyes meeting Lucy's with a directness that took Lucy's breath away.

"Well, this is Mr. and Mrs. Russell, and they tell me they have been praying for a daughter for a very long time. What if your wish and their prayers could be the answer for you all?"

Alice looked up at the nun. "What about Mr. and Mrs. Perkins? Won't they be sad?"

"Oh, yes, dear," the nun hastened to assure her. "But they have the twins, and Mr. and Mrs. Russell have no children."

"Will I have a room of my own then?" This, she directed to Nardo, who nodded. "And toys of my own? Not ones I have to borrow from the twins?"

A smile twitched at Nardo's lips. "Toys of your own," he confirmed.

Seemingly satisfied with Nardo's answers, Alice turned her attention to Lucy. "And you will be my forever Mommy? No givebacks?"

Lucy dropped to her knees to be more on the child's level. She suddenly realized what hardships her daughter had suffered and witnessed in just five years. "I promise…forever and a day," she managed.

Alice seemed to consider this. She looked up at Nardo and then back at Lucy. "You're very pretty," she said softly.

"So are you," Lucy replied as tears filled her eyes and began to spill over.

Alice looked taken aback at the sight of Lucy's tears and placed her hand on Lucy's shoulder. "Don't cry," she whispered, and then brightened. "I know. Would you like a hug?"

Unable to form a sound, Lucy held out her arms and nodded. And as her daughter wrapped herself around her, her warm body shaping itself to Lucy's, Nardo knelt and wrapped his arms around them both. "How about I take my two best girls for ice cream?"

Alice squealed with delight, broke away, and ran for the exit. "Come on," she shouted. "I know the bestest place."

Nardo took hold of Lucy's hand as they hurried to catch up with their daughter.

CHAPTER TWENTY-ONE

Sarasota, Fall 2022

Chloe

*I*nstead of the gala being held in January to take advantage of the arrival of tourist season, Chloe had convinced Tilda to reset the date for November. "The money we could raise is needed now, not months from now," she had reminded Tilda.

"There's so much to do," Tilda groaned. "I'll have to reschedule everything and make sure all the suppliers and caterers can make the switch. That could take some time. Oh, and the printing—invitations, programs, posters, ads for the newspapers, not to mention—"

"Well, now that I've persuaded my publisher to postpone my book for several months, I can help. What do you need?"

Tilda thumbed through the list she kept on her phone. "Do you think you might organize the silent auction? There are a number of items, including those Nana Rose donated, that really should be assessed by professionals. We would want to make certain the opening bid is appropriate to the value of the object."

"I can do that," Chloe agreed.

"Perfect." Tilda was clearly warming to the idea of moving up the date for the event. "I stored everything in the vault at Ca' d'Zan. Ian can show you how to access that, and you can probably lay everything out there in the game room. Ian's team can set plywood on sawhorses or something." She glanced at Chloe. "Uh-oh, you have that look I've come to recognize. The one that says you don't want to be a bother."

"Well, Ian is trying to get the renovation back on track and—"

"Storing everything in the vault was his idea. And do not tell me it would be a hardship to spend your days working in the same space as the oh-so-gorgeous Dr. Flanner." She clutched her hands to her chest with a dramatic sigh. "Yes, the brush of his hand, the sound of his voice, the late nights—"

Chloe burst out laughing. "All right, enough." She was relieved and delighted that Tilda seemed to have gotten over her crush on Ian. Lately she had been full of chatter about a young reporter for the local newspaper she had met, gushing over how he had these wonderful ideas for feature stories about Chloe and her book. "I'll get started making an inventory of the auction items today," she promised. "I assume there are more to come?"

Tilda nodded. "I'll send you the full list so you can keep track of what's here and who we still need to pester to make sure they come through with whatever they promised. In the meantime, I'm late for an appointment, so I'll text you later to see how things are going with the inventory—and the romance," she teased.

Chloe couldn't deny that working in the mansion was going to be a welcome change of pace and that working in close proximity to Ian was a chance to deepen their relationship. She'd convinced herself anything serious was out of the question. Their lives ran on different paths, so how could that sort of long-distance thing ever work? On the other hand, there was no reason not to enjoy a bit of flirtation, perhaps as they danced on the terrace under the stars serenaded by the orchestra Tilda would hire for the gala. Or maybe a kiss as they stood high above everything in the tower of the mansion looking out at the sunset?

"Oh, for heaven's sake, Chloe. Get a grip." She shook off her romantic fantasies, gathered her things, and set off. She'd never organized a silent auction although she had participated in many, and the opportunity to work on something totally different from her usual research and writing was invigorating.

To Chloe's surprise, when Ian showed her to the place where Tilda had stored the items for the auction, there were stacks of boxes in all sizes. "This is a lot of stuff," she said.

"Yeah. I kind of mentioned that to Tilda, but apparently she has this idea of combining stuff into themed gift baskets…. She didn't talk to you about that, did she?"

"No, but it's a good idea."

"I had the guys set up the game room, and I can assign one of them to help move anything you need. Some of these boxes weigh a ton—books, I think. What else do you need?"

"I really don't want to interrupt your work, Ian. Are you sure using this space is okay?"

He grinned. "Seems to me like it might be *fun*." He was leaning casually against the doorframe, his arms folded as he looked at her. They had come a long way in the few months that had passed since the day they first met—the day when she'd seen by his expression that he rarely considered the possibility of work being fun. Chloe couldn't help being pleased about the way things had developed. "As long as my project doesn't keep you from yours," she replied, "I'd be grateful for the help."

"How about I get you started by moving a few of these cartons to the game room, then when you're ready for more, just ask Jake."

"Jake, the policeman?"

"Yeah. He had some vacation time coming and volunteered to spend it here, helping out however he could. Right now I've got him painting the trim in the tower guest room." He chuckled. "Trouble is, he's so good and works so fast, it's hard to keep him busy."

Chloe took another look at the pile of boxes. "Well, I'll certainly be glad to have his help."

"Okay. I'll check back with you later." He started to leave then looked back. "You wouldn't want to catch some dinner later? There's a new group playing downtown at the tiki bar by the marina. I understand they're pretty good."

She waited for him to add some business reason for the invitation—the group might be a good choice for the gala, or he wanted to talk more about ways they might use the gala to raise the funds they needed for the restoration. But as the silence between them bordered on uncomfortable, Ian added, "Or not. Just a thought."

"I'd love to," she fairly shouted as he reached the stairs.

He hesitated and then said, "Okay then. It's a date."

By midafternoon Chloe had made good progress sorting through more than half the boxes. She had discovered that several of them held large baskets Tilda had obviously accumulated to fill with a variety of goods. She was surprised at how instinctively her mind worked to form natural connections. These would all work together for a gourmet-themed basket, and those could be combined to tempt the sports enthusiasts.

"This little guy almost got lost in the shuffle," Jake said as he placed a small box on the table Chloe was using to open the containers and record each item.

"Those are the things Tilda's grandmother donated," she said, recognizing the box. "Let's see what we've got." She carefully opened the flaps that had been folded into each other and began removing the items, each wrapped in several layers of tissue. "Oh, how lovely,"

Chloe exclaimed as she peeled tissue away to reveal a beautiful hand-painted fan. She flicked it open and flapped it lightly at Jake.

"That's a beauty, all right. Not sure the ladies go for that sort of thing these days though. With air conditioning, seems like they're always looking for a sweater or shawl to take the chill off." He chuckled as he waited for Chloe to open the next item.

"A shawl," she squealed. "Look at this, Jake."

"My wife would sure take a shine to that," he said, gently fingering the raised embroidery.

Chloe laid it on the bed of tissue and prepared to open the next item. It was small but heavy for its size. She unrolled it from its cocoon of paper and held up a small silver bud vase for Jake to see.

"Needs a good cleaning," he said.

Chloe was examining the base for a maker's mark. *Tiffany*. "This is a real treasure, Jake. No basket collection for this piece—it will bring a good price on its own."

"Small as that?"

"But look at the unusual design of it and the Tiffany mark and…" She ran her fingertips over the smooth surface of the silver. Jake was right that it needed a proper cleaning, but once it was brought back to its original condition? Her fingers touched a rougher area and she moved to the window, hoping the piece had not somehow been damaged. Squinting, she held it up to the light.

M&J

Forever

Images flashed through her mind. The archives… Toby showing her an article…. Lucinda Conroy arrested for stealing….

"A vase," she whispered. "A small silver Tiffany vase." She turned to Jake. "I have to go." She snapped a couple of photos of the vase then quickly rewrapped the treasures, including the vase, from Tilda's grandmother and placed them back in the box. "Please see these are put somewhere safe, Jake. I'll explain later."

She ran down the main stairs and out the rear exit, tossing off a hurried, "Later, Darcy," when the older woman seemed inclined to want to chat. She ran all the way to the archives and arrived breathless and soaked in sweat. "Is Toby here?" The receptionist looked up, frowning at Chloe's appearance.

"I'll see if he's with someone," she replied as she picked up the receiver. "It's Ms. Whitfield," she said when someone responded. "She seems to be in a bit of a state," she added, covering her mouth and the receiver.

"Tell him I'll only take a few minutes," Chloe urged.

"He's on his way," the receptionist assured her. "Perhaps you want to sit?"

Chloe was far too excited to do more than pace. When Toby finally came through the door that led to the archives, she said, "I think I may have found the vase."

Toby needed no further explanation—although it was evident by her expression that the receptionist had no idea what vase she was talking about. "You found out where it's hidden?" Toby's eyes popped with excitement.

"I found the vase," Chloe repeated, emphasizing each word.

"Holy moly," Toby whispered. "How can you be sure it's really... That is, we'd have to..." He shook off further thought and took hold of her arm. "Come on back. Let's check the files and see if we can find a drawing in Mr. Jefferson's inventory."

"There's an inscription," she told him and described it.

"M&J? Mable and John," he said. "Has to be."

Over the next hour they scoured the records kept by the Ringlings' butler. "If we knew when they acquired the piece," Toby said, "this would be easier."

"It could even have been before they moved into Ca' d'Zan," Chloe replied. "Do his records go back that far?" She turned a page and ran her finger down the list of items and froze. "Toby, look."

Silver bud vase in the tulip design; Tiffany; inscribed M&J Forever.

The entry also listed the measurements of the piece, but Chloe hardly needed that information once she saw that the butler had included the inscription.

"Toby, this is the vase my great-grandmother was accused of stealing."

"And it was donated for the gala by Tilda's grandmother?"

Chloe nodded. Her mind tumbled with details she could not piece together.

"Let me scan a copy of the entry," Toby said.

"I have to talk to Tilda." And as he handed her the copy, she added, "Please keep this to yourself, Toby, until we can figure out how…why…"

"Of course," Toby assured her. "Good luck."

But although she had asked Toby to remain silent, she needed to talk this through with someone before she saw Tilda, and the only someone she trusted was Ian. As she hurried back to the mansion, she texted him.

Meet me at the cottage as soon as you can.

His response came at once. On my way.

But when she reached the cottage, Tilda was there. "Oh good, you're here," she said as Chloe came up the front walk. "I have the best news and just had to tell you in person, so I took a chance that— What's happened?" Tilda rushed forward, her expression one of concern. "Please tell me it's nothing to do with the gala."

"Let's go inside, Tilda. Ian is on his way over."

"Oh, my stars," the younger woman wailed. "It *is* about the gala. And just when I got three major businesses to sign on as sponsors, meaning we've covered all the costs of staging the event and anything we bring in through ticket sales and the auction is gravy as Nana Rose would say. *Please* tell me—"

"That's wonderful news, Tilda. Your father is going to be so proud of you and so grateful for the way you've pulled this entire event together." Chloe tried to reassure Tilda as she led her inside the cottage. "Ian will be delighted as well." She set her things on the kitchen table and began filling glasses with ice. "How about a nice tall glass of fresh orange juice?" She didn't wait for Tilda to agree.

The screen door squeaked.

"Ah, here's Ian," she said with relief. But if she'd thought his presence might calm Tilda, she was mistaken. He looked as concerned as his assistant.

"What's happened now?" His voice held all the frustration that came with weeks of one disappointment and mishap after the other.

"I have something to show you both," Chloe said, indicating Ian should join Tilda and her at the table. She gave them the digest version of unwrapping the items Tilda's grandmother had donated for the auction. "Something about it seemed familiar, and then I saw the inscription." She held up her phone to show them the photo she'd taken.

"You found the missing vase?" Ian's eyes widened in surprise.

"Wait a minute," Tilda said. "That vase was a wedding present from my great-grandfather to my great-grandmother. Nana Rose thought because it was from the period—not to mention made by Tiffany—it would bring a good price at the auction. How could you possibly..." She started shaking her head. "No. That is not the...You cannot think my grandmother would..." She leapt to her feet. "No!"

"No one is accusing your grandmother, Tilda, but the fact remains that this vase was once part of the inventory at Ca' d'Zan." Chloe showed them the copy of the inventory and then the other photos she had snapped of the vase. "How do you explain the inscription?"

Tilda enlarged the photo with her fingers, then leaned back and smiled. "M&J? Martin and Julia—Nana Rose's parents, my great-grandparents. Clearly there was more than one of these vases made." She lifted her glass.

"Or Mable and John," Ian said softly. He thumbed through the photos Chloe had taken, including one of the maker's mark on the bottom of the piece, then looked again at the inventory. "The serial numbers match, Tilda."

Tilda's hand shook, and orange juice sloshed over her fingers. "No way," she whispered.

Gently Chloe removed the glass from Tilda's hand and handed her a napkin. "Let's not jump to conclusions. There are other possible explanations. For example, perhaps whoever stole the vase sold it or pawned it, and your great-grandfather bought it. I think we need to talk to your grandmother, Tilda. We need to see if she recalls anything more."

"Absolutely not," Tilda shouted, then burst into tears. "Daddy will never forgive me if I bring even a hint of scandal on the family's name. Please, don't do this to me."

Chloe's heart went out to Tilda. The young woman had spent much of her life trying to gain her father's approval, and with the work she had done to raise the funds needed to replace those that had been rescinded, she had come closer than ever before to succeeding. Bill Tucker would not be happy about this turn of events. Chloe pulled her chair closer to Tilda's and tried to console her. "There has to be a way to put this all right," she said. "Please, Tilda, let me speak with your grandmother in private."

"At least for the moment, there's no reason to involve your father or anyone else, Tilda," Ian said. "In fact, as long as the vase is returned to its rightful place…"

"You won't tell Daddy?"

"I see no reason why I would," Ian assured her.

Chloe stroked a lock of Tilda's hair away from her wet cheek. "This does not have to affect the gala in any way. It's simply one less item for the auction—no biggie."

Tilda stared down at her hands. "All right. I'll call Nana Rose, but I want to be there when you tell her."

"Actually, you should tell her why we need to meet. It would be cruel to simply spring this on her."

Tilda nodded. She fingered the copy of the inventory report. "Can I take this with me?"

"Of course."

"And maybe send me the photos?"

Chloe picked up her phone. "Done," she said as she tapped out the message and attached the photos.

Tilda stood. "I'll let you know when and where…and if," she added. "Nana Rose might well refuse."

"Understood," Chloe replied as she accompanied Tilda to the door. But she couldn't help wondering what they would do if Tilda's grandmother refused to believe them.

To everyone's surprise Tilda's grandmother took the discovery of the vase in stride. "I always wondered about it," she admitted. "My mother gave it to me on my thirteenth birthday—made a bit of a show of the gift. I noticed my father and grandparents seemed upset. There were looks exchanged, if you know what I mean. Mama told me Daddy had given her the vase on their wedding day." She held the vase up to the light. "That night Mama and Daddy had a huge argument, and Daddy left. He was gone for days. It was not the first time. Theirs was a tempestuous and unhappy union." She closed her eyes briefly before continuing. "The truth is I always felt the vase was somehow tainted. I couldn't explain it, but that's why eventually I just put it away."

Chloe leaned forward. "Did you ever hear your parents—or grandparents—speak of a woman named Lucinda Conroy?"

"Lucy? Oh my, yes. Whenever Mama and Daddy argued—and that was often—Mama would shout, 'Well then you should have married Lucy.'"

"And you knew that to be Lucy Conroy—a performer with the circus?"

Rose nodded. "Once I was older and my parents divorced, I was sure it was because of her. Daddy worked for Mr. John Ringling, you see, and I always suspected he had an affair with this woman."

Chloe bit her lip to stop herself from providing details. It was important to let Rose tell the story in her own time. "But it ended? Perhaps when he met your mother?"

"Oh, he and Mama practically grew up together. No, there was a scandal involving this circus woman. I think she was arrested for stealing something from Ca' d'Zan."

"This vase." Tilda said. "But then how did Grandfather Marty get it back, and why wouldn't he have returned it to the estate?"

Rose studied the inscription on the vase for a long moment. "Now that I think on it, I once overheard my grandfather tell Daddy that…" She blinked and pressed her lips together.

"Tell him what, Nana," Tilda prompted.

"He said 'that woman' should have listened to reason…something about a baby." Her eyes widened in understanding. "I think Lucy was pregnant. The scandal would have been more than my grandparents could abide. They would have done anything to avoid gossip, and they were quite wealthy. What if they tried to pay her off?"

"Yes," Tilda interrupted. "What if they tried to pay her off?"

"But Lucy was accused of stealing cash in addition to the vase," Chloe said.

"But what if she refused?" Rose suggested.

"And they framed her," Ian, who had said little since their arrival, added.

"Oh, that poor girl," Rose said softly. "Imagine what she must have gone through."

They were all silent for a long moment, and then Rose said, "If Lucy was pregnant by my father, and if she had that child, then—"

"You have a half sister." Chloe's heart was racing. Her grandmother and this woman might be related.

Tears pooled in Rose's soft gray eyes. "I always wanted a sister," she whispered. "I used to pretend…" Her voice trailed off, and she sank back in her chair, thrusting the vase at Ian. "Please take this and make sure it gets back to its rightful place at Ca' d'Zan, Ian."

"I'll take care of that," Tilda's father said as he strode across the room and took the vase from his mother-in-law. None of them had realized he had returned, and Chloe wondered how much he had overheard.

"Really, Mother Rose, we can hardly afford the questions that are bound to come with returning this. Collections are carefully cataloged and if this suddenly reappears…"

Rose rolled her eyes. "My son-in-law—much like my grandfather—is terrified of scandal." She straightened in her chair and eyed Bill Tucker. "And what do you suggest we do, Bill? Continue to perpetrate a lie that is now decades old and possibly ruined the life of an innocent young woman?"

"I— We—"

Ian stood. "A detective with the Sarasota police is doing some work at the mansion. I trust his discretion, and he would know or could certainly find out the legality of all this. Before we take any further steps, let's find out where we stand."

"Excellent," Rose agreed, then turned her attention to Chloe. "Tilda tells me you have done a good deal of research on Lucy Conroy, dear. I believe you are related to her?"

"She is my great-grandmother."

Rose's eyes brightened with hope. "And that of course presumes you have a grandmother or grandfather descended from her?"

Chloe nodded. "Grandmother," she murmured.

"Is it possible…?"

"I'm not sure," Chloe replied.

As in I'm not sure what you are asking, but this is a conversation I cannot have until I speak with Grandma Alice.

She gently squeezed Rose's hand. "Will you give me some time?"

Rose nodded. "Thank you for coming—all of you. Tilda, dear, you have shown rare courage, and I am so proud of you." Then with a deep sigh, she turned her attention to her son-in-law. "Sorry, Bill, I fear there are skeletons in the closets of my family." And with that she took her cane and left the room.

CHAPTER TWENTY-TWO

Newark, June 1945

LUCY

*P*apa is coming home!" Alice repeated the ditty she'd set to music as she danced around the bookshop.

The war was finally over, and every day thousands of soldiers and sailors poured into the city. There were victory parades, and the usually somber, rushed citizens of New York were given to smiling and laughing and even hugging with abandon.

As she finished hanging bunting in the shop window, Lucy watched her daughter—now a lively nine year-old—accept Seymour's invitation to waltz with him. How long had it been since she'd danced with a man—with her husband?

Never, she realized.

That night at Ca' d'Zan she had promised him a dance, but it never happened. In the years since then, they had had little inclination for dancing. The years had been hard, and now for the last four, Nardo had been overseas fighting the enemies of freedom, liberating those taken prisoner and tortured in labor or even death camps.

"We should go," Seymour said as he collected his hat and walking stick and turned out the shop lights. "The train will be arriving soon and we do not want to miss it, do we?" He tweaked Alice's nose.

"Mama, come on," she shouted. She left the shop and started

skipping down the street.

Lucy linked arms with Seymour and followed, calling out to Alice to wait while Seymour locked the shop's door. They joined the throngs of others all headed to the subway for the ride into the city. On the way someone popped the cork on a bottle of champagne, and everyone cheered as it overflowed with foam. At the station they moved as one from the crowded cars to the platform and on up the stairs where they spread out like ants escaping their nest to find the train that would bring their loved ones home.

Alice led the way. "I think I see him," she shouted as she took off running. "Papa!"

It was as if the throngs of people parted, allowing the little blond girl to make her way through. Lucy hurried after her, looking back once at Seymour. "Go. I'll catch up," he urged. And with that one quick look back she had lost sight of her daughter. "Alice!"

Her heart pounded with the fear that something might happen to her beloved child even on a day like this where it seemed nothing bad could ever happen again. Finding it impossible to see past the swarms of uniforms and civilians, all seeming to be on the same mission, she stepped onto a bench and scanned the scene for some sighting of the red, white, and blue ribbon Alice had insisted Lucy add to her straw hat, the ends streaming down her back.

"Mommy!"

Lucy heard the call, and despite the platform being filled with any number of children and their mothers, she knew that voice. "Alice!" She waved her hand wildly above her head. "Over here!"

But Alice was not alone. She was clutching the hand of a soldier and chattering away as she pointed to Lucy and dragged him through the hordes of others.

Lucy stood frozen on the bench as Nardo came toward her. He was thinner, his face lined with the weariness of war. But then he smiled and held out his arms, and as if they were once again flying in midair, she leapt from the bench and he caught her. He buried his face in the curve of her neck and swung her around. "Lucinda," he whispered—the name he still called her in private.

"Nardo." She traced the curve of his lips with her fingers. "Is it truly you? Are you—"

"It is over, Lucinda—the war, the past—a new beginning, yes?"

"Yes," she agreed happily and kissed him.

Finally, he set her on the ground, but he kept one arm around her and turned to look down at Alice. "And who is this beautiful young lady you sent to find me?"

"Oh, Papa," Alice chastised. "You know it's me. Now come along. Mr. Seymour has planned a special surprise." She grabbed Nardo's free hand.

"Bossy little thing, is she not?" Nardo laughed as he allowed himself to be pulled forward. "Takes after her mother," he added and tightened his hold on Lucy.

Seymour had indeed planned a surprise. Once they returned to their neighborhood they were greeted by their landlady, neighbors from the apartment building, and other shopkeepers along the street. Maria and Luigi had set out a spread of food on tables placed along the sidewalk in front of the bookstore, and a trio of musicians heralded their arrival with patriotic music. Alice's schoolmates were there and showered Nardo with confetti. Their landlady, whose nephew had died in France, greeted Nardo with teary eyes and kisses on each cheek.

"You are too thin," she declared. "We will see to that." Taking his hand, she pulled him toward the buffet. "Eat," she urged.

Lucy stood back and watched as the woman fussed over him, filling a plate to overflowing and insisting he eat. She watched him as he obliged by stuffing food into his mouth.

The party continued until dusk, the musicians shifting from patriotic tunes to popular songs of the day—background to the chatter and laughter and relief of the war being over. But when she heard a waltz, Lucy set aside the piece of cake someone had handed her and looked around for her husband. His back was to her as he stood with the other men from the neighborhood toasting the day with raised glasses of beer. He had removed his uniform jacket and hat, opened his collar, and rolled back his shirtsleeves.

Lucy tapped his shoulder, and when he turned to her, she said softly, "I believe I once promised you a dance?"

CHAPTER TWENTY-THREE

Brooklyn, November 2022

CHLOE

The gala was scheduled for the thirtieth. Chloe planned to spend Thanksgiving with her family and surprise her grandmother with the invitation to return with her for the gala. She also planned to do a bit of research. Tilda's grandmother had given her a man's inlaid ivory hairbrush. "This belonged to my father," she told Chloe. "Perhaps you can have it tested for DNA? I suspect writing mysteries, you have connections for that sort of thing?"

She did, but the gesture still surprised her. "Why?"

Rose sighed. "Because, my dear, if in fact your grandmother and I are half sisters, I would find great joy in knowing that. Of course, she may not feel the same, and rest assured I would never insist on pursuing a relationship that made her uncomfortable."

"I was stunned," Chloe told Ian later that evening as they sat on the terrace watching the sunset.

"Do you have a way to follow up on it?" he asked.

"Not immediately. I mean, most of my contacts are in New York, and with the holiday and all…"

"Perhaps Jake knows someone here in Florida. My guess is these things take time, but if you could get the ball rolling before you head home for Thanksgiving, perhaps by the time you return with your grandmother, you'd have the answer."

Chloe smiled. One of the things she had come to admire about Ian was the way his mind worked in logical patterns while hers tended to dance around the edges of a situation until finally she found some way. "Would you ask him for me?"

"Sure." They watched as the sun slipped behind the horizon. He reached over and took her hand. "I was thinking. How would you feel about my coming with you? I'd like to meet your family." Before she could find words, he continued. "Then maybe we could head to Santa Fe for Christmas—or after. My mom is driving me nuts asking questions about you."

"You said she's a fan of my books," Chloe replied with a nervous laugh.

Ian turned to her and cupped her face in his hands. "She's more interested in getting to know the woman her son has fallen in love with," he said in a voice thick with emotion. "I don't suppose there's a chance…?"

Words froze in Chloe's throat, so she did the one thing that seemed natural. She leaned in and kissed him.

"Is that a yes?" he asked.

She kissed him again.

"I'm definitely liking this new way of communicating," he whispered, and this time he pulled her fully into his arms and kissed her back.

A week later they were seated around her parents' large dining room table, her sister's children hanging on Ian's every word with undisguised adoration, while her sister and mother were not far behind. Only Grandma Alice seemed to hold full approval in reserve.

"How long have you known this professor? He doesn't seem

your type—quiet and serious." Grandma Alice had insisted she and Chloe would finish the last of the dishes while everyone else was gathered around the television watching football. Chloe had not been fooled at the transparent effort to get her alone and quiz her about Ian.

"Several months," Chloe replied. "Don't you like him, Grams?"

"I just met the man." She continued drying the crystal Chloe was handwashing. "I don't want you rushing into anything just because—"

"I'm an old maid," Chloe teased.

Grams pursed her lips. "I'm trying to be serious here," she grumbled, and then she sighed. "It's all the talk at dinner about the Ringlings and the circus and—"

"You're thinking of your mother," Chloe said, drying her hands and embracing Grams. "I'm sorry we were so insensitive."

"Sentimental drivel," Grams replied. She sat at the kitchen table watching Chloe return the glasses to the cabinet. "I hardly think of her at all. I mean, she was not really my mother, was she?" She drummed her fingers lightly on the table.

Chloe set the last glass in place and closed the cabinet door, then took a seat next to Grandma Alice at the table. "I want to tell you about my latest book," she said.

"I'm fine, Chloe. There's no need to distract me by changing the topic. We can talk about my mother—my real mother."

"Good. Because she's the inspiration for the protagonist in my next book, and I've learned some things that may help you understand why she did what she did."

"You can call it what it is, dear. She abandoned me."

"What if she didn't? What if Lucille O'Connor Russell was in fact Lucinda Conroy?" She went on to explain the idea for DNA testing. "So, I need something of yours for the test as well as something belonging to Lucille Russell, if you have it. If my guess is right, then the results will prove that Lucille was in fact Lucy Conroy—your mother—and there's every chance that the test of Martin Sutherland's DNA will prove him to have fathered both you and Rose Sutherland—in that case, your half sister."

For a split second Chloe saw hope flicker across her grandmother's face, but it was gone almost before it registered. "Don't be ridiculous," she fumed.

"But what if…?" Chloe persisted.

"My life is not one of your novels, Chloe." Grams rose from her chair, took a moment to gain her balance, and then left the room. On her way she brushed past Ian.

"Everything okay?" He took Alice's vacant chair and wrapped his hands around Chloe's.

"I've put my foot in it this time," she said. "I thought…I mean I guess I wanted…" Two large tears plopped onto the back of their joined hands.

"Look, it's a shock. I mean, just the idea of it has to be. Give her time to work through it," Ian advised. "In the meantime, how about we take a walk?"

"It's freezing out there."

"That's probably why we have coats and scarves and mittens. Besides, it started snowing half an hour ago, and my guess is you didn't even notice." He stood and pulled her to her feet. "Come on. Fresh air will clear your head."

"I thought you weren't that kind of doctor," she teased as she took coats from the hooks in the back hallway, handing him one and pulling on another. "Ian and I are going for a walk," she shouted, answered by a chorus of groans that apparently had to do with the football game rather than her announcement.

Once outside she hooked her arm through Ian's and turned her face up, opening her mouth to catch the falling snow. He did the same, and suddenly all the intrigue of Ca' d'Zan and DNA disappeared, and they were just two people walking in the snow.

She gave him a tour of the landmarks of her childhood—school, church, library. They stopped at an all-night diner for hot chocolate, and by the time they got back the house was dark except for the front porch and hall lights.

"What time is it?" Chloe asked.

"Nearly one," Ian replied. "Do you think your dad is waiting in that dark living room to give me a tongue lashing?"

"More likely to be Grandma Alice," Chloe said. And suddenly she was right back to where she'd been before Ian persuaded her to go for a walk.

Once inside they hung their coats on hooks to dry, and Ian followed her upstairs where his room was at one end of the hall and hers at the other. He kissed her and smoothed her hair away from her forehead. "Tomorrow's a new day," he whispered.

"I know. It'll all work out." She traced his lips with her finger. "Thank you," she added, then headed for her room. "See you in the morning."

"Chloe?"

She turned, and he covered the short distance between them and embraced her. "Been trying to find the right time to say this all day," he murmured. "I love you."

It was as if the weight of everything she'd been dealing with over the last several months was gone. She felt lighter and at the same time more anchored than she could ever recall feeling.

He loves me! Oh sure, he said he was falling, but this is so much more, isn't it, God? I mean this is without doubt. This is love.

"That's really a relief, Dr. Flanner," she said, "because I'm pretty sure I love you—have loved you for months now."

He grinned. "So that first day?"

She giggled, recalling how they'd gotten off on the wrong foot—for her quite literally.

A door opened, and they looked around to see Grandma Alice.

"Oh good," she said. "You're finally back. Well, come on in. I have some things to show you." She was still fully dressed, and when they entered her room her bed was covered with a variety of clothing and objects. "Will any of this do?" she asked.

"For what?" Chloe was mystified.

"For that DNA testing, of course." Grams glanced at Ian and rolled her eyes. "Really, young man, I hope you know what you're getting into. You seem quite the stable sort, while I expect you've noticed by now that my granddaughter's head is in the clouds much of the time."

CHAPTER TWENTY-FOUR

Newark, June 1960

LUCY

*L*ucy and Nardo watched with enormous pride as their daughter accepted her graduate degree. She had lived at home while attending New York University, helping out in the bookshop Seymour had left to the family in his will. But Lucy understood that everything was about to change. Alice was anxious to travel, and she had accepted a job teaching at a small college in upstate New York. She had found the love of her life in a young man she'd met while on a spring break trip to Florida. That year she came home filled with stories of this boy, the son of teachers in the public schools of Tampa.

The family's connection with Tampa raised long-buried concerns for Lucy. What if Alice got it in her head to try and explore her past there living in the orphanage? So many times over the years she and Nardo had lain awake discussing whether or not to tell Alice that Lucy was her mother in every way including by birth. But always they had awakened the next day to the sunny greeting of their beautiful child and wondered why they would ever consider bringing any conflict into the life of such a happy and contented person.

And so the years had passed. Alice knew she was adopted, knew about the time in the orphanage—even had some foggy memories of the foster family she'd gone to live with after the fire. But in all her years she showed no curiosity about her birth parents—who they were, why they had given her up for adoption. Once she reached her teens, if anyone brought up her past, Alice simply deflected the question and changed the subject. Lucy accepted that to mean Alice was content with what knowledge she had. And what good could possibly come of confusing her with the truth? Even with the changing mores that came with the advent of the sixties, a story like hers—pregnant without benefit of marriage—could raise eyebrows of disapproval.

And when Alice came home late one night, knocked on her parents' bedroom door, and announced she was engaged, that sealed the deal for Lucy. Alice would marry and have children of her own. Why on earth would anyone think of coloring the lives of future generations with a past as sordid as hers? No, she and Nardo were much respected by friends, neighbors, and their customers who had made the small bookstore one of the most successful in all of New York.

Lucy would leave the past where it belonged—in the past. The future was what counted, and she was thrilled to see her daughter's future explode into everything her mother had ever dreamed of for her.

CHAPTER TWENTY-FIVE

Ca' d'Zan, November 2022

CHLOE

*T*ilda had settled on a Roaring Twenties theme for the gala, and judging by the guests who filled Ca' d'Zan's Grand Court and spilled out into the ballroom and onto the wide terrace overlooking Sarasota Bay, she had hit the jackpot. The young woman was positively glowing with the pride of accomplishment, and for once, it did not seem to matter if her father shared her delight.

"Have you seen the bids on the auction items so far?" she gushed as she and Chloe stood watching the guests. "They are way beyond anything I dreamed. You did a great job of putting the baskets together, Chloe." She leaned closer and added in a whisper, "Nana Rose is very excited about meeting your grandmother. Is she here?" She scanned the room, seeking a likely candidate.

"Not yet," Chloe hedged, knowing the truth was that Grams was still back at the cottage, having refused to come once Chloe told her what the DNA testing had revealed. Her grandmother's reaction had been anything but the satisfaction Chloe had expected. While Tilda chattered on, eventually drawing Toby into their circle, Chloe recalled the earlier scene with Grams.

"So the DNA proves that Lucille Russell was actually Lucinda Conroy and, more to the point, both your birth and adoptive mother.

Furthermore, your birth father was indeed Martin Sutherland, who married Julia Gordon and fathered a daughter—Rose."

Grams went quiet, and the expectant smile she'd worn evaporated. Her lips thinned to a hard line, and she turned away, staring out the window of the cottage.

"Grams, you have a half sister," Chloe had said softly. "Rose. She's Tilda's grandmother, and she'll be attending the party tonight."

Nothing.

"Grams? She wants to meet you, and—"

Grams wheeled around, her eyes wide with alarm. "This woman knows? This Rose person? She knows about me and my mother and—" She actually shuddered and wrapped her arms tightly around her body as if trying to prevent herself from breaking apart.

Idiot, Chloe thought.

Ian had warned her that she was giving her grandmother a great deal of new information about her past and her life. The life she had always believed to be one thing and now would forever be something else.

"Come sit down," Chloe urged, guiding her grandmother to a chair, then kneeling next to her. "Forgive me, Grams. I was just so excited to have finally solved the mystery of your past—of your real mother. I didn't think."

"No, you did not," Grams replied, her expression fixed with anger. She stood, her posture ramrod straight. "I would like to return home as soon as possible if that could be arranged—tomorrow, I assume. I know you need to attend this party, so all I ask is that you make no further attempts to connect me with this information you have managed to uncover." She turned her back, fingering the frame of the photograph of Lucinda that Chloe had had reproduced as a surprise. "You should get ready and go."

And Chloe had done as she wished, leaving the gown her grandmother had planned to wear hanging on the back of the bedroom door. "I'll be back as soon as—"

"You are the guest of honor at tonight's event. You will stay and do your duty, young lady." And with that Grams had gone into the bedroom and closed the door.

The festivities surrounded Chloe—people laughing, chattering, calling out greetings to new arrivals. The band Tilda had hired was excellent, the vocalist good at engaging guests to come onto the dance floor that had been set up at one end of the terrace. Darcy was managing the silent auction, leaving Tilda free to handle any unforeseen emergencies. It was all very exciting, only Chloe was not in the mood for celebrating. She saw Ian engaged in conversation with Bill Tucker and other members of the board. For once Tilda's father looked pleased to be in Ian's company. The work on restoring the mansion was back on track and now there would be no worries about paying the bills.

At least one of us has achieved what we set out to do, she thought as she sought out a quiet corner outside to collect her thoughts. She owed her grandmother an apology, and yet she so wanted her to be a part of this evening. She thought about the fun they had shopping for gowns on Black Friday, chortling over price tags slashed by more than half. Grams had looked so elegant in the dark blue V-neck chiffon with its elbow-length lace sleeves and sequined bodice, and she'd been pleased when Chloe insisted on buying it for her along with shoes and a silver clutch purse.

"Well, aren't I something?" she'd said as she modeled the outfit for Chloe's parents.

My parents—how will I ever explain all this to them?

"Chloe?" Ian was crossing the terrace with two flutes of champagne in hand. "I've been looking everywhere for you."

Forcing a smile, she accepted the glass. "I needed a moment."

"Bill wants to make some sort of presentation. Tilda is beside herself because it's not part of the plan. I think it involves you."

The band started playing a slow dance, and he took her glass and his and set them on a small table, then held out his hand to her. "Dance with me?"

They moved into the rhythm of the music as if they had shared many dances. She was aware of the admiring glances of others on the dance floor. They made a striking couple—Ian, tall and athletic, wearing a 1920s-style tuxedo that might have been tailor made for him, and Chloe wearing a one-shoulder, floor-length silk jersey gown in a shade of aqua that was perfect with her copper-colored upswept hair.

"You look beautiful," Ian said. "But sad. What's happened?"

She told him the story. "When Grams agreed to the DNA testing, I thought that meant she was ready—that she'd be thrilled to finally know. What I failed to understand was how the truth would stir up the past and raise questions—mostly about why Lucy never told her the truth." As the dance ended she added, "I've made a real mess of this, Ian."

"Maybe not," Ian said. He pointed to the doorway where a gray-haired woman in blue stood.

"She came," Chloe whispered.

"Shall we?" Ian offered Chloe his arm and together they went to greet Grandma Alice. "Welcome," he called out when they got close. He gave Grams the smile that Chloe suspected had been setting hearts aflutter most of his life and said, "I thought I had found the prettiest girl here, but now..."

Grams laughed. "You are quite the charmer, young man. Would you get me a glass of that champagne, please? I want to have something in my hand when the toasts begin." Once Ian left, she turned to Chloe. "About earlier—"

"You're here, and that's all that matters," Chloe interrupted. She clasped hands with her grandmother. "You do look fabulous."

"This old thing," Grams teased, then sobered. "So, where is this Rose?"

"You're sure? I mean we don't have to do this tonight. Perhaps tomorrow—somewhere quieter and more private?"

"Oh, for heaven's sake, child, you can be most exasperating. First, you're all gung ho to do this, and now you're hedging? I never knew you to lose your nerve."

Just then they heard the unmistakable clink of silver on crystal calling everyone's attention to the bandstand where Bill Tucker stood next to an easel that held a covered object.

"If I could have everyone's attention," he boomed through a microphone that squealed in protest. He stepped away and then tapped the mic with his fingernail and began again. "Is everyone having a good time?"

Chloe thought perhaps in his college days Bill had been on the cheer squad. He had that kind of over-the-top enthusiasm. A chorus of approval was the response.

"Until now," someone shouted, and everyone laughed.

"I'll keep it short," Bill promised. "First, I'd like to introduce the person responsible for this evening's event. Tilda? Get up here," he shouted.

Toby and a couple of the other volunteers she'd recruited to help manage the evening pushed Tilda forward. Once she was onstage, her father wrapped his arm around her and kissed her forehead. "This young dynamo is my daughter, and some of you might have bristled at the idea of hiring a member of my family to manage something as grand and important as this gala. But here at the Ringling we have a policy of hiring the best, and I think you will all agree that tonight's festivities could not have been better. Not only are we having a lovely time, but I am also pleased to say we have raised all the funds needed to complete the restoration of this treasured home. So, join me in raising a glass to the museum's new event planner, Tilda Tucker."

Tilda's smile was like a spotlight as the surrounding guests raised their glasses and shouted in unison, "To Tilda." And Chloe was pleased that finally, Tilda had achieved the one thing she'd sought her entire life—the approval of her father. But she hoped going forward Tilda would aim higher and realize what an amazing young woman she was, and how many people had seen that all along.

"We are not done," Bill continued as Tilda left the stage. "Most of you are aware that it has been our privilege to have the celebrated mystery author, Chloe Whitfield, staying here on the grounds these last several months. She has become a member of our little community—pitching in when Hurricane Dennis threatened last summer, freely giving of her time to visit schools and bookstores this autumn, all while working on her next novel, which will be set right here at Ca' d'Zan. I give you the lovely and exceptionally talented Chloe Whitfield."

Chloe glanced at her grandmother, whose smile was worth any advance or award she'd ever received for her writing, then made her way to the stage, where Bill handed her the microphone. She hadn't prepared any remarks, but she'd been in similar situations dozens of times.

"Good evening," she said. "When I first arrived at Ca' d'Zan, I will admit I had a moment's thought that coming to Florida in July might not have been the smartest move I ever made."

The audience chuckled.

"But the welcome I received here was one I wouldn't trade for anything. Darcy Prescott, Pete Willis, Jake Helton, Toby Jensen, and Tilda—dear Tilda." She was surprised to feel emotion well as she looked at the young woman who had become a close and trusted friend. "They all made me feel at home—a part of the Ringling community, and they all played a role in the story I will tell in my next novel."

She paused, her gaze settling on Ian, who stood with her grandmother. "But there is one person who has been so instrumental in the work I've accomplished here that I plan to dedicate this new novel to him. Please join me in raising a glass to your museum's executive director, Dr. Ian Flanner."

The applause was deafening, interspersed with whistles and cheers as the crowd called for Ian to come on stage. Chloe noticed he took a moment to complete what looked like a fairly serious conversation with her grandmother before striding forward.

Basking in the applause along with Chloe and Ian, Bill finally raised his hands, calling for silence. "There's one last bit of business before we all get back to the party," he said, reclaiming the microphone. "There is the matter of restoring the name and reputation of a member of the extended family that was the Ringling circus troupe to its rightful place in the story of this place. Ian?"

To Chloe's surprise, Ian crossed the stage to the covered easel. He cleared his throat, and Chloe saw him look back at Grandma Alice, who nodded. "One of the foundations of this museum—beyond the art collection and this house—is the colorful history of the circus and the people who made that story their own. Over three-quarters of a century ago, there was another party held here at Ca' d'Zan—John Ringling's last grand soiree. On that occasion he had enlisted the talents of one Lucinda Conroy—the star of his show—to thrill the guests with her trapeze act. That day, in honor of Mister John's seventieth birthday, she and her partner, Bernardo Russo, went beyond their usual high-flying act. On that occasion Lucy Conroy performed a triple somersault, a feat only one other woman in the world had performed at that time."

He went on to briefly tell the story of Lucy's false accusation and subsequent disappearance as well as the need to assume a new identity. "But because of the solid investigative work completed by Ms. Whitfield and members of our staff here at Ringling, we are pleased to once again honor Lucinda Conroy and her performance partner, Bernardo Russo, as respected members of the Ringling

Museum story. To do the honors, I would like to invite Lucy's daughter to the stage—Mrs. Alice Russell Whitfield."

Ian moved to the short flight of steps leading from the dance floor to the stage and held out his hand to Grandma Alice. She was regal as she crossed to the easel and removed the covering to reveal a vintage circus poster featuring Lucinda Conroy flying through the air with Bernardo waiting to catch her. The audience once again burst into applause. Chloe saw tears fill her grandmother's eyes and stepped forward to embrace her.

Meanwhile, behind them, Bill had grabbed the microphone from Ian. "Happy endings, folks. That's the bottom line here at Ringling. Now I think Tilda has opened the dessert buffet, so go fill your plates and come back for the fireworks."

The partygoers drifted away, and Bill left the stage to accept the kudos of his friends and colleagues, leaving Ian, Grandma Alice, and Chloe standing in front of the poster.

"Isn't she lovely?" Grams ran her finger over her mother's image. "She was always so lovely...so kind. I wish I had known. I wasted so much time thinking she'd abandoned me when she was there the whole time. Why didn't she ever tell me?"

"Some things are impossible to know, Grams."

"Would you ladies like some dessert?" Ian asked. "Happy to serve."

"I'll come with you," Chloe said. "Grams, you'll be all right here?"

"I'm not incapable of taking care of myself, Chloe. Go...and if there's something chocolate, I'll take that."

Chloe laughed and hugged her grandmother before taking Ian's hand and following him through the clusters of guests to the dessert buffet.

"Okay," she said as they filled a large plate with a selection of goodies, "how did you ever persuade her to agree to do the unveiling...to be introduced as Lucy's daughter?"

"I just told her what was on the easel. I didn't want it to come as a shock, given what you'd told me."

"But she agreed to be introduced as Lucy's daughter?"

Ian shrugged. "I asked if that would be okay, and she said sure."

While Chloe took the desserts back to where Grams was sitting enjoying the music, Ian went to get coffee for them. The evening had turned cool—for Florida—and the fireworks show was about to begin. She had just sat down when Tilda hurried over. She looked distressed.

"What's happened?" Chloe asked.

"Sit down, dear girl," Grams added, indicating the chair next to hers.

"I have to go," Tilda said. "Nana Rose...I think...I mean, she just...one minute fine...then collapsed...what if..."

Ian arrived with the coffee and immediately took charge. "I'm calling 911. Chloe, find Pete and let's see if we can get Tilda's grandmother away from the crowd here."

"Pete and Darcy are with her now," Tilda said tearfully. "She was at our table and—"

"What can I do?" Grams was already on her feet.

"Come with us," Chloe urged. "We can stay with her while Ian and Pete direct the EMTs."

It wasn't until they had reached the now conscious but clearly unwell Rose and assured her the ambulance was on the way that Chloe remembered her grandmother and Rose were meeting for the first time. To her surprise, Grams took the chair closest to Rose and held her hand.

"Rose? It's me—your half sister, Alice. You need to hang on, because you and I have much to talk about."

Rose grasped Grandma Alice's hand. "Our father was a first-rate scoundrel," she murmured.

"I won't disagree," Grams said, "but fortunately, from what I know, neither of us seems to have inherited that trait." A siren sounded in the distance, and they all looked up. "Can they get here—I mean all the way here?" she asked Tilda.

"I think so."

Grams turned her attention back to Rose. "With any luck at all, there will be several calendar-worthy young hunks fussing over you within minutes, so stay calm."

Rose managed a laugh, and Chloe could not recall when she had loved her grandmother more.

Blessedly, most people seemed unaware of the excitement. Everyone had moved out to the terrace to watch the fireworks lighting up the clear night over the dark waters of Sarasota Bay. To the accompaniment of oohs and aahs, the EMTs arrived, did some preliminary checks of Rose's heart rate and such, and then transferred her to the ambulance for the ride to the hospital.

"Do you want me to come?" Grandma Alice asked her.

Rose nodded. "In the ambulance," she added.

Grams glanced at Tilda and her mother who both nodded. "We'll follow in Dad's car," Tilda said. "Ian? I really need to go."

"Of course. Go. We've got this covered. Text us when you know something."

Following the grand finale of the firework display, the guests were taken back to their cars using the electric carts the museum used to transport visitors from one part of the expansive campus to the next. The band packed up, and the caterers cleared away everything to do with the food, dishes, linens, and rented tables and chairs. In what seemed like no time at all the terrace was deserted except for Ian and Chloe, who were making a final check to be sure nothing had been left to chance—no candles left burning, no handbags or such left behind.

Chloe sat on one of the wicker chairs that normally lined the terrace and unbuckled the high-heeled strappy sandals she'd worn all evening. Ian pulled a chair opposite hers, took hold of her bare foot, and began massaging it. "Tired?" he asked.

"Exhausted," she admitted. "But it was a wonderful evening. Everything went perfectly.... Well, up until Rose..."

"I had a text from Tilda. Apparently, the diagnosis was dehydration. They've started intravenous fluids, and she should be discharged tomorrow."

"That's a relief." Chloe took out her phone to check for a message from her grandmother. "Grams is staying with her," she said softly. "Says they have a lot of catching up to do."

"So, all's well that ends well."

Chloe relaxed in the chair and looked up at the almost full moon casting a light on the water that reminded her of a road. "And speaking of endings," she said, "next week I fly back to New York."

I thought I made a mistake coming here, and now I don't want to leave.

Of course, she would never say that out loud to Ian. He might take it the wrong way— think she was more like Tilda than he knew. Of course, her feelings went beyond a girlish crush on the handsome professor. This was love of the forever and happily ever after variety. They needed more time, of course, but...

She realized he'd been talking while she was lost in thought.

"So, what do you think?"

"About endings?"

"About us *not* ending," he said, focusing on massaging her foot.

"How would that work? You have an important—and exciting—job here and I—"

"Can work anywhere as long as you have a functioning laptop. I know it's only been a few months, and maybe I'm way off base here but—"

In one single motion, Chloe pulled her foot free of his grasp and leaned forward and kissed him. "You're not off base," she murmured. "In fact, you just hit a home run."

Ian grinned. "Your grandmother is going to be so pleased."

"I don't understand."

"Well, at Thanksgiving when I was at your parents' house, she kind of cornered me. She's not one to beat around the bush, as you well know."

"What on earth did she say to you?"

"In effect she asked what my intentions were. I told her my intentions were to figure out a way to get you to stay on in Sarasota—give us a chance."

"And she said?"

"She rolled her eyes and tapped her wristwatch, then muttered, 'Clock is ticking' and walked away." He chuckled, then sobered immediately as he tucked a strand of Chloe's hair behind her ear. "And tonight, when I saw her with Rose and thought about all the years they might have had, I realized she was right. I love you, Chloe, as in spend-the-rest-of my-life-with-you kind of love. So, what if you came home with me for Christmas…meet my mom and brothers and their wives and kids. See how it feels."

For a writer, she was suddenly bereft of words to say how much she liked that idea—liked the whole idea of a rest-of-my-life kind of love. "Okay."

"Okay?"

"Yeah, okay," she repeated, grinning. Already she was imagining how they would tell their kids and grandkids the story, how they would all laugh at her inability to put words to one of the most important offers she'd ever had.

They were married the following spring on the terrace of Ca' d'Zan with both families and their growing list of friends all present. Just after New Year's Ian had persuaded Chloe to agree to the purchase of a run-down 1920s cottage in the historic neighborhood of Laurel Park. The place had been painted a garish green with red trim, the windows boarded over with plywood, and the front porch and steps sagging. But Ian had promised by the time she returned from her book tour she wouldn't recognize it. Chloe was skeptical. She loved the location and the historical ambience of the setting. They could walk to pretty much everything they could ever want—theaters, bookstores, restaurants, coffeehouses, the downtown farmers market—and best of all they were just blocks away from Tilda's place. But the cottage needed a *lot* of work, inside and out.

Ian enlisted Tilda and Toby to help him keep Chloe from seeing the final renovation until after the wedding, and they took their role to heart. Tilda's father and the board even got involved, presenting the couple with a wedding gift of a night spent in the tower guest room of the mansion. Once the reception dinner had been devoured, the cake cut, and the bouquet tossed, Grandma Alice and Rose herded everyone away, and Ian and Chloe had the place to themselves.

This time they watched the sunset from the Belvedere Tower, then sat cross-legged on the floor and opened the gifts Darcy and Pete had made sure were piled in the guest room. Around midnight they raided the kitchen for second helpings of the food they'd been too busy to enjoy during the reception and then took the elevator to their special honeymoon suite.

When Chloe woke the following morning, the sun was streaming into the room, and from above her in the tower she could hear Ian whistling. Clutching her robe around herself, she climbed the stairway and saw her husband setting out a breakfast of fresh orange juice, coffee, and huge slices of wedding cake.

How she loved this man!

"Good morning," he said and kissed her before leading her to the table. "I thought perhaps after breakfast, we might drive up to—"

"Stop right there," she cautioned. "The only place we are driving to is our home. I want to see how you managed to salvage what was a disaster, even though I know you are a master at restoration."

He grinned and dangled a set of keys at her. "Keys to the castle," he teased. "Our castle. It's not Ca' d'Zan, but—"

"Just eat your cake and let's get going."

Chloe didn't recognize the quaint little house. Ian parked on a side street, and she walked right past their house without realizing it. "Where is it?"

Gently he took her arm and turned her back the way they had come. "There," he said.

The property had been transformed, the garish green covered over with a pale aquamarine accented with white and peach details. New windows and front door. A transom over the front door fitted with a stained-glass panel. A front porch where two pristine white rocking chairs seemed perfect for morning coffee. A yard filled with native vegetation and towering palm and oak trees.

"There's a mango tree in back," Ian told her as he unlatched a wrought iron gate and led the way up the front walk. "And of course, citrus as well—oranges, lemons, limes."

He unlocked the door, then scooped her high in his arms and carried her over the threshold.

"Welcome home, Mrs. Flanner," he said.

She felt a bit as if her head were on a swivel, so much was she turning it to take in every detail. "Put me down," she pleaded, and when he did, she went from room to room drinking in the perfection of it all, uttering little squeals of delight at each new discovery.

"So, you like it?"

"I love it," she exclaimed.

"It's not Ca' d'Zan," he said.

She wrapped her arms around him and looked up at him. "Ca' d'Zan is beautiful, but the history and memories made there were not always so wonderful. This is a place that practically dares anyone in residence not to be happy. Come on. Let's call our families and friends and tell them to get over here. Let's start making those memories today."

Ian grinned. "As Grandma Alice might say, 'Clock is ticking.'"

ANNA SCHMIDT is the author of over twenty works of fiction. Among her many honors, Anna is the recipient of *Romantic Times'* Reviewer's Choice Award and a finalist for the RITA award for romantic fiction. She enjoys gardening and collecting seashells at her winter home in Florida.

Doors to the Past

Visit historic American landmarks through the **Doors to the Past** series. History and today collide in stories full of mystery, intrigue, faith, and romance.

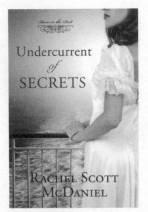

UNDERCURRENT OF SECRETS
By Rachel Scott McDaniel

As an event and wedding coordinator for the 100-year-old steamboat *The Belle of Louisville*, Devyn Asbury needs to win a contest to revive the old steamboat. Then Chase Jones shows up with a mysterious torn photo from the 1920s. A century earlier, Hattie Louis, the adopted daughter of a steamboat captain, is everything from the entertainment to the cook. When strange incidents occur aboard the boat, Hattie's determined to find the truth. Even if that means getting under First Mate Sterling Monroe's handsome skin.

Paperback / 978-1-64352-994-3 / $12.99

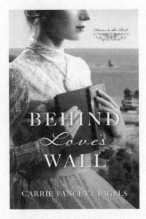

BEHIND LOVE'S WALL
By Carrie Fancett Pagels

Two successful women, a hundred-and-twenty-years apart, build walls to protect their hearts. Modern-day Willa, a successful interior decorator, is chosen to consult for the Grand Hotel's possible redesign. She discovers a journal detailing the struggles of a young woman, Lily—which reveals dark secrets. The renowned singer wasn't who she pretended to be. As Willa reaches out to Lily's descendant, a charismatic and prominent landscape artist, she lets down her guard. Should she share the journal with him or once again erect a wall as she struggles to redesign both the Grand Hotel and her life?

Paperback / 978-1-63609-069-6 / $12.99